Lucilla Andrews was born in Suez and qualified as a nurse in one of London's large teaching hospitals. With her expert knowledge of the nursing world, she has become a popular writer of nurse romances, joining her technical knowle... to her understanding of ... the medical professio...

Also by LUCILLA ANDREWS

THE SECRET ARMOUR
THE FIRST YEAR
A HOSPITAL SUMMER
NURSE ERRANT
THE YOUNG DOCTORS DOWNSTAIRS
THE NEW SISTER THEATRE
FLOWERS FROM THE DOCTOR
A HOUSE FOR SISTER MARY
THE HEALING TIME
HOSPITAL CIRCLES
MY FRIEND THE PROFESSOR
THE PRINT PETTICOAT
THE QUIET WARDS
RING O'ROSES
HIGHLAND INTERLUDE
EDINBURGH EXCURSION
SILENT SONG†

and published by Corgi Books
† to be published by Corgi Books

The Light in the Ward

Lucilla Andrews

CORGI BOOKS
A DIVISION OF TRANSWORLD PUBLISHERS LTD

THE LIGHT IN THE WARD

A CORGI BOOK 0 552 09501 X

Originally published in Great Britain
by George G. Harrap & Co. Ltd.

PRINTING HISTORY

George Harrap edition published 1965
George Harrap second impression 1965
Corgi edition published 1966
Corgi edition reprinted 1967
Corgi edition reprinted 1969
Corgi edition reissued 1974
Corgi edition reprinted 1975

Corgi Books are published by Transworld Publishers, Ltd.,
Cavendish House, 57–59 Uxbridge Road, Ealing, London, W.5.

Made and printed in Great Britain by
Richard Clay (The Chaucer Press), Ltd., Bungay, Suffolk

CONTENTS

1. A Flat from Francine   7
2. A Quiet Night in Albert   22
3. Breakfast with George   36
4. Nurses look Identical at Night   48
5. Albert is not so Quiet   61
6. Charles turns King Cophetua   74
7. Everything happens in Casualty   85
8. Mrs Shaw asks for Help   97
9. Andrew forgets his Medicine   108
10. Andrew turns Neighbourly   118
11. Hospitals cannot work Miracles   130
12. A Picture in a Newspaper   142
13. Tiny writes me a Letter   156
14. Albert sounds like Albert again   165

CHAPTER ONE

A FLAT FROM FRANCINE

My cousin Francine's telephone call got me out of night nurses' breakfast that morning.

'Cathy, don't you have an odd night off to-night?'

'Yes. Thank the Lord.' I yawned. It was Tuesday. Tuesday in our hospital was the first day of the new week. Albert, my ward, had been on accident take-in for the last week. The week-end had been unusually fine for early November and produced bank-holiday-type traffic. We had been admitting road casualties the entire week-end, and Monday had lived up to its reputation of being the heaviest day and night of the week. That was why our hospital week began on Tuesday, since it gave the students who worked in rota on weekly shifts as Casualty and Theatre dressers six days' experience before facing Monday. 'I intend to spend most of the next thirty-six hours sleeping. Why?'

'Do you still want to live out?'

'Of course. When I can find a flat near enough that won't take my whole salary in rent even if I share it.' I closed my eyes, since I could talk as well with them shut, and they were feeling nearly as weary as my feet. 'Have you heard of one?'

She said casually, 'You can have mine for three months from to-day, if you like. Rent free.'

I woke up smartly. 'What did you say?'

'I'm offering you my flat, darling. I've just decided it might be fun to go with Daddy on his lecture tour after all. He flies to New York from Manchester to-morrow. You know I told you last week he wanted me along with him. My visa's all fixed. So why shouldn't I go?'

I said, 'I thought his secretary had cancelled your plane ticket.'

'I've just rung to tell her to uncancel it. She'll manage. Now, listen. I want to drive up to Daddy to-day, but still haven't packed, and I'm not going without fixing about my flat. I hate leaving it empty. There's no time to sub-let, and anyway tenants are murder. They'd wreck it. That's why I thought of you. Do you want it?'

Her mews flat was just across the river from St Martha's, my hospital. It was a dream of a flat, and a very expensive dream at that.

'Francine, I'd love it! Are you sure you don't mind lending it?'

'Cathy, don't be dumb! Why else should I offer it to you? Use it as your own, and if you want one of your girls to share, go ahead. Only do try and get in to-day. I don't want to make any song and dance about being away. That's just asking for burglars.'

That was reasonable. 'I'll see Matron as soon as possible. I'm sure she'll understand, and as I'm a fourth year she'll have nothing against my living out. When do you want me over?'

She said she would like the place to herself while she packed, and was quite happy to have me move in during the afternoon, after she had gone. 'I'll hide the keys in the usual place. If Matron is sticky, ring me. If not, I'll take no news as good news. Now, down to details; forward my mail to Mother in New York—you know her address; I'll deal with my tradespeople; I'll leave my car in Manchester. The two garages needn't bother you. Charles is using one, and I've sub-let the other to the new tenant in the flat on my right.'

'Francine, this is all very efficient.'

'Darling,' she protested, 'you career girls are even worse than men! You seem to think any female who doesn't hold down a job has to have her head stuffed with cotton-wool! I think that's all—and I must rush as I can hear Charles shifting his car and I want to talk to him. Have lots of fun here——' and she rang off.

Charles was her only brother. He was eight years older than Francine. She was twenty-three, I was a year younger. Charles had been in London throughout my time at Martha's. We met roughly once a year at Francine's flat. When we met he greeted me as the love of his life, and in the intervals ignored my existence. I seldom forgot his. I was not in love with my cousin. I merely enjoyed thinking about him in the same way as I enjoyed thinking about chinchilla coats. Both were splendid material for day-dreams, but had no real connection with my life. I shared a surname with my cousins, and had a stronger physical resemblance to Francine than was often found in sisters, but we lived in different worlds.

My father as a young rector had married his rural dean's daughter. His identical twin had qualified at Martha's, and then married an American girl studying at the London School of Economics. The year Charles was born my aunt had inherited an astronomical number of dollars from a Texan great-uncle who had died a bachelor, and in his long lifetime had the handy knack of always drilling for oil in the right places. He had chosen my aunt as his heir out of a host of great-nephews and nieces, simply because she happened to be his favourite and long-dead sister's only grandchild.

My uncle was now Professor of Tropical Medicine in a northern teaching hospital. He had always insisted to my parents that his wife's money had never affected his career, but of course it had, since he had been able to afford to specialise without having to bother about the low salary hospitals paid embryo specialists, as he had never had to support his family, or pay for his children's expensive educations. His private life had been affected even more plainly. His marriage had remained superficially intact only because neither party was interested in the prospect of a divorce. They saw very little of each other. My uncle was devoted to his work, and, when he remembered them, his children. His wife, after openly admitting she found small children boring, and teenagers unbearable, was now apt to write petulant letters to my mother complaining how seldom Charles and Francine visited her permanent home in New York. 'They know I cannot tolerate your terrible climate! I declare I do not understand why Charles insists he just has to work in London, when his own mother lives in New York.'

Charles was on the boards of a whole row of City companies. I was never very clear what he did, but he obviously enjoyed doing it. Francine found this as puzzling as her mother, but, as she was very fond of her brother, she was prepared to write off his habit of working regular and often long hours as an excusable weakness. 'Obviously a streak of Daddy coming out in him.'

That particular streak had only once come out in her. She had started nursing in my set at Martha's the year after her first London season, and after ending her second—or it might have been the third—engagement. I never could remember which, and had long stopped trying to keep count of her affairs, since she got engaged and unengaged about twice a year. I remembered that specific one ending, because just after she had spent a few days at my home. My new uniform arrived while she was there. We were the same height and build, so it had fitted her as well as myself. It had been the sight of her head in a Martha's cap that had done the trick. She announced she had always wanted to do something worthwhile. She was bored with *la dolce vita*. There was medical blood in her veins. She knew, she just knew, she had a vocation. 'Nursing is so romantic! I must ring Daddy! He'll know which string to pull!'

She was not the first girl to take up nursing after a broken engagement, or to imagine it a romantic occupation. I had several friends in the former category, including one Meg Harper, who had later won a gold medal. And most of us had once pictured ourselves gliding softly up and down dimly lit wards, laying cool hands on fevered brows, followed by the admiring glances of grateful, and exclusively male, patients. In my set's first week in the Preliminary Training School we had practised soft glides in our crackling new uniforms until Sister P.T.S. informed us tersely we were training as nurses, not fashion models. Her staff nurse, a pale, prim young woman who modelled herself on the pictures of the youthful Miss Nightingale, and whom we called for obvious reasons Little Flo, warned us non-stop of the horrors ahead. 'Come along now, nurses! Hurry! Faster—faster—or you will be in real trouble when you reach the wards! Nurses! Never let me see you carry a glass of water in your hand again! That could mean a trip to Matron's Office once you reach the wards! Remember, everything—even a teaspoon—must be *on* a saucer, on a tray!'

We adored Little Flo, and thought her a big laugh until we really did reach the wards and found her advice very useful. I started in Robert Ward, Francine in Matilda. Sister Matilda was a youngish woman with a square, muscular figure and the reputation for being the toughest thing in skirts or trousers in all Martha's.

Bridie Sullivan, another girl in my set and since one of my great friends, was sure Matron had sent Francine and herself to Matilda to test the voltage of their lamps. 'And who could blame the poor old bag,' added Bridie, 'what with Little Miss Money's debbie past and myself having tried modelling, the stage, and art school before deciding I had to be a nurse.'

Francine had walked out for good after three weeks in Matilda. Bridie was still with us. Matron had offered to move Francine to another ward. Her offer had been refused. 'How can you bear to stay behind in this hell-hole, Cathy?' my cousin had demanded.

I was happy to be left behind, but not with the reputation she had managed to leave behind after the P.T.S. and those three weeks. As we looked alike, more so in uniform, and had the same surname, whenever I moved to a new ward in my first year the sister had a way of looking me over and saying, 'Oh, yes, Nurse Newenden,' that made my blood run cold. Bridie advised me to pin a notice on my apron bib. 'Not *that* Newenden. The poor relation.' Time ironed things out, but I had a very tricky first year.

Francine flew off to visit her mother after leaving Martha's. She was away about a year, then had a row with her mother, and another with her then current fiancé, an American, handed

10

back his ring, and returned to London. That was when she bought a long lease on her present flat.

Charles was at her house-warming party. 'Cathy, my dear! Wonderful to see you! You must dine with me! May I ring you?'

I said certainly, without expecting him to do anything of the sort, which was just as well, as he did not.

He was on my mind when I left the telephone booth after Francine's call. He lived in a block of service flats a few minutes' walk from Francine's mews. I wondered how much, if anything, I would see of him when he came to collect or put away his car. The top of his head from a window? Probably.

George Martin was standing with his back to me a few yards down the corridor, gazing at one of the busts with which it was lined. I stopped at his elbow. 'What's the matter with him?'

He looked round. 'Oh, it's you. I knocked his ear off last night and bust it. I've just stuck it back. It show much?'

'That crack's a bit obvious. And the chip. Have you got it?'

'No.' He was smiling. 'I stood on it.'

He was one of the orthopaedic housemen. He was the right build for orthopaedics. He was six foot three, with shoulders that balanced his height. I asked how he had managed to knock over the bust.

'Leant against it when I was talking to one of the chaps after our rounds last night. Damn thing went over. We took the bits of ear along to the plaster theatre and got it back in one piece. I hoped it would be good enough. You don't think it is, Cath?'

'Not if some one looks closely. I tell you who could make a better job of it—Bridie Sullivan. She did some pottery when she took her art course, and she's quite good at sculpting.' I patted the stone face. 'The poor old boy looks one-sided. Let's shift him round a bit—that's better.'

We walked on together. He asked me to ask Bridie for her advice. 'Tell me what she says to-night.'

Albert was an acute male orthopaedic ward. George was our houseman. We saw each other nightly in Albert, and had been seeing each other in our off-duty for the last eighteen months. Our friends were convinced we were 'good friends.' We were, if not in the way they assumed. 'Not to-night. Have you forgotten I'm off?' And I went on to tell him of Francine's call.

He had been to a few of her parties with me. 'Whose ring has she chucked back this time?'

I shrugged. 'As far as I know she's between affairs.'

'Then why the quick getaway?'

'Maybe she just wants to see something of her parents?'

George said maybe, but on past showing he doubted it. 'So

she's handing you her flat with no strings?'

'Apart from looking after it—yes. And she doesn't mind if I share it.'

'Will you?'

I thought this over. 'That might be more fun. Snag is, whom do I ask? I'd like Bridie, but she thinks living out is crazy, as it means getting up earlier. I like the rest of my set a lot, but I'm not sure I'd want to live on my own with any of them.'

He said slowly, 'Then how about Meg Harper? I know she's not in your set, but you seem to like her, and she's a sensible soul.'

'George, that is a brilliant idea! Meg'd be perfect! You are clever.'

He flushed. 'Just thought it might do.'

I looked at him in some surprise. He was not usually so easily embarrassed, but then I did not usually pay him compliments. Our relationship, if unexciting, was very pleasant. I liked having him around. He was attractive without being too good-looking, and had the easy-going temperament of so many big men. He never lost his temper, or appeared to have strong feelings about anything but rugger and food.

Tuesday was his free evening, so I invited him to supper. He said he would bring a bottle of wine.

'Do that.' We had stopped at one of the many side-doors to our park. 'George, I must go over for a clean apron before I ask the Office for a date with Matron. This one was clean an hour ago, but Bridie spilt tea on me at breakfast.'

'Don't forget to ask her about that ear. The Dean'll have a stroke if he spots the chip. He's got an obsession about those chaps. Expect he doubts we'll treat him with proper respect when his time comes to join them if he doesn't make us toe the line now.'

'Probably.' He was holding but not opening the door. 'George, I must go.'

'Sure.' But he did not move. 'Cath, I hope you'll be all right on your own in that flat. It's pretty quiet in that mews, and Francine's furniture is hellish valuable.'

'I won't be on my own if Meg joins me. You know I'm going to ask her, and I expect she'll say yes,' I reminded him. 'George, I must go, as I have to be back in the Office before half-past. Any requests to see Matron after that have to wait until the next day, and I promised Francine I'd get in to-day.'

Matron saw me at ten. She said she understood my desire to live out, and had no objections to it despite the short notice, but she did not wish me to spend all that day packing and moving, as I had been given the extra night off to compensate for having my last nights off curtailed, and needed to rest. 'Take a few things with you to-day, and each day until your next batch of nights off, when you can move the rest. And if for some reason your cousin should return earlier than she at present anticipates, then you can always move back to the Nurses' Home.'

I looked for Bridie when I got back to the Home. She was in the bath wearing a scarlet plastic mob-cap and chain-smoking. 'Will you shut that door, girl! Home Sister'll kill me if she smells this smoke.'

I sat on the edge of the bath and gave her my news. She said making his lordship a fine ear would be no trouble at all, and she couldn't wait to hear how I enjoyed living it up with the other half. 'And how long will it be before Little Miss Money changes her little mind?'

'Your guess is as good as mine, dear.' I coughed. 'Bridie, how can you stand this atmosphere?'

'My last packet. I'm back to Robert to-night. When I'm through this lot I'm giving it up!'

Robert was a chest ward. After working in Robert most nurses gave up smoking. Bridie was now one of our very few heavy smokers. I congratulated her on all the money she was going to save, and left her soaking and smoking.

Meg Harper was away on nights off and due back that night. I left a note in her room, then went back to mine, packed a suitcase, set my alarm for mid-afternoon, and fell asleep as soon as I was in bed.

The short winter afternoon was beginning to fade, it was raining fitfully, and much colder than it had been that morning, when I let myself out of the silent Night Home. I got a bus immediately. The rain left off when the bus deposited me at a corner about twenty yards from the entrance to the mews.

Francine's flat stood between two others over a row of private lock-up garages. The left-hand flat was rented by a youngish American married couple, both journalists and away a good deal. The right-hand flat had recently changed hands. For some reason the garage beneath it was included in Francine's lease.

Her flat had a bright-blue front door crowned with a row of bare orange window-boxes. There was an orange plant-tub beside the door in which she always hid her keys. I looked round before digging for them. The mews was quiet, the only other visible occupant a youth in overalls working under the bonnet of a car up the far end. I had found the keys and smoothed the top earth before he emerged. 'Not much of an afternoon, Miss Newenden,' he called. 'Lot more rain coming—and it's not getting any warmer.'

'It certainly isn't!' I called back, amused, and rather

reassured for Francine's sake by his error. Then I let myself in.

A steep, narrow, white staircase ran straight up from the door to the little hall above. The hall was all blue—walls, ceiling, and carpet. The long, low front room was gold and white, Francine's bedroom varying shades of rose, the spare bedroom yellow. The kitchen was scarlet and cream. Every room had fitted carpets. There were enough built-in cupboards in the two bedrooms to house the wardrobes of my entire set, and sufficient food stored in the kitchen to last a three months' siege.

It was a beautiful place, but a show place, not a home. It was a very chaotic show place that afternoon. The surprised me. Francine was very untidy, but she had an excellent daily help. That reminded me that Mrs Withers, the help, was one person we had forgotten to discuss. Then I found a note half buried under forgotten cosmetic jars and used cleaning tissues on Francine's dressing-table.

'My wretched Mrs Withers,' wrote Francine, 'broke her ankle yesterday. She will be away ages, but that doesn't matter now, as you won't want the expense. Other things I forgot; if any domestic problems crop up, contact Charles's secretary. Number on pad by telephone. Help yourself to anything in the kitchen; it won't keep. And don't stand any nonsense from the new man next door right. He has done nothing but complain ever since he moved in. Wish I had never agreed to let him have the garage—it would serve him right to have to keep his precious car outside. Sorry about the mess—had a wonderful party last night—know you won't mind coping. F.'

The kitchen was littered with empty bottles and dirty glasses. It must have been a very good party and had probably gone on most of the night, as her parties usually did. The Americans, and the last tenants on the other side, had been incredibly tolerant about noise, and in any case generally came to Francine's parties, probably in self-defence. I wondered why she had not dealt with this new neighbour in that way. I had the impression from her note that he was on his own. Or had he refused the invitation? If he had, Francine would have been out for blood. She was not used to refusals from men.

I dealt with the kitchen, then the rest of the flat; cooked a supper that would not be ruined by waiting if George was late, then had a bath.

The bathroom was all mirrors, black marble, gold knobs, and rather hideous. The knobs did amuse me, but in playing with them I turned on the shower accidentally and drenched my hair. Of course, there was a hair-drier. I did not feel like sitting under it, so I rubbed my hair damp-dry, then let it hang out to

14

finish off, instead of switching it up as I usually did, which made me look more like Francine's twin than ever, since she was now growing her hair and it was just below shoulder-length.

The telephone rang while I was dressing. It was Charles's secretary to ask if I was safely installed and if my cousin could call in on me for a few minutes when he put his car away. 'At around ten to seven, Miss Newenden. That will suit you? Thank you.'

I was curious as well as pleased by this unexpected civility. Perhaps Charles only wanted to show me that as Francine had left me with a good many very expensive possessions, he would be keeping an eye on them. Yet his polite warning was still a nice gesture. I finished dressing, did my face with much more care than I would have taken for George, and was rather glad I had wet my hair, since it gave me an excuse to keep it down, and from Francine I knew Charles liked his girl-friends to have hair floating round their shoulders. She had also told me he only liked brunettes, which was reasonable, as he was nearly as fair as Francine and myself, but I ignored that. That was not difficult, because I was a night nurse, had had only three hours' sleep since seven o'clock last night, and a very heavy night in Albert. I was now having that vague, and only unpleasant when one has to work, sensation that affects normal people who sleep at night when they stay awake until the small hours. I drifted round the flat in a kind of enchanted haze in which it was quite easy to imagine the flat really did belong to me, and Charles was coming to call because he really wanted to see me.

I was in the kitchen some time later when I heard a car being garaged below. The sound seemed to come from directly under the flat, but in case it was the difficult neighbour I went into the unlighted sitting-room to look down from the front windows. The room light was off, because, despite my haze, turning off lights in unused rooms was a habit that had been ingrained in me first in childhood, then in hospital, where Home Sister was quite as adamant as my mother on the subject of electricity bills.

There were three street lamps in the mews. The nearest was some way off. The neighbouring flats were still in darkness. It was now raining hard, and all I could see of the man who had closed one of the garage doors below before I got to the window was a turned-down hat and raincoat. He looked the right size for Charles, but, remembering the many dates Charles had failed to follow up, I waited. It might be the new neighbour.

Then he rang my front-door bell. I pushed up the window. 'Don't wait in this rain!' I called. 'Come on up.' I closed the window, as the rain was blowing in, and went out to the hall, turning on lights. 'Isn't it a wretched night——' and I gaped. He was not Charles.

The telephone rang. The man on the stairs said, 'I'll wait while you answer that, Miss Newenden.'

Obviously the new neighbour; obviously he did not know Francine well. No one who did ever mistook us for each other at such close quarters. I looked him over covertly as I picked up the receiver, guessing George was calling to say he would be late.

'Cathy, my dear,' said Charles's voice. 'How are you?'

Momentarily I forgot the stranger. 'Fine, thanks, Charles. How's with you?'

'A disappointed man, my sweet. I had planned to skip a very dull business dinner. My secretary says I mustn't. Do forgive me, but I'll be too late back to look in. You know how these things happen!'

I certainly did. 'Sure. Thanks a lot for ringing.'

'Not at all. As this was my idea, I wanted to be sure all was well. I'm afraid you must feel you've been so rushed into all this.'

I was feeling too vague to remember just what Francine had said that morning. 'What was your idea, Charles?'

'Your having her flat, my dear! What else? Didn't Francine tell you?'

'I can't actually remember.'

'You poor dear! Aren't you on night duty? No wonder! When do you go back to work?'

'To-morrow night.'

'That's too bad. I hoped we might have a date. Never mind. I'll be in touch.'

He sounded more sincere than I had ever heard him. That could have been wishful thinking, and had I been alone I would have made myself some strong black coffee and thought it over. But the man on the stairs was waiting.

I said, 'I'm sorry about that—oh, no!' Again, the telephone was ringing.

He said drily, 'After you have dealt with that one, if you would be kind enough to disconnect your receiver for a couple of minutes while you let me have my key, I should be grateful.'

I did not know what he was talking about. 'I'll be as quick as I can,' was all I said.

This time it was George. Matthew was having a crisis, and though he was officially off, being a Matthew houseman, there was no hope of his getting away. I was sorry for him, but glad for myself, as it meant I could have an early night.

16

I replaced the receiver. 'I'm so sorry. What did you say you wanted?'

'My key, please.' His tone struck me as unnecessarily curt. I could not help having those calls. 'I've just called at Mrs Shaw's. She said she left it with you this morning.'

'Not with me, I'm afraid. I think you are mistaking me for my cousin, Francine Newenden. I'm Catherine Newenden. Francine is away and has lent me her flat.'

He came up the remaining stairs. He was taller than I had thought, being nearly George's height. He was much older, thinner, and darker. He looked at me closely, then his expression relaxed slightly. 'Yes, I did take you for the other Miss Newenden. I can now see the difference, though you are quite uncannily alike. Your cousin? You could be sisters.'

I gave my inevitable reply to that inevitable remark. 'Our fathers are identical twins, and we take after them.'

'Interesting.' He was now studying me with almost clinical interest. 'I must apologise.'

His manner, though far from forthcoming, was much more civil. I liked his voice. It was very deep, and he slightly accentuated his r's in a rather attractive way. 'I should apologise too. I thought you were my cousin Charles. That's why I asked you to walk in.'

'I see.' He introduced himself as Andrew Lairg, the new tenant next door right. His name struck a vague chord, but before I could place it he again asked for his key.

'Which key, Mr Lairg?'

'My latchkey. My only latchkey.' He paused, as if expecting some reaction from that. I had none, and was silent. 'Did your cousin not tell you Mrs Shaw left it here?'

I shook my head. 'I'm sorry, but who is Mrs Shaw?'

From his expression he was not sure whether I was being tiresome or plain stupid. 'My cleaning lady.'

I stifled a yawn. 'Excuse me—and she's supposed to have left it here? With Francine? Your only key.'

'That's so. It's my only key—since your cousin lost my spare last Saturday.'

'She did?' I was suddenly much more awake. I knew Francine much too well. 'How was that?'

'Your cousin offered to let in some furniture for me. Mrs Shaw doesn't come on Saturdays, and had mentioned the subject to your cousin. I had to go to work and was grateful. She let in the furniture and locked up after, then unfortunately mislaid the key that evening. As it happened, I was delayed until late evening, there was a party going on here when I returned, so I waited until the morning to collect my spare. It

couldn't be found. Since then, not having had time to get
another pair cut, I've left mine with Mrs Shaw. She arrives in
the mornings before I leave, and as I have to pass her home on
my way back, I've stopped by for it. Apparently this morning
she was called home for some domestic crisis about an hour
after I left, and as she was worried about missing the laundry,
your cousin again offered her help.' He paused briefly. 'Mrs
Shaw said nothing about your cousin's going away.'

'She made up her mind rather suddenly.'

'Indeed? What time did she leave?'

'I'm not sure. I think some time this afternoon.'

'Has she gone far?'

'She's driving up to Manchester and flying to the States to-
morrow.'

His eyebrows shot up. 'On the spur of the moment? How?
One can't fly to the States without a visa, passport, plane ticket.
That all takes time.'

'I know. But she's got all that,' I replied absently, my mind
occupied with thoughts I could not share with a stranger. Francine was no girl to be neighbourly without motive, and she had
a very bitchy streak. She had probably offered to help with that
furniture to get him to her party. If he had refused, or not
turned up, he never had a hope of getting that first key back.
Francine frequently 'lost' other people's property after they had
annoyed her, and she had a fixation about keys. The day after
she walked out of Matilda the linen-room lock had had to be
forced and a new one fitted. I never knew if Sister Matilda had
connected that with Francine. I had—instantly. I remembered
the time she locked Luke in our garden shed after a row with
him when we were children; and the telephone call to our home
one Easter holiday from the hostess with whom Francine had
been staying until she arrived unexpectedly on our doorstep.
She had detested that hostess, and the poor woman had lost her
car keys. They never turned up, nor did the ones for our garden
shed, and Matilda linen-room. I would be very surprised if this
man's keys turned up. But I could not tell him that. She was
my cousin, I was living in her flat, and though I did not like
her, I was fond of her.

I had to make a pretence. I asked him to take off his raincoat
and wait in the sitting-room while I searched.

He wore a dark professional suit. The cut and cloth were
good. I was mildly curious to know what he did for a living.
Only mildly, as the urge to sleep had returned and was making
me more light-headed with every passing minute. I kept stifling
yawns as I opened drawers and looked inside every possible
object.

He asked, 'Late night last night?'

'Yes. All night actually.' I was on the point of explaining I was a night nurse when he said drily, 'I hope it was a good party.'

That annoyed me, and annoyed I always turn dumb. If he wanted to think me a carbon copy of Francine he could go ahead. I was sorry for the inconvenience this was causing him, but it was beginning to irritate me quite as much. Francine, if she could see us now, would consider it a splendid giggle. One of these fine days I would take great pleasure in telling her my opinion of it.

He watched me constantly and in silence. I found both very disconcerting. I had the impression he was aware I was putting on an act and was waiting to see how long I could keep it up. He had a clever face. It was strong-jawed and angular. His eyes were very good. They were that rare very dark blue, and extremely shrewd. He was not a man I would have chosen to annoy, but that would have had the opposite effect on Francine. She enjoyed ruffling people, which was another reason why she had been such a disaster as a nurse.

I said, 'I'll have a look in the kitchen,' and left him to brood over the sitting-room. He had other ideas. He walked into the hall.

I glanced at him covertly as I attacked the kitchen drawers. In another time and place I would have found his appearance interesting and wondered not only about his job, but if he had a wife, and if not, why not. I guessed him somewhere in the late thirties or early forties. Most men of that age were married. From all that Mrs Shaw talk, there did not seem to be a Mrs Lairg around at present, but she might be away, like the American journalists. Not that her presence would have stopped Francine making a pass at her husband, had she been so inclined. Francine had quite a yen for husbands. Yet I could, now I had met him, understand why for once Francine had drawn a blank. Just as one could sense at sight if a man was interested in one, so one could sense the reverse. He did not like our physical type. I did not hold that against him. He was not my type. I merely wished he would stop making me feel like a butterfly on a pin.

I had finished in the kitchen. He said, 'Miss Newenden, shall we now end this farce?'

I did not know what to say to that, so said nothing.

He went on, 'You're not going to find those keys, are you?'

I shrugged. 'I've looked everywhere. I'm sorry.' I had a belated hope. 'I've not looked in that tub outside. I'll get an umbrella. They might be there. That's where Francine left hers.'

'I'll be very surprised if they are.'

I agreed with him. That was another thing I kept to myself. I was back with muddy hand but no keys in a few minutes. 'I'm really sorry about this, Mr Lairg.'

'Frankly,' he said, 'so am I. I've had a long day, and I have a profound dislike of practical jokes. And don't tell me this isn't some kind of joke,' he added impatiently before I could tell him anything, 'or that you have ever had any intention of letting me have my keys. That's been obvious.'

'I haven't hidden them—if that's what you think? Honestly! Why should I?'

'I didn't say you had hidden them, merely that you knew you were not going to find them. As for why—don't ask me!' He picked up his coat. 'I can't interpret such moronic teenage behaviour. I can only presume it amuses your cousin and yourself, possibly because you haven't enough to occupy your minds.'

I was more than annoyed, I was angry. 'I'm not a teenager! I'm twenty-two.'

He was on the stairs. 'Then isn't it time you grew up?'

'Mr Lairg. I've said I'm sorry. You are being most unfair——'

He cut me short. 'If I am I apologise. You must admit that while the loss of one key might have been a genuine mistake, the loss of both is, to say the least, peculiar. As both are lost, I'll have to make the best of it.'

'How?'

'I'll break a window. There's a ladder in my garage. Had you forgotten that?'

'How could I know it was there? I've only just moved in.'

'So you've said.' He was at the front door. 'I'm sorry if this spoils your wee joke.'

'It's not my joke!'

He said slowly, 'You are an even better actress than your cousin, and she was magnificent on Sunday. I congratulate you both.'

'Why do you have to assume I'm acting?'

'My dear young woman, don't keep asking me why. I'm only a physician, not a psychiatrist. Good night.'

I stared at the closed door. Physician. Lairg. I know that name. Why? Something Meg said. When? I reached for the telephone and rang Henry, the senior night Casualty porter. Henry knew everything about every one even dimly connected with Martha's.

'Lairg, Nurse Newenden? Do I know of a Dr Lairg? A Dr Andrew Lairg?' Henry was shocked. 'And didn't he take over from Sir Joshua not ten days ago! And wasn't he our S.M.O.

eight—no, I tell a lie—it'll be nine to ten years back? Always a one for hearts he was, even in them days. Mind you, he was Sir Joshua's Senior Registrar afore that. To think I mind him well when he was a student lad, and here he is back on the staff, a real pundit and all. What makes you ask, Nurse? They're not shifting you to the heart block from Albert?'

'No.' I closed my eyes. 'No. I just thought I knew his name, but couldn't place why.'

'Well, no,' said Henry reasonably, 'you'd not have much call to, would you? Not stuck up in Albert along of all your ortho-paedic lads.'

I heard the sound of glass breaking as I put down the receiver. It was still pouring with rain. And he was a pundit in my own hospital. Dear Francine, I thought, dear, dear Francine! Of course, she knew, but to have told me would have ruined her splendid giggle. Also, though I had never yet allowed myself to admit it to myself, she had never quite forgiven me for surviving a Martha's training. One way and another she had had quite a busy day.

CHAPTER TWO

A QUIET NIGHT IN ALBERT

I SLEPT late next morning. When I left the flat to collect more of my belongings from Martha's a man was fitting a new pane of glass to one of Andrew Lairg's front windows, another man a new lock on the front door. Upstairs there was the hum of a vacuum-cleaner and above it a woman's voice '. . . like as I said to the doctor, if it's not the one thing it's another when you got kiddies.'

In the Night Home Meg was awake and writing letters in bed. She wanted a few days to think over my offer, since, like Bridie, she was unsure living out was worth the trouble. 'I've never minded the all-girls-together atmosphere as much as you, Cathy.'

'It's not the girls I mind, it's the lack of privacy. It's sheer heaven not to feel Home Sister or one of her stooges brooding over my every move. Though it has its little snags.' I told her about last night.

'Cathy! You're joking, of course! Not our Dr Lairg?'

'I suppose it might be another with the same name.' I described my neighbour hopefully. 'Have you seen him? Does it fit?'

'It does. He came in one night last week. Didn't I tell you?'

'Yes. One morning at breakfast. That was why his name rang a bell. Remember? At the time I didn't even know old Josh had retired.'

Sir Joshua Billings had been Senior Consultant Physician to Martha's and head of our cardiac firm for the last twenty years. He had a coronary a few months ago. This had produced an immediate rumour that he was first dying, and then bound to retire. He had then made an excellent recovery, and the rumours had stopped. His department was five blocks from Albert, and his name only came up there when some one used him as another example of the old medical maxim that specialists always suffered from the diseases in which they specialised. I had been very surprised when Meg told me the old man had retired without any fuss and handed over to one of his former Senior Registrars.

Meg said now, 'Josh pulled a few strings to get Lairg back

from Edinburgh. The post was advertised, of course, but, as always, it was fixed behind the scenes. Josh thinks this Lairg a very bright lad.'

'He looks bright, but no lad.'

'He's thirty-eight. The right age for one of our junior pundits.'

'Thank God,' I said, 'he's a junior.'

'But still a pundit.' She looked worried. 'He may not be best pleased by this.'

'He wasn't! Nor was I! Wasn't my fault. And as he's so bright, he should have remembered the dangers of spot diagnosing—or given me a proper chance to explain. He didn't. He was foul! He just assumed I was another debbie Francine type and gave me hell! He said it was time I grew up—and needed something to occupy my mind!'

'Cathy! No! What if you have to work with him?'

I smiled. 'He'll probably have a coronary, and then the back-room boys will have to pull more strings to replace him.'

'My dear, I'm serious!'

'Right—then let's look at it. I was a bit het up last night, but now I've had time to think it over I can't see it'll matter much, if at all. I'll be safe in Albert until I come off for my final month's holiday, and then I'm booked for midder. When have we had a cardiac case in Albert? Or needed any kind of pundit physician at night? He won't come near my block; I certainly won't go near his.'

'But you'll be living side by side in that mews.'

'And how much do London neighbours see of each other unless they want to be neighbourly, which I don't? After last night, and what I can guess of his previous set-to with Francine, I don't see him banging on my door to borrow milk and tea.'

'Perhaps not.' She smiled reluctantly. Meg took hospital life very seriously, which was another reason why she had won her gold medal. 'Still, avoid him as much as possible in the mews, and don't go to and fro in outdoor uniform. That would be asking for trouble.'

'Oh, no! Do you mean that?' She did. 'Hell! Our outdoor uniform may be hideous, but it does guarantee one a seat on the most crowded bus, or being shoved to the head of the longest queue. Think of my poor feet!'

'Think of your poor future. Don't forget he's a pundit, dear. Pundits have Matron's ear, and although the board may think it runs Martha's, as we all know, it's the pundits who tell the board what to do.'

'You're not suggesting he might complain to Matron about last night?'

She said, 'I don't know him well enough to know what he'll do. I do know men can be as petty as women, and sometimes even more so, when they feel their dignity had been upset. One thing, Cathy, for God's sake don't talk about this to anyone else! The grape-vine would adore the story of a pundit being forced to climb a ladder and bust into his own flat in pouring rain. It would get back to him at once, and he would know who to blame. Do take my advice.'

'I will. But it's a pity. It would make such a fab. story, and serve him right for spot diagnosing!'

Meg was always giving me advice, and most of it was good. She was a reserved, clever girl, three years my senior in age and hospital time. We had met for the first time last year on nights in Casualty, and after a slow start had got along very well. She was now one of the three senior staff nurses working as Night Assistant Sisters. Every one tipped her as a future Matron of Martha's. She had the right qualifications—her gold medal, brains, a talent for administration, and a strong anti-men complex. She was a tallish, shapely brunette, with heavy features that could look strikingly attractive when she wore the right clothes and colours, but as she had a poor fashion sense she generally looked lumpy. Her legs were beautiful. They had saddened the Casualty dressers. 'How can a girl with those legs be such a chip off the old ice-block?'

Meg had frozen up before she came to Martha's, and by now would long have got over that broken engagement had she not allowed her immediate reaction to the break to grow into a habit. In her first year she had refused all dates and concentrated only on work. By the time she was half-way through her training she had acquired her present untouchable reputation. Our students cared no more than other young men to be constantly refused, and so left her alone. George said he would sooner have made a pass at Sister Matilda. 'A chap would get some reaction from Sister Matilda, if it were only a straight right to the jaw. Meg Harper just looks through a chap.'

Her manner had put me off, in common with all my colleagues, until I worked with her. She was a very good senior, who always did her own work and was happy to carry her juniors when necessary. I had been warned never to mention men to her, as men, but once we got to know each other she had relaxed sufficiently to talk about her broken engagement, and I had told her all about Charles. She had not met either of my cousins. She had been on nights in the theatre during Francine's three weeks in Matilda, and though I had tried to get her to one of Francine's parties, she had refused flatly.

She asked if there was any significance in Charles's suggesting Francine lent me her flat.

'If it was his.' After my sleep I had remembered that telephone call from Francine in full.

Meg's eyes widened. 'Are they both nuts?'

I laughed. 'Francine's more spoilt than a nut. She had an odd upbringing, shuffling from school to school and nanny to nanny. As for Charles—he's no nut. He just has a knack of always saying the right thing at the right time. He doesn't expect me to believe him.'

She pressed her lips together. 'He could be dangerous.'

'Not Charles! He's a dish—but a harmless dish! I think he's heaven, but I would never take him seriously.'

I thought that would reassure her, but she continued to look put out. 'Then there's hope for the faithful George.'

'George is only faithful from force of habit—as I've told you! I'm his status symbol. Every houseman has to have a bird or die of shame. I do until he finds some one he likes better.'

'You'd hate it if he did!'

Her vehemence surprised me until I remembered she was tired, and fatigue made her crochety where it made me lightheaded. 'I don't think so. I do think it's time I let you sleep. See you to-night—and do join me. Incidentally, it was George who gave me the idea.'

She flushed. 'Why should he do that? He barely knows me?'

'He's seen you around for years. He was very keen on the idea. Think it over.'

I had a quiet day at the flat and slept most of the afternoon. Two ambulances turned into Casualty yard when Bridie and I crossed the road from the Home for our supper. Matthew and Matilda Wards were on accident take-in.

Joan French, the Matilda senior, groaned at our news. 'No! I've got a foul headache. Why were cars invented?'

'Because Henry Ford detested horses,' replied Bridie.

Joan cursed Henry Ford, and the table was silent. The first meal of our night was always quiet, just as our breakfast in the morning was the noisiest meal in the hospital day. After the register Joan walked with me to the orthopaedic block. 'If Sister Matilda pitches into me to-night I'll throw something at her. You are so lucky to have Albert, Cathy.'

Albert had quietened down since the night before last. Sister Albert was having a half-day. She was nothing like as fierce as Sister Matilda, but, as always when a ward sister was off, there was a holiday atmosphere in the ward.

The senior day staff nurse was in charge for the evening. The men should all have been in bed by the time the night staff arrived. She apologised for a third still being up. 'We were so anxious to watch some special boxing-match on television.'

All the bed-patients were listening to the sound broadcast over their wireless head-phones, some sewing, knitting, making baskets and rugs, while tuned in. Their injured limbs were extended in plaster, or strung up in traction splints. There were men in high beds, but most in beds of normal height. Nearly all the beds had fracture boards under their mattresses; three had their foot-rails removed to make room for the extra boards necessary for very tall men. Chalmers and Webb were six foot five; Tiny Ellis, in bed three, the tallest man in the ward, was six foot seven. His right leg was in plaster from above the hip to the ankle. His right femur had been broken in two places, he had had eight below-knee fractures, and lost over one hundred and eighteen square inches of skin when he crashed his father's Citroen. Tiny was twenty-one and training as a chartered accountant. He was the ward expert on football pools.

Albert was only really tidy when Matron or a teaching round was expected, but even then it lacked the a-human perfection of a tidy medical ward. At night it looked what it was—a human repair shop. It was a forest of pulleys, wires, lifting-straps, hitched crutches and sticks, suspended steel pins, buckets of weights, bed-cradles, and plaster. The smell of plaster, of plastic mackintoshes, ether, tobacco, and men, was omnipresent, no matter how many windows were open. Smoking was now officially much frowned on throughout the hospital, but Sister Albert and our consultant, Mr Franks, refused to enforce the non-smoking rule strictly. We were told not to encourage the habit, but if an injured man needed the help of a customary cigarette, then a cigarette he could have.

Sister Albert was in her forties. She had been happily married to one of our pathologists for the last fifteen years, and as they were childless had returned to full-time nursing five years ago. She lived out, mixed with the other sisters only at meals or sisters' meetings, and was considered by us the most normal sister in the hospital. She could be strict, but was always fair and had a strong sense of humour. A ward atmosphere was invariably a reflection of the ward sister's personality. Albert had a very pleasant atmosphere.

Roughly 90 per cent of our men were road-accident victims. Until their injuries the vast majority had been in good health. Once they were over the shock and immediate post-operative period, as they were injured but not ill, their spirits returned to normal long before their bones healed. As most of them were young men, Albert was generally a gay and often downright rowdy ward. I loved it.

26

When I had gone off duty yesterday morning the three men in the beds directly opposite the table had looked moribund. Now all three were listening to the fight, their fists clenching and unclenching, and sometimes stabbing the air unconsciously, as they enacted the commentator's description.

Staff Nurse Jenkins was a gentle, prim girl, given to talking in the third person. The men called her 'Nurse Listen with Mother' behind her back, but were seldom irritated by her 'we's' because they were so grateful for her gentleness.

She looked round smiling. 'We are enjoying ourselves! I hope this excitement won't keep us awake, and that our London boy wins. We are all so certain he will, apart from Tiny. He seems to favour this young American. We can't think why.'

Nurse Player, the night junior, sat facing us across the table during the report. As senior, I sat on the right of the report-giver. Player caught my eye, looked away quickly. I looked at my hands in my lap.

Since night nurses generally knew more about the ward patients than any of the day nurses, we were both certain Tiny was running a book on this fight. Tiny opened a book on anything from which surgeon would be the first to walk in on a given morning to the type of injury of the next patient to occupy an empty bed. 'Rained this afternoon, and now it's a fine night. H'mmm! That'll bring the ton-ups out and off. What'll I give you for a fractured skull? Ten to one? Do you mind, chum! That's odds on.'

It was a strict hospital rule that any form of betting was forbidden in any ward or department of Martha's, and a rule we would have had to enforce, if we knew about it officially. The men were very good about never actually discussing it in front of us, but Player and I knew what was going on at night, as that was our job. As the maximum stake Tiny ever took was two shillings, and as it gave the men a great deal of fun, and kept Tiny's mind off the still-strong possibility of losing his leg, we kept the matter to ourselves. I often wondered if Sister Albert knew. I suspected she did, but like ourselves preferred not to know. I was quite sure Nurse Jenkins did not. The poor girl would have been shocked to death.

Albert had thirty-two beds. The detailed report on every patient took approximately twenty minutes on a quiet night, and could take up to an hour after a heavy day of admissions, transfers, and operations. Nurse Jenkins had reached Duncan Rose in Seventeen when the ward winced and, almost to a man, moved their hands to their right eyes. She was on Professor Brown in Twenty-seven when a concerted groan interrupted her.

27

'Dear me,' said Jenkins sadly, 'I am afraid our boy must be losing.'

The Professor removed his ear-phones, and turned gravely to his right-hand neighbour. 'Poor lad! I was much afraid of this after he had that cut eye in the sixth.'

I glanced over my shoulder. In Four, Tiny was beaming.

When Jenkins left us the television viewers returned in their wheel-chairs and on their crutches and sticks. Kevin and Hubert, both young stevedores, one from Glasgow, the other from Jamaica, were our only patients with arm injuries. They had come in on the same day from the same docks with identical injuries to opposite arms. They were in One and Two. They had not met until they found themselves in Albert, and had become enormous friends, and were very proud of having two good arms between them. They were wonderful at helping us, and after trundling in all the wheel-chairs, and then putting the empty chairs neatly away in their row to the left of the balcony door, they vanished to the kitchen to put on the milk and water for the first round of night drinks, while Player and I got the remaining up-patients to bed.

Duncan Rose was a charge-hand butcher in a pie factory not half a mile from Martha's. He was twenty-eight, and heavily built. He had smashed a knee-cap playing football for his firm. It had been wired yesterday. He had looked quite comfortable as he listened to the fight, but suddenly he was sitting stiffly upright, gripping the sides of his bed.

I went over to him. His eyes were too bright, and his face too taut.

'Poor Mr Rose! Knees can hurt a lot, and I think yours now is.'

'Playing me up a bit,' he muttered. 'It'll go off. I don't want nothing. It'll go off.'

'Yes. But I think you should have something to help you.' I took his pulse. It was the pulse of a man in real pain, and there were beads of sweat appearing on his forehead and upper lip. I looked at the prescription sheet in his bed-ticket. He had an injection in hand. I flicked shut his curtains. 'I'm going to get you something to take it away.'

'No.' He grabbed my arm. 'I don't like taking stuff, Nurse. I'll be all right—oh, dear—oh, dear——' He gripped me now with both hands and leant his head against me. 'Oh—dear—dear—dear——'

I said quietly, 'I know you don't like taking things, my dear, but you really need it.' I dried his face with his towel. 'I'll get Nurse Player, and we'll give you an injection. Can you let go—that's it.' I had to untangle his hands. 'I'll be very quick.'

28

He could not move now. He stared at me with the petrified stare of a human being in great pain. He could no longer waste breath in words. He did not groan, or thrash about; it is the fear of pain that causes those signs. When pain itself takes over the possessed scarcely dares breathe.

I took his bed-ticket, hurried down to the kitchen for Player, unpinning the Dangerous Drug cupboard keys from my bib pocket as I went. She collected the ordered drug, D.D. book, and a small hypodermic tray while I scrubbed up. We checked the script together, and the ampoule label as I assembled the syringe. She came with me to his bedside.

He was sitting as I had left him. Player rolled up one pyjama sleeve, bent his arm and the elbow for him. 'Can you just go limp, Mr Rose?'

When the injection was given she removed the syringe in a kidney dish, and herself. I stayed with Rose, one hand on his shoulder, the other holding his hand. I did not say anything until the pain began to let go and he began to cry.

Some minutes later he moved his head from my shoulder and lay back. I wiped his face with his damp face-flannel. He dropped his arm over his eyes. 'You must think me real soft, Nurse.'

'No, Mr Rose. You didn't cry in pain. This is just reaction, not softness.'

He let his arm fall on the pillow. 'It is?' I nodded. 'It often happens.' 'Was that why'—he jerked his thumb at the drawn curtains—'that why you shut out my mates?'

'I thought you might like a little quiet.'

'That's a fact, Nurse. Ta.' He closed his eyes. 'Ta. Much obliged.'

His pulse was settling after the injection. I left the curtains round him a little longer, then opened them quietly as he had dropped off to sleep. The men in the beds on either side looked at him anxiously, then jerked their thumbs up at each other. 'He'll be right as rain, Nurse,' one muttered, 'after a good kip.'

Professor Brown in Twenty-seven lowered his book. At eighty-two he could still read without glasses. He shook my hand. 'Welcome back, Nurse Newenden. Your substitute last night was a most excellent gel, but, as we all agreed, she was not our Nurse Newenden. Have you had a good rest?'

Momentarily, my mind went back to this time last night. The thought amused me, yet now seemed nothing to do with me. The flat, Charles, that nonsense about the keys, even my neighbour turning out to be a pundit, seemed to concern another girl in another life. Not myself, in this my real life. I said I had had a fine rest. 'And how about you, Professor? Staff Nurse Jenkins

29

told me about your little walking tour round the hospital. Not too tired, I hope?'

He was a retired zoologist, our oldest patient in the ward, in time as well as age. He was a slight, neat Edwardian, with thick white hair, the aquiline face of an old Roman, and old-fashioned manners that enchanted the entire Albert nursing staff. The other men were very fond of him, but they did not call him 'grandad,' as sometimes happened with elderly patients in a mainly youthful ward. They called him 'the old Prof.,' or occasionally, when not thinking, 'sir.' 'A proper old gentleman, the old Prof.,' said the ward. 'One of the real old school. And no side to him neither. Aren't many like him left—and more's the pity.'

He had been a widower since before I was born. He now lived alone in a small country town forty miles from London. He paid monthly visits to the British Museum, and on his last visit had stepped off a pavement on a wet day before he noticed the oncoming lorry. The driver had swerved magnificently, which was why the old man was alive. He had come in very shocked, with three broken ribs, a perforated right lung, and a cracked pelvis. Those injuries would have been serious at any age. At eighty-two they had the Professor on the Dangerously Ill list before he was off his first stretcher trolley.

I had worked two months on days in Albert before taking over at night. On the Professor's first evening George had confided gloomily, 'He's bound to get pneumonia—and probably a lung abscess as well. Then he'll spring a pulmonary, or a coronary—or just a stroke. What else can you expect at his age? And, of course, his kidneys'll play up! You know what these old boys' kidneys are like if you give them half a chance! He won't get away with cracking his pelvis without every bladder complication in the book.'

The Professor had made a swift and uncomplicated recovery. He said he had survived four years as a soldier in one war, six, mainly in London, in another, and refused to be more than inconvenienced by a few broken bones caused by his own care-lessness. He was determined to be sufficiently well by mid-December to satisfy the airline with whom he had already booked that he could be safely flown to Australia to spend his first Christmas for twenty years with his only child, now a grandmother, in Melbourne.

Australia was one of the few countries he had not visited. He was as enthusiastic as a schoolboy about his long-saved-for trip, and loved flying as much as he detested sea-travel. 'I am queasy on a calm day in harbour, my dear. Yet take-offs and touch-downs I enjoy.'

'Doesn't flying frighten you, Professor? It does me.'

He said, 'My child, when you get to my age death has taken so many of your friends that you cease to look on it as anything but another friend waiting to claim your friendship. I trust not too impatiently. There are a great many more things I want to see and do in this world before taking a long look at the next.'

He had never slept well, as he no longer needed much sleep. He enjoyed breaking his nights with cups of tea and little chats. That was when I heard all about his affairs. He lived alone from choice. 'My daughter is always asking me to join her out there. But if I went I should never come back, and I feel I'm a little old to transplant successfully. I enjoy my quiet life—my few friends—and there is so much to be done in my garden. Would you credit this, Nurse? In my half-acre this summer I pulled up four thousand eight hundred and seventy-two bits of bind-weed! Whole place is riddled with the wretched weed. But there's no getting rid of it permanently unless you dig the whole plot over to a depth of twenty feet—a little beyond me now!'

Often, with him, I forgot the sixty years between us. Something in the ward would strike me as funny, and when I caught his eye I knew he was as amused as myself. He did not talk down to us, or the other men. He never pretended to be a day younger than his age, nor did he use his age as a weapon, as some old people I had nursed. It was just a fact that occasionally annoyed and more frequently amused him. He was the first old person I ever met who did not make me feel vaguely guilty at being young in his presence.

Night Sister arrived early for her first round. 'This is the one quiet ward in your block, so I am starting here, Nurse Newenden. How is that man with the knee?'

I told her we had given Duncan Rose that injection. 'Good. Nasty things, knees. Painful. And I do not,' added Night Sister firmly, 'approve of pain. How about the others?'

We went slowly round all the beds. On the way out of the ward she said, 'I am expecting a telephone call—oh!' The night bell on the duty-room telephone was buzzing discreetly. 'That may be Dr Lairg for me. I left word I was starting here. I'll take it, Nurse.'

I waited until I heard her 'Yes, good evening, Dr Lairg. The Night Superintendent speaking——' then closed the door and waited in the corridor as etiquette demanded, feeling irrationally irritated. I wished the man had not intruded into this, my real world. Then I realised it was also his world.

'Why so peeved?' George had walked in.

I jerked my head at the door. 'Just waiting for my boss.' He smiled and went on into the ward. In our men's wards the housemen did not have to be escorted on their rounds; in the women's words they had to have a chaperon only when actually examining a patient. That rule also applied to Registrars (unless one was standing in for the Senior Medical or Surgical Officer), the many itinerant pathologists coming and going from the various laboratories, and all the male students. Our few female students we all welcomed with joy, since they never needed chaperons. There were at present only four women among the seventy-odd residents, and none were on the surgical side. St Martha's, while officially open to women students, had never yet appointed a female house surgeon. Women, said authority, made excellent doctors, but were not, alas, physically strong enough to stand the long hours of theatre work. This was a theory that gave great pleasure to all the theatre sisters and theatre nurses, in more ways than one. The marriage rate in the theatres was higher than in any other department, being around 98 per cent.

Our Night Superintendent ranked as Matron at night. She insisted on being addressed by the old title 'Night Sister,' which made life a little confusing for the patients, as she had two full junior sisters working under her as well as the three senior staff nurses. The junior sisters we talked of as Miss So-and-so officially, and called 'Sister' to their faces. Night Sister held strong views on old traditions being observed, and etiquette. This attitude was shared by Dr Barnes, our S.M.O., but not always by Mr Simmonds, the S.S.O.

The consultants seldom appeared in the wards at night, and when one did it was a bad sign. A D.I.L. patient in the cardiac block must be in a bad way now if our Dr Lairg was in the hospital.

George joined me at the table. We screened this at night, leaving gaps between the screens at each end, so that we could see up and down the ward. As he sat down he knocked the pulled-down overhead light and set it swinging. I caught it. 'Did you see we gave Rose that quarter? Can we have something else in hand?'

'Sure. His ticket here—thanks.' He opened it at the prescription sheet. 'His second night. Will he want anything stronger than codeine?'

'He will. The second night is often worse than the first. There's no lingering anaesthetic to help. He's bound to have more pain at dawn—and Night Sister does not approve of pain —and nor do I. If you ask me, the only people who say pain refines the character are those who have never felt it, or seen it.'

'Come down off that soap-box, Cath.' He wrote obediently. 'This do you?'

It was the houseman's job to do most of the ward writing at night, and the night senior's to remind the houseman what needed to be written, after being briefed by the day report. Later the Registrar checked on the houseman; frequently the S.S.O. checked on both. If anything was overlooked George got it from Joe Briggs, our Registrar, Joe from the S.S.O., and myself from Sister Albert.

I put on my glasses. 'Not much to-night. Mainly Path. Lab. requests and two X-rays.'

'Right.' He glanced up. 'What have you got those on for? Where are the ones with slanting blue rims? I like them.'

'These are my new pair. Don't you like the black? I think they are rather chic.'

He studied me, shook his head. 'Not for you. Too high-powered. They make you look intelligent.'

'Thanks very much.'

'I said something wrong? Sorry. Sorry about last night too. How's the flat?'

'Fine.' I stood up. 'Move over, George. Here's our Mr Briggs.'

Mr Briggs wore a long white coat. George's was short. Some of our Registrars were very conscious of the length of their coats, but not Joe Briggs. He told George not to shift as he would not have time to sit down. He was on Casualty call for the night. 'And Cas. has been calling me every ten minutes since my shift started.'

George had gone by the time Mr Briggs had seen all the men. He checked through the notes while on his feet. 'That's that. Thanks, Nurse.'

'Thank you, Mr Briggs. I hope the rest of your night is quieter.'

'A kindly thought, Nurse Newenden. I wouldn't bet on it.'

The Senior Surgical Officer arrived for his round an hour later. 'Quiet as a morgue. Did you slip them all knock-out drops in their bed-time milk, Nurse Newenden?'

Mr Simmonds was a temperamental man, at times very much the Big Doctor, at others anxious to be one of the lads. He liked women, particularly blondes, and laid an automatic arm along the back of my chair as we sat down. 'Tell me the secret of your technique, dear Nurse.'

We all knew he hoped we thought him the biggest menace in Martha's. In fact, despite his wandering hands, we felt as safe with him for ourselves as we did for our patients in his charge as S.S.O. He was a very competent and unusually kind surgeon. He cared genuinely for the patients as people, and would work tirelessly for them. He never took an unnecessary chance, nor

33

was he in any hurry to reach for his knife. The less experienced students might grumble at the routine dullness of his operations, but every girl who nursed his patients, should she herself need an op., would rather have it performed by our Mr Simmonds than any other general surgeon in Martha's, pundits included. In ninety-nine cases out of the hundred his patients' recoveries were as undramatic as his technique. For that, we were happy to indulge his little ways, especially as they were so harmless. I now simpered coyly to please him, then told him about Rose's pain and asked after Tiny.

He said soberly, 'May be trouble there. Still no below-knee union to any of those fractures, and we're not happy about that skin graft.'

'Do you think his leg may have to come off below the knee eventually, Mr Simmonds?'

He grimaced. 'If he doesn't heal there'll be no alternative. We won't take it off as long as there is a ghost of a chance, and for quite a while after. Mr Franks doesn't like amputating, and nor do I. There's nothing like an amputation for making one feel like a butcher. You look at the amputated limb; you think, by God, I did that—I've crippled a human being.'

'Only because you had to.'

'Yes. The fact remains'—he tapped his chest—'when you have to do it, it was your hand holding the knife that did it.' He looked over his shoulder between a chink in the screen to Tiny's bed. 'Twenty-one, the poor young bastard!' He was silent a few seconds, then he asked, 'And who else is worrying you?'

When he had gone Player said we were going to run short of milk as Hubert and Kevin had used two quarts for their cocoa.

'Two? Did they bathe in it?'

She shrugged. 'Can I try and borrow from Matilda?'

She returned with three quarts and the news that Matilda had just admitted another female 'road.'

From the ward windows overlooking the theatre block we saw the lights go on in the Orthopaedic Theatre. They were still alight when Meg came round at two to collect my first written report for Night Sister. (The second was collected at six.) The girl in Matilda and two men in Matthew had been operated on; the Orthopaedic Theatre had just finished.

I asked if she knew why Andrew Lairg had come in.

'The Mat. Unit had a blue-baby prem.'

'Had?' I asked quickly.

She nodded. 'An hour ago. We moved her into Christian. The new incubators there are wonderful. It wasn't any use. She obviously had an enormous leak. The father was in a terrible state. I must say, Dr Lairg was very good with him and the baby.'

'What about the mother?'

She said slowly, 'It's hard to tell. If anything, she seemed relieved. She's got five others.' She looked round the ward. Player hovered at the far end by the wheel-chairs. 'Would you say Lairg looks all buttoned up?'

I thought this over. 'Very much so. Why?'

'Night Sister was talking about him. Keep this to yourself, as she told us not to spread it, but his wife was killed in a car crash when he was a Registrar. He was on duty at the time. The cops rang the hospital.'

'Meg, no! Any kids?'

'None. They had only been married a year.'

'Oh, God!' I felt faintly sick. Having worked in Casualty, I had seen the faces of husbands who had been given that kind of news. 'The poor man! Was she one of us?'

She shook her head. 'Night Sister said she had some money. She didn't work. She was very fair and very pretty. Night Sister thinks she was about twenty-five when it happened. She was driving some friend. They were both killed.'

'When he was a Registrar? That'll be some time back?'

'Ten years. Night Sister is surprised he hasn't married again. I said perhaps he now prefers being single, having got used to it. Some people,' she added defiantly, 'don't have to have a sex life.'

'He wouldn't have to marry for that. Meg—I wish this hadn't happened, and not for the obvious reason only. It's making me feel so guilty about disliking him.'

She said, 'From the little I've seen of him I'd say he would much rather be disliked than pitied. And you told me you felt he didn't like you.'

'He certainly did not!'

We looked at each other. The same thought must have struck us both, because she voiced it. 'You and Francine may remind him of his wife. He probably hasn't lost the habit of resenting all blondes for being alive after she was dead. Lots of patients' relatives have told me something like that, and, in a much lesser way, from my own experience I can understand it. It's only very recently that I've found I have been able to look at men with my ex-young man's colouring without wincing. I think,' she added, 'that what with one thing and another the less you can see of our Dr Lairg the better. Now, we must stop gossiping and tell me about your men. Night Sister wants me to do her round up here.'

CHAPTER THREE

BREAKFAST WITH GEORGE

THERE was a note from Charles sitting in the flat letter-box. He thought I would like to know his father and Francine were in New York, and he would like me to ring him, if possible this morning. 'I would ring you myself,' he wrote, 'but I might disturb your sleep.'

I was rather touched and very surprised by his thoughtfulness. He was the first non-medical man in my life to appreciate that night nurses actually slept in the daytime. And it was nice of him to tell me my uncle and cousin had landed safely, even if he had never bothered to keep me informed of their movements before. But then I had not been living in that flat before. He probably guessed that knowing Francine I was feeling very insecure about my tenancy, and that it would reassure me to know she was across the Atlantic.

I re-did my hair and face before ringing him. That was the effect he had on a girl. His secretary answered. She had a high, cool voice. 'Mr Newenden is expecting you, Miss Newenden. I'll put you through.'

'Cathy,' said Charles a few seconds later, 'this is very sweet of you. Will you do something for me?'

'If I can.' I was half amused, half disappointed, guessing all he wanted was some errand.

'Dine with me to-morrow night before you go on duty. I gather that's possible, as you are a senior nurse.'

'It is—but how did you know?'

'Darling, I made it my business to know. Will you?'

'Thank you—yes. This is very kind of you, Charles.'

'Darling,' he said again, 'as you must know, kindness is about the last motive any man has for asking a pretty girl to dine with him. What time may I call for you?'

I knew the odds against his keeping that date, but found the fact that he had gone to a certain amount of trouble to make it enchanting, and a little peculiar. It was still very much on my mind when I changed into uniform in my room in the Home that night. Bridie put her head round the door. 'Save my life with a ciga!'

'Not sure I can. Oh—yes.' I found two in an old packet in a

drawer. 'I thought Robert had finished you?'

'Honest to God, girl! It's a close thing!' She swung her legs over the arm of my chair, inhaled deeply, and began to cough. 'You should have heard those poor souls this morning at dawn! Twenty-one advanced carcinomas of the lung all coughing the remains of their lungs up together! Scared the living daylights out of me! I'd to keep reminding myself a third are non-smokers.'

'But when did they give up smoking?'

She waved that aside. 'Don't you start. I've enough hell from Basil Barnes every night.'

'For your own good.' I switched up my hair, pinned on my cap. 'He's cut it right out.'

'Has he not! And to think he was once a fine-tempered S.M.O. with no stomach on him at all and a kind word for all nurses! But there he was in Robert last night trying not to bite his nails, and worrying about his weight, and taking me apart for being a weak-minded female. "The figures for women are going up," he says, "and we'll not be able to do anything for you." So then I asked him the figures for men with fatty degeneration? And is obesity no problem at all? And what about all the anxiety states? And the tranquillisers we hand out to the non-smokers in shovels?' She smiled placidly. 'Was he mad at me!'

'Poor Basil B.! But watch it, Bridie. He might report you to Night Sister for insubordination.'

'He'll do no such thing! He's too busy trying to save me from myself. And what do you think he told me about the new heart pundit? Now, not a word of this to anyone, Cathy——' and she gave me the story of Mrs Lairg's fatal accident. 'Have you seen the man? A dreamboat, no less! No doubt at all he must be still in love with her, and that's why he looks so haunted.'

I opened my mouth to contradict the dreamboat, and haunted, then closed it without a word. The S.M.O. might not know Bridie's tongue. I did. With the best of intentions in the world she was incapable of keeping quiet about anything.

She asked about the flat. 'Has Little Miss Money returned yet?'

'She's in New York. Charles let me know.'

'Charles—? Ah, I have him! Her brother. Is he around?'

She was intrigued by my answer. 'And what does he want, dating you? As if I couldn't guess.'

'Actually,' I said, 'I'm honestly not sure. I would be, if we were not first cousins.'

'What's that got to do with it? Is there a law that says a man can't make a play for his own cousin?'

37

I hesitated. 'No. But Charles is no fool. I'm too close to home. He wouldn't play around that close.'

'Would you be willing, if he was?'

I thought this over, then rather reluctantly had to shake my head. I held up my right hand.

Bridie studied my hand sadly. 'Cathy, you've no conception the beautiful friendships that hand of yours has ruined for me.'

In my second year I fell down the Children's Block stairs and broke two small bones in my right hand. I had that hand in plaster for a month and was put on 'dry sick duty.' That meant I could not get my hands wet, which ruled out ward work. I had spent the whole month chaperoning in the daily ante-natal clinics in our Maternity Unit. After hearing all day, every day, 'But, Doctor, it was only the once!' from often shocked, terrified girls of my own age and much younger, I got the message. If it needed to be underlined, I heard the obstetric registrars equally frequent, 'I'm sorry, my dear, but once is enough, and I'm afraid there is no such thing as a totally safe contraceptive or "safe" period. If there was, most of us here would be out of work.

That month had left its mark on my set as well as myself. The girls said that whenever they found themselves alone with a man about to switch off the lights, as the gloaming was so much nicer, they remembered my right hand, and the lights stayed on.

At supper two other girls swore our whole table to secrecy, then told us about Andrew Lairg's wife. They all seemed to share Bridie's view on him, which I found mildly interesting, since he did nothing for me personally. I kept that and his being my neighbour to myself and was grateful for Meg's advice. The man had set the grape-vine buzzing enough as it was. I had now lost the inclination to add my story, and could not help feeling rather sorry for him. He must hate being a talking-point, particularly in this context. Then I remembered he was a pundit, and so was unlikely to hear this present buzz. Of course, it would reach his pundit colleagues, but they would certainly not pass it back to him for a good laugh, as they might well have done had they heard he had been shinning up a ladder in the rain.

Joan French was absent. She was warded in Nightingale, the sick nurses' ward, with flu. Meg went to Matilda in her place, which pleased her so much that she was still telling me of the joys of having live patients to fuss over instead of office forms when we reached Matilda and I went on alone up to Albert without being able to get in my news about Charles's invitation.

Sister Albert was on duty, and all the men were in bed. There had been no changes made in the ward that day, and the night was as quiet as the previous one. While Player, helped by Kevin and Hubert, did the first drink round I did a long and very sociable round of the men, hearing their day's news, admiring again their many photos of their wives, children, girl-friends, cars, and motor-bikes; helping out with their handiwork, and very much enjoying the rare pleasure of not being in a hurry.

Duncan Rose said his knee was trying to give him gyp, but it was no worse than a toothache. He took the two tablets I offered him without a protest. 'You know your trade, Nurse. Ta.'

Donovan, in Nineteen, was sunk in gloom. I asked, 'Phantom leg playing up, Don?'

'Nah. Foot's tickling. Just wants a good scratch. That's all.'

Kevin hovered with the trolley on which he was collecting the empty cups. 'Would you like me to be away down the Kennington Road with a wee feather to do that for you, laddie?'

The ward was intrigued by Donovan's missing leg. Donovan himself had accepted his injury with great courage. His left leg had been amputated above the knee by his own motor-cycle when he ran into the back of a double-decker bus. His phantom leg had caused him considerable pain at first, as phantom limbs can, but it was now beginning to fade. When he had pain from it it seemed sited closer to his stump. Usually he enjoyed discussing this in detail with ourselves and his fellow-patients. Not now. 'Lay off, Jock,' he mumbled.

Kevin, with the sensitivity of one patient for another, ambled on with an amiable nod. I waited a few moments, then asked, 'Maureen been in to-day, Don?' Despite his surname, he was a born Londoner. 'Cor! Not her! Reckon she's got herself something better to do.'

Maureen was his girl-friend. From the coloured photo on his locker she was a plump, pudding-faced red-head. She was a packer in the same pie factory as Duncan Rose. The day girls told us Maureen was a sex-pot. 'When she walks up the ward on visiting times even the D.I.L.'s reach into their lockers for hair-cream.'

I suggested she might not be well, as there was a lot of flu in our area.

Don looked at me bleakly. 'And a lot of phones, Nurse. Her mum's got one and all. She could have let me know.' He scowled at the ceiling. 'She didn't come in yesterday neither. Can't say as I blame her. Not much cop to her now, am I?' He smiled without humour. 'Can you see Long John Silver doing the twist? Reckon as I'll get my "Dear John" any day now.'

I had not met Maureen, but from the day girls had heard she

had been a very faithful visitor. There was a chance that she might be trying to drop him—unfortunately that happened fairly often to patients who had suffered mutilating injuries like his—but that did not tie up with her regular visits and all he had previously told me about their relationship. 'Maybe her mother's phone is out of order? Have you tried ringing her?'

His face set. 'I'm not pushing meself if she's not keen, Nurse.'

'Don, surely there's no harm in ringing?'

He shrugged and looked at the ward clock. 'After hours now. They shoved the portable along to Matilda this evening.'

'It's back now. I saw it in the duty-room when we came on duty.' I looked at the time. Officially the patients were not allowed to make private calls over the portable telephone after nine at night. 'Night Sister shouldn't be in for another half-hour at the earliest. I'll draw your curtains and then push it up, and you ring her mum. The poor girl may be ill herself. Isn't it worth a try?' I hurried down to the duty-room before he could protest, then pushed the unwieldy portable phone quickly up the ward, plugged it in by his bed, and drew his curtains. 'Have you got enough change? Then get on fast. Night Sister'll kill me if she walks in now.'

A few minutes later he pushed back his side-curtains. He was beaming. Maureen was at home and in bed with a bad sore throat. Yesterday she had lost her voice. 'Cor, you should hear her croak, Nurse! Sounds like she swallowed a load of gravel. Seems she didn't want her mum to ring me yesterday as she was afraid I might think she was real bad and start fretting. Had to fetch in the doctor and all. She'll not be back at work all week, he says, but when she gets up he don't reckon as she ought to visit me here, as she might fetch me her sore throat. Thanks a lot for letting me make that call, Nurse. She said as I was to tell you you're a real doll!' He reached into his locker for his dressing-gown. 'Can I stretch me leg, Nurse? Not had much exercise to-day.'

He did not need the exercise, but he did need to let off steam. I helped him up, handed him his crutches. 'Don't be up too long. Remember Night Sister.'

Albert was very pleased for Don. We had men of all ages, types, and from assorted backgrounds, but within a few hours of being in the ward they all turned into Albert. Albert on occasions spoke with one voice, even if the voice had mingled accents. Albert had been upset by Maureen's non-appearance. Albert now drew a sigh of relief and waited to discuss Don's successful love-life with him in bawdy terms as soon as Player and myself were out of hearing. Albert never uttered the mildest of doubtful remarks in front of us, or ever used any form of bad language. Bridie said she adored nursing men, but found it a constant strain as she always had to watch her own language. 'They'd be so shocked by one small damn. There's no doubt, girls, that to a sick man there's only two kinds of nurses—the sinners and the saints. Will you just tell me now—is my halo straight?'

When I went into the kitchen a little later Don was sitting on the draining-board, balancing himself by propping his good leg on a newspaper across the kitchen table. He was cheerfully drying up the cups Kevin was washing with his one good hand. Hubert was arranging the dried cups on the early-morning tea-trolley, and keeping an eye on his private brew of cocoa.

'Gentlemen,' I said, 'I'm sorry, but your party must break up in five minutes. All right?'

Don grinned, jerked a thumb upward. 'Won't you have some cocoa, Nurse?'

'I'd love some, thanks—but can you imagine what Night Sister would say if she walked in and found me drinking cocoa with the ward main lights still on and the three of you still up!'

'That'll be the day, eh, Nurse!'

I left them to it, knowing they would leave the kitchen, and leave it spotless, directly the five minutes were up. Don was in bed, and Player drew back his curtains as ten finished striking. By half-past half the ward was asleep. An hour later only the Professor was awake.

I offered him a hot drink.

'No, thank you, my dear. I am very comfortable. I shall drop off directly.' He held his watch in my torch-beam. 'Night Sister and the surgeons are very late. Trouble?'

'It's beginning to look like it. I don't know where. I can guess Matthew or Matilda, as they are on take-in.'

The old man sighed. 'Dear, dear! Bound to be more youngsters.'

'At this hour, I'm afraid so.'

He said, 'One doesn't appreciate the true meaning of the road-accident figures until one is in a hospital ward.' He looked up the sleeping ward. 'All these youngsters. So very sad. Yet this is so seldom a sad ward. There is so much laughter, so much courage.' He was silent. Then, 'I have observed that courage is the one light in this ward that never goes out. I have observed that on the darkest nights. It has a lovely light, my dear. I am grateful to have been in a hospital ward again and to have refreshed my memory on that score. This is a good place in which to work.'

'I think so too, Professor.'

41

He fell asleep about twenty minutes later. I walked over to a window overlooking the theatre block. The General and Orthopaedic theatre floors were both working. Player was at my elbow. 'Where is every one, nurse? Not one round yet.'

'By the look—they are all in the theatre.'

'No.' She had turned. 'Here's Mr Martin.'

George came in quickly. He had a mask round his neck, his white coat was limp, his eyes were bloodshot. He said Matilda was a shambles. 'They admitted four girls, just after nine.'

'Girls only? No boy-friends?'

'No. The girls were out together. They are student teachers or something. They live in a hostel. One of them had a car, it was their half-day, so they drove down to the country. They had a front off-side blow-out on the way back in on that clearway just beyond the new flyover down the road from here.' He frowned at me, but as if he was not seeing me. 'The cops say they must have been doing around seventy. Car was airborne. Total write-off.'

I winced. 'How are they?'

'Not dead yet. All on the D.I.L. The two in the back may make it. The other two haven't a flaming hope in hell. God'—he caught his breath—'you should see Matilda now. They've got them in end-beds. And just about every one's there. Fatso [Mr Franks], the S.S.O., Joe Briggs, even Basil Barnes—one of the girls in the back is a diabetic—Meg Harper, another Night Ass. coping with relatives, plus a couple of extra juniors. The lot. And I've got to get back, so let's get things over here.'

I went round with him, then we had to return to the table for the writing. 'Only forms to-night.' I put on my glasses. 'I'll fill in the unessentials later. Ready? Path. Lab., first. Dawson; grouping, white blood count, haemoglobin content. The same for Jennings, Ellis, McKay, Chalmers.' I removed each form once he finished. 'Now, X-rays. Straight for Thomas, Wiseman, the Prof., Donovan. Portable up here—Smith, B.W., Jackson, Sims, Ellis. That's all. No notes. No ops. to-day or admissions.'

'Thanks, Cath.'

I walked with him into the ward corridor. Player sat at the table to listen for our men.

'All their parents in Matilda?'

He nodded. 'And the head of their college and a Home Sister type.' He dug his hands in his pockets and hunched his shoulders. 'God, Cath! Those two up front really caught it. They had safety-belts. They hadn't bothered to put them on.' His voice grated with a mixture of rage and despair. 'The kid in the passenger seat went face first through the windscreen. Sliced it off.'

'George—no!'

'Yep. No eyes—nose—nothing. We've had to shove in a tracheotomy-tube. And half her head's gone. We had to work on it before we could let her parents near her. Looks like a head. Half is dressing.' His voice shook. 'I've done that for a chap before. Not a girl.' He paused. 'Know what I did just before I came in here?'

I shook my head helplessly.

'Picked her father off the ward floor and carried him out to the duty-room. And he hasn't seen what she really looks like.' He paused again. 'I know we've got to keep her alive. I hope to God she doesn't last long.' He turned and walked away. He was twenty-four. From his walk he could have been older than Professor Brown.

I went back to the table. I told Player what he had said. We sat and looked at each other in silence.

Night Sister arrived fifteen minutes later. As she left the S.S.O. walked in. 'I'm doing Mr Briggs's round, Nurse. How are they?'

After his round I asked about the Matilda admissions.

'All four are still alive, Nurse. Only God knows why.'

Night Sister did her own 2 A.M. round. She looked very grave. At six one of the Night Asses. arrived in her place. She told me two of those girls had died. Two mothers and one father had been admitted with shock. The girl with diabetes was expected to recover; the fourth girl had collapsed in the last hour. She was nineteen, the same age as the girls who had died. The diabetic was twenty.

Our breakfast was unusually quiet that morning. Although Martha's was large, as the night staff was so much smaller than the day, sooner or later at night we all heard if something out of the ordinary was going on in one particular ward. What had happened in Matilda was unhappily not all that unusual, apart from one aspect. Those girls had been students; we were student nurses. We knew how they had felt on their half-day yesterday. There had been other half-days when we had piled into some one's car and driven out of town. The 'there but for the grace of God go I' thought was very present at the breakfast tables.

Meg did not come in to the meal. One of her two colleagues told me she had gone straight to bed, and that one of the Matilda empty beds had already been filled by a girl with leg injuries returning from a party in her boy-friend's car. He was in Matthew with four fractured ribs.

George was waiting by one of the stone busts a few yards from the dining-room door. He was not in a white coat. He looked as if he had had no sleep for weeks and would get none now if he went to bed.

He said, 'The S.S.O. has told me to get out for an hour. Want a lift home on the scooter?'

'If you aren't too tired?'

'I'm tired of my own bloody company. Meet you outside in five minutes.'

'Make it ten. I've got to change.'

He was sitting on the scooter in front of the Night Home steps when I got down. He wore a skid-lid, goggles, and leather jacket. He handed me a spare helmet in silence. I put it on over my headscarf.

The lights were all in our favour, and we reached the mews in a few minutes. The scooter bounced over the cobbles to the bright-blue front door. I removed myself. He switched off the fuel, hitched the machine on its stand. 'Repulsive shade of blue!'

It was a gay blue, but a morning when gaiety jarred. I unlocked the door. 'You've lots of time. Come and have some coffee.'

The door on the right opened as I spoke. George, bending over the scooter, said, 'I can use some coffee after that party last night.' He was more upset by those girls than I had ever known him to be. It was not until I saw Andrew Lairg's expression as he glanced from George's back to myself that I remembered there was more than one kind of party.

'Morning, Miss Newenden.' He was now looking at my skid-lid as if surprised it was not a policeman's helmet. 'Good party, I presume.'

He was not asking a question, he was stating a fact.

I let it go, returned his greeting, and went indoors. George followed me in, closed the door, then pushed up his goggles. 'What's he doing here?'

'Lives next door.' I went up to the kitchen, filled the kettle. 'Had breakfast?'

'Not hungry.' He went into the sitting-room to look out of the front window, then came back. 'He lives next door? You know who he is?'

'Yes, Andrew Lairg.' I switched on a hot plate and the grill. 'Francine's sub-let him her other garage.'

'Does he know you're at Martha's?'

'No. Just Francine's cousin and obviously another debbie type.'

He removed his helmet and goggles. 'Hence the dirty look?'

'Yes.' I put bacon on to fry and began cracking eggs. 'Can you eat two or three?'

He said petulantly, 'I've just told you I'm not hungry.'

I ignored that and made it three eggs. Then I toasted six slices of bread.

He took himself round the flat while I cooked. He called from the spare room, 'Why haven't you told him you're a Martha's girl?'

'Long story.' I made the coffee. 'Come and eat.'

He appeared in the kitchen door. 'I wish you'd lay down that bloody lamp, Cath. I don't want any food.'

'Nonsense! You've got to work. You can't do that on an empty stomach. Sit down.'

'I wish to God you'd stop bullying me,' he grumbled, but sat at the place I had laid on the table. 'That's the worst of nurses. They will push a chap around.'

I let that one go too. He had to hit some one after last night, and it might as well be me.

The coffee was too strong, the bacon not crisp enough, the eggs were underdone.

I offered him the toast. 'No doubt you'll break your teeth on it, but try it.'

He scowled. 'You don't have to humour me.'

'Oh, yes, I do. You're bigger than I am. In your present mood if I don't you'll probably clout me.'

He stared, then smiled reluctantly. 'Am I being that haema-dementic?'

'Plus, plus. It's mostly lack of blood sugar.'

He pushed aside his empty plate. 'It isn't, and you know it.' I said nothing. 'I can't get that girl with the face——' He shuddered, suddenly leapt up and shot out to the bathroom. He was away some time. He looked very pale when he returned. 'Sorry. Wasted that food.'

'Just as well you had it to bring up.' I had made tea. 'Have this. It's less sickly than coffee.'

'Thanks.' Though very pale, he was now feeling much better and at last able to talk about the girl without a face. 'Know something, Cath? I had never believed in euthanasia until last night. I would have given her the works, had it been up to me. Instead we had to shove in that trachy-tube—we borrowed a tent from the medical side—we wasted hours when every one knew we hadn't a hope in hell of doing any good.' He helped himself to half the sugar-basin. 'I asked David Simmonds why.'

'George! That must have fixed things!'

'It did.' He smiled wryly. 'He asked me who I thought he was, God, or just a bloody surgeon? Then he asked how many patients I thought would come into Martha's or any other hospital if they thought surgeons were going to turn into murderers

45

when they thought fit? He said if I had homicidal tendencies I had better get the hell out of medicine, but fast! And that it was too bad I had been born too late and in the wrong country, as the Nazis could have found a good job for me in one of their extermination camps. He really gave it to me, Cath. Shook me. I never thought David Simmonds had such strong views on the subject.'

'I've heard him on it. I'm sure he's right, if not about you. I'm all for stopping pain, but no more than that. Even when some one looks obviously booked they can recover. You must have seen the apparently incurable cured. I have. Dozens of times.'

'That's what your pal Meg Harper said.'

'Did the S.S.O. take you apart in front of her?' I was surprised, as this was unusual for Mr Simmonds.

'No.' He coloured. 'I was rather shaken afterwards. She gave me some tea, and I sort of had to talk so told her about it. She was—rather nice.'

'She is—underneath. As I've told you.'

'Yes.' He was silent for a while, then he asked, 'Who turned her into an icicle? You never told me that. One of our chaps?'

'Some man she was engaged to before she came to us.'

'What happened?'

'I don't know all the details.' That was true. Meg had never told me her ex-fiancé's name. 'It broke up.'

He gave me an oddly thoughtful glance. It was odd, as he was not normally a thoughtful person. But last night had jolted him badly, and though he was now looking better there was something different about him. It was as if he had suddenly grown up. I had seen that happen over-night to other men, and girls, in hospital.

When he next spoke it was about Andrew Lairg. Hugh Devine, the junior cardiac houseman and his greatest friend, had told him of Mrs Lairg's death. 'Don't pass this on, Cath. Basil B. only briefed the cardiac chaps so that they wouldn't put their foot in it with Lairg.'

'I won't. But it's all round Martha's already.'

He shrugged. 'Trust the grape-vine.' He looked in the direction of Andrew's flat. 'Bit of a turn-up for the book, his living next door. You see much of him?'

'No.' The thought of Hugh Devine prevented my enlarging on that.

'Probably just as well. Hugh says he seems a quiet sort of chap and quite decent for a pundit. But you never can tell with pundits. Most of them are bastards under the skin. They have to be, or they wouldn't have got to be pundits. The rat race is a kid's romp compared to what goes on behind the scenes for a top job at Martha's. Lairg's done all right, getting back over so many heads.'

'He couldn't just have done it by his brains?'

'Brains help, but a man needs more to make him a pundit. Think of the competition. A man,' said George, 'needs brains, a one-track mind, a strong streak of the bastard, and a hell of a lot of luck.'

'What about his wife?'

'Hell, Cath, no one gets it all ways.' He smiled not unkindly. 'Not even pundits.'

CHAPTER FOUR

NURSES LOOK IDENTICAL AT NIGHT

UNTIL the moment Charles arrived I more than half expected he would cancel our date.

'Cathy, my dear,' he said as I opened the front door, 'you look more enchanting than ever.'

I found that delightful even though he could not see me properly, as I had my back to the light. He had a taxi waiting. 'My way of avoiding the evening parking problem.'

When Francine avoided any problem I thought her irresponsible. When Charles did the same I thought it showed his good sense.

He was not quite so fair as Francine and myself, his features were less regular, and his eyes were brown. He was tall, slim rather than thin. He could afford an excellent tailor, and had one. He was far and away the most elegant man I had ever seen, much less been dated by. But although he had so many obvious attractions, the one that loomed above all others was his attitude to women. He gave any girl in his company his whole attention, treated her as if she was ultra feminine and desirable and there was nothing on earth he would rather do than be with her. That dinner was as good as, if not better than, the little dinners with him I had thought up in my day-dreams. Yet the very expensive restaurant, the hovering waiters, the superb food, and his being so nice to me were so like my day-dreams that I kept having the notion that I had been through it all before.

I had forgotten my watch and had to have it on duty. We went back to the flat for it before returning to the hospital. As Charles held open the door of the waiting taxi for me Andrew Lairg drove up.

'We're just leaving,' called Charles.

Andrew stuck his head out of his window. 'It's all right, thanks. I don't want my garage. I'm going out again.'

When we drove off Charles asked, 'How are you making out with him? Well, I should imagine. Isn't he a doctor?'

'Yes. He doesn't know I'm a nurse.' I explained why not, in detail. I thought he might be amused. He was not.

'There are times when my spoilt brat of a sister should be spanked! Of course she took his keys! She told me he had

48

refused her invitation to her party. I am sorry we let you in for this, my sweet.'

'It wasn't your fault.'

'It was. I told you, I suggested she lent you the flat. Don't you remember? Or did my precious sister tell you it was her idea?'

'Actually—yes.'

'Darling, you know Francine. Once she likes an idea, she promptly persuades herself and anyone handy that it was hers.'

That was true. And as this seemed a moment for truth, I asked why he had thought of me.

He said slowly, 'I thought it was time you and I got to know each other. You don't mind?'

'No.' My heart was suddenly making such an absurd noise I thought he must hear it. 'I'm glad. It's a lovely flat.'

He kissed my hand. 'You are very sweet.'

He did not touch me again that evening. I found that far more disconcerting than a passionate embrace, which would have been the least a good many men would have expected after the kind of dinner he had just given me.

My hands were still shaking when I changed into uniform. I reminded myself of all I had said to Meg and Bridie; of his legion of brunette girl-friends; of all Francine had told me of the difficulty he had keeping gold-diggers out of his hair, and how bored he was at never having met any woman who knew how to say no to him. Had he been bored to-night? He had not mentioned another date. He had just been so damned nice, as if he really did want to get to know me better. That was soothing in one way, but quite the reverse in another. I sailed over to the hospital a good two feet above the ground.

Night nurses with permission to skip supper had to be in the dining-room in uniform when the register was called. Night Sister opened the book as I arrived. I answered my name, then noticed absently that Meg was missing, Joan French still the only absent senior, but there were three empty places at the junior tables.

After the register Night Sister read out the list of nightly changes. Player was having nights off. Mary Eccles, her usual relief, was on as Albert junior, which would please Tiny. Mary was a very tall, very slim girl, two sets senior to Player. She had near-black hair, huge brown eyes, a very white skin, and was without question the best-looking nurse in Martha's. We had scores of pretty girls. Mary Eccles was beautiful. And what was more important from my angle, she was an excellent junior.

Night Sister's voice droned on. 'Nurse Sullivan to the Office, please. Nurse Davids to Robert Ward.'

49

I glanced at Bridie, mouthed, 'Where's Meg?'

'Flu.' She fingered an imaginary lace bow beneath her chin. 'Call me Sister.'

I could not call her anything, as Night Sister was looking at me. 'Nurse Newenden, Sister Albert has asked for an extra junior for to-night. I will do my best to help you, but as I am short of juniors, until I hear the full hospital report I cannot tell whom I can spare.'

'Thank you, Sister.' I looked across the room to Mary Eccles. She seemed as surprised as I felt. She came over directly after grace.

'What's going on in Albert, Nurse Newenden? I thought we were quiet.'

'So did I.' I turned to Bridie. 'Do you know why we want an extra?'

'I do not. I had no idea at all they were promoting me, though I knew Meg Harper was running a temp. and moved into Nightingale this evening. Nightingale now has eleven day girls and five night warded with this flu. A plague, no less.' She waited until Mary moved back to her own set, then added, 'Guess who I happened to meet in the park on my way over?'

'Not Basil B.?'

'Himself.' She grinned. 'To be honest, he was not hiding behind a bench for me. He'd been over to talk to Home Sister about Joan French. The poor girl's not at all well.'

'I'm sorry about that. More than flu?'

'Pneumonia. And she's not the only one. Tom Orme's another. So poor Basil can't be away for his free week-end seeing that his S.M.R. [Senior Medical Registrar] is on the S.I.L. in Jenner.'

'Tom Orme? From this flu? It must be an ugly bug.'

'It is. But I'm not sure that's the only reason. Do you know what Tom Orme has been doing? Walking round with one hundred and one and giving himself a full dose of aureomycin, because he didn't want to report sick, as it should be his week-end on as acting-S.M.O.! And the man's a physician!'

'Trust a physician to play the fool with his own health! Are many of the boys sick?'

'Seven residents so far. Five are physicians.'

Mary Eccles caught me up on the orthopaedic stairs. She did not talk, but her silence was not unfriendly. She was a naturally quiet girl, and we often worked whole nights without exchanging more than a few words. I found this rather restful, and so did the men, with the possible exception of Tiny, who was at present in love with her. Last month he had been badly smitten by one of the day girls, another good-looking brunette. Despite

Mary's lovely face, she did not have the rest of the ward sitting up and panting as Don's Maureen was reputed to do. This had at first surprised me, but when I mentioned it to George he said it made sense to him, as Mary was so staggeringly attractive that he personally would never dare make a pass at her, or ask her for a date. 'She must have queues to choose from. I don't dig queues. And when I take a girl out I don't want to have to wear knuckle-dusters to keep off the wolves.'

We were on the last flight up to Albert before I broke our silence. 'Obviously we've some one who needs a special. There was no one ill when I left this morning. Weren't you in Matthew last night? Was there any talk of Matthew overflowing into Albert?'

'No. But that might have happened to-day.'

'Or be one of our tenth days springing something.'

She asked, 'Who are on their tenth?'

'Let's see—Chalmers, Dawson, Sims. Could be any of them——' I opened the outer door to Albert. 'It's quiet. Much too quiet.'

She looked up the corridor into the strangely still ward. 'It could be a medical ward.'

She was right. The whole atmosphere of Albert had altered. The quiet was tense and very unnatural. We left our spare clean aprons with our cloaks in the changing-room, and walked on into the ward. Instead of the usual smiles and 'Here they come —our night nurses!' the men nodded at us unsmilingly, like polite strangers. The sight of Mary made Tiny brighten momentarily, then he looked at the curtains drawn round Twenty-four.

The bed stood directly opposite Sister's table and was generally occupied by the patient needing closest observation. Dick Yates, who at eighteen was our youngest patient and had come in last Monday, had been in Twenty-four when I left that morning. He was now in Twenty-seven. His face was subdued. I took a quick look round, since we frequently had general posts to fit in emergency beds. Only thirty-one beds were visible, thirty-one subdued faces. Professor Brown was missing, but as he had been doing so well he had probably been transferred. Then we saw his bed-ticket lying across the open report book on the table. A scarlet D.I.L. label was clipped to the ticket.

There was the whispering hiss of oxygen from behind the curtains, and then Sister Albert's voice, 'Another little injection, dear. It won't hurt. Now.'

Mary and I looked at each other. Then I moved the bed-ticket, and we read the entry against the Professor's name in the report. He had had a coronary after tea. I was used to shocks on duty, but that one had me very close to tears. I did not hear

Mary's murmured question until she touched my arm and pointed to a name in the report. 'Who's this Dr Lairg?'

I blinked, and took a grip. 'The new heart pundit.'

'Where's Sir Joshua?'

'Retired.' I replaced the ticket, as we could hear Sister returning.

She apologised for delaying us, unrolled and buttoned her sleeves, and put on her cuffs before taking her seat. 'Sit down, Nurses. Just the two of you?'

I told her what Night Sister has said.

'I hope you get help,' said Sister Albert, 'as otherwise you will have to manage the ward alone, Nurse Newenden. Nurse Eccles must special Professor Brown. I will report on him first, as my day nurse is waiting to be relieved.'

The news of the Professor's changed condition had been cabled to his daughter in Melbourne. Sister said, 'I wish Mrs Gunning lived in this country. She should be here to-night. He has been very confused and asking for her.' She looked at the curtains. 'He is a very tired old man to-night. He should have some one of his own with him, but as we know, he has no other relatives in this country. We must try and fill that gap as best we can. Don't leave him at all, Nurse Eccles. If you require anything call Nurse Newenden.'

When she dismissed Mary she added, 'One thing I must tell you, Nurse Newenden—expect Dr Lairg in later.'

'Dr Lairg, Sister?' I echoed sharply.

Not unreasonably, she misunderstood my reaction. 'That is the name, Nurse. Were you not aware Dr Lairg has taken over from Sir Joshua? Well, he is being his own Registrar for to-night, Dr Norton being unwell. Dr Lairg has at present gone home to pack a bag, but will be back in the hospital by ten. So you can expect him to do his own Registrar's night round.'

I felt weak. 'Isn't that unusual, Sister?'

'A little. Not all consultants are willing to return to night work. Mr Franks has done this once or twice. Now—on with the others.'

At last she closed the book, flicked down the neatly folded corners of her apron skirt. 'I will have another look at the Professor before I go.'

He had been heavily sedated and was now asleep, propped in a sitting position by his pillows and the bed-rest. His white head was tilted sideways, his profile hidden by the oxygen-mask. He did not stir when his pulse and blood-pressure were checked. He was barely breathing. The little green rubber bag attached to his mask fluttered as if it held a trapped butterfly. Watching him, my throat was tight. He seemed to have shrunk. His hands were thin as paper. He looked utterly exhausted, and very, very old.

Sister looked down at him, her face sad, yet resigned. She patted one of his hands gently, then moved away. I followed to escort her from her ward, a strict point of Martha's etiquette. She said nothing until we were in the small corridor.

'It's a wonder this hasn't happened before.' She looked back into the ward. 'There are many worse ways of dying.'

She was right, but I was not yet ready to reconcile myself to what from her manner she obviously considered inevitable. 'You think this time he won't be able to get over it, Sister?'

She said frankly, 'My dear, I'd be only too delighted, but he is now a very ill and very old man. He has been very strong, but he is barely over his accident, and has so recently had to make such withdrawals on his reserves of mental and physical strength that the store must be very low. After constant withdrawals everything runs out, including the will to live. His attack was very severe. I thought it was going to kill him. Dr Lairg considered it one of the most severe in even his experience. I must admit,' she added reflectively, 'that while I have every confidence in Dr Norton, I was relieved to have his consultant present. The young men are always so anxious to rush in and use all our fine new machines. I agree with Dr Lairg. The heart-rest machine has its great uses, but in my view, it would have been most unkind as well as unnecessary—as Dr Lairg put it—to use the machine on Professor Brown.'

I did not agree. I would have been willing to do anything to keep my old friend alive. He so enjoyed life. He was not yet ready to slip out gently, as they all seemed to assume. But I could not say that to my ward sister, particularly when her views had the backing of a pundit. So, as always to a senior in those circumstances, I said, 'Yes, Sister. I see, Sister.'

When I returned to the ward alone Kevin and Hubert were out of bed and helping each other into dressing-gowns. 'You leave the drinks to us, Nurse. And if you are wanting a wee hand lifting the lads,' said Kevin, 'we'd like it fine for you to give us a shout.'

'Man, that is so right.' Hubert's lilting West Indian voice was soft as a song. 'Is the old Prof. real sick, Nurse?'

'Not very well. But sleeping.'

They had been in hospital long enough to translate that as very ill indeed, without its being underlined by Mary's presence behind those curtains. They shook their heads and removed themselves quietly to the kitchen. Tiny beckoned me. 'Can I have Nurse Eccles to sit and hold my hand the night the pearly gates open for me?'

I forced a smile. 'As I hope you'll be around ninety at the

53

time, you had better take that up with your future wife. How's the leg?'

'It's O.K., thanks.' He caught my apron skirt. 'The old boy's pretty bad, isn't he, Nursie? Why couldn't he have had his trip first? It's so hellish unfair. And don't tell me these things happen,' he added impatiently, 'as I know they do. What I want to know is—why?'

'Tiny,' I said quietly, 'I'm just a nurse, remember?'

'But don't you ever wonder why?' he demanded.

I looked down at his belligerent face. He seemed much younger than the year between our ages. 'Obviously. Even nurses are human.'

'Then how can you bear to be a nurse?'

'Sometimes, Tiny, I've wondered that myself. Now, let me look at your leg.'

There was a window cut in the lower part of his leg plaster round the area of his skin graft. The dressing was going to need changing. I promised to come back to him directly I had the other men settled.

The others were as upset about the Professor, as disturbed as Tiny, but, being mostly older, rationalised their impatience with fate as irritation with their own helplessness. 'Wish they'd get a move on and give me a tin leg,' grumbled Don. 'Then I could give you a bit of proper help. I got two good hands and all.'

Sims, in Twelve, was always slipping down his bed. He was only five foot seven in height, but weighed fifteen stone. 'You best leave me where I am for the night, duck. You'll do yourself a mischief if you tries to shift me alone. I'll manage.'

'Not in that uncomfortable position, you won't. I can get you up.' I removed his pillows, then pulled his bed away from the wall, got behind the head, climbed on the foot-rail, leant over, grasping with both hands the top of his long under mackintosh. 'Hang on to your lifting-straps. Ready. Up—now.' I leant back, using my whole body's weight as a lever and taking all the strain on my back muscles. His mattress shot up the bed.

Sims was torn between admiration and the conviction that I must have given myself a hernia. 'Slip of a girl like you shifting me, duck. It's not right. And how's the old boy?' he added in a stage whisper. 'Packing it in, is he? Shame! And him dead keen on going on his holidays. Here—duck—you give him some of me chocs. I got lots more, and I've seen as he's like my old dad with a sweet. A rare one for a sweet is my old dad. Bad as a nipper. You take this lot over to the old Prof. and tell him Simmy says to keep his chin up.'

The Professor was too far under for me to tell him anything when I left the chocolates with Mary. She showed me his quarter-hourly pulse and blood-pressure chart. 'No change,' she murmured uneasily.

'No.' I took his pulse, stood watching him, then glanced round instinctively. She offered me the chart again. I shook my head. She was a good junior, but not yet sufficiently experienced to understand my movement. Generally one was in one's third or even fourth year before one learnt to recognise the presence of death. Not death in the dying, but the shadow of death on a patient's face, lying across a bed, standing by a patient, or, occasionally, waiting in a ward doorway. I had seen the shadow too often to dismiss it as imagination; I could not have described it; I could recognise it, just as I could recognise what certain little restless movements invariably meant. The old man was barely breathing; his pulse was nearly untakable. It could be said he was as still as death, but I found his stillness reassuring. I saw nothing round his bed, and the look in his face was only—to me—the look of sheer exhaustion.

I seemed to be in a minority of one. George walked in while I was still settling the men. 'I haven't come for my round yet, Nurse Newenden.' He waited in the middle of the ward, and when I joined him warned me to expect a visit from a pundit.

'Sister warned me our Dr Lairg'd be in. I can't say I'm looking forward to it—except for the Prof.'s sake. But, thanks.'

'Not talking about him. Fatso.'

'Oh, God! Not him as well!'

'Why not? This is Fatso's ward. He's very low about the old boy. Wants to pay his last respects and so forth.'

'George,' I snapped under my breath, 'he's not dead yet! People can get over coronaries.'

'Be your age, Cath, and remember his,' he reminded me not unkindly. 'It's a tough break, but he has had a good innings.'

One of the pathologists on call arrived ten minutes later, disappeared behind the curtains. On his way out he stopped in the open doorway of the sterilising-room. I was setting a dressing-trolley for Tiny's leg. He had taken a sample of the Professor's blood for another clotting-time check. 'I'll ring down the result, and unless I hear to the contrary be back in an hour for the next. I doubt it'll have more than academic value.'

I closed the lid of the instrument steriliser with a slap. 'How do you think he looks, Doctor?'

'Booked, I'm afraid,' he said and walked on. 'Booked' was Martha's jargon for moribund.

Mr Franks arrived with the S.S.O. as I was finishing Tiny's dressing. 'Don't let us disturb you, Nurse. Carry on. Carry on.'

After looking at the Professor the S.S.O. took him round the other men. They stopped with Tiny, talking football pools as I drew back his curtains. 'Can't follow those permutations,' said Mr Franks. 'They tell me you are the expert, lad. You must give me some tips. And how's the leg now? Better after the dressing. Going to have something for it to-night? That's right. Nothing like a good sleep.' He tapped Tiny's head. 'You'll do, lad. You've got the right stuff up here. Sleep well.'

Fatso was a large, stout man with an enormous laugh and gentle voice. In the corridor he faced the S.S.O. and myself. 'Bad business about the old man. Should have enjoyed seeing him walk out of here. Still—can't expect miracles. Well, David —whom do you want to show me next? Night, Nurse. Thank you.'

They had just gone when Night Sister telephoned. 'Is Mr Franks still with you? And how is Professor Brown? I see. And your ward? Managing all right? I am afraid I have no spare junior yet. Fortunately Albert is not busy—apart from the Professor.'

I had not stopped running since I took over. 'No, Sister. Thank you, Sister.'

'Nurse!' called Tiny's voice. 'You're wanted!'

Mary wanted another oxygen cylinder. 'When you've time. No hurry. This one has just started its last third.'

In our medical blocks, in the theatres, and their attached recovery-rooms, oxygen was laid on in pipelines. In the surgical wards we still used individual cylinders, since surgical patients in general seldom required continuous oxygen for the same length of time as medical patients.

'I'll get one now.'

I pushed an empty wheeled cylinder-stand from the sterilising-room into the little corridor. The spare full cylinders stood in a permanent stand against the wall opposite the fire-buckets, like a row of penguin sentries with thin green collars. There was a creak of bed-springs and lifting-straps, as the men awake in the beds by the door sat forward to watch.

The first of the broad wing-nuts holding the metal stand-bands in place came off easily. The second refused to move, even when I used a spanner.

'Must be jammed against the thread,' Tiny hissed. 'Clock it one, Nursie.'

I did not want to do that as it would wake the rest of the ward. 'I'll try again, Tiny.'

'Let me have a go, Nurse,' said a quiet voice at my elbow. 'May I have the spanner, please?'

'Thanks.' It was only as I handed it over that I realised whom I was speaking to. I stood back watching my next-door neighbour, now disguised in a Registrar's white coat over smooth pundit's suiting, with very real apprehension. This moment might have seemed funny beforehand, or perhaps in retrospect. Not now.

He removed the nut, shifted and fixed the cylinder into the stand. 'Good evening, Nurse. I'm Dr Lairg. I expect Sister Albert told you I am doing Dr Norton's work to-night and would be in to see Professor Brown?'

My jaw dropped behind the mask I had put on for Tiny's dressing and since forgotten, even when with Fatso. That would have given Night Sister a stroke, as wearing masks while escorting pundits was one of the many things she considered shameful etiquette. Luckily Fatso was far too sensible and easy-going to bother over that detail, and knew that wearing a mask was second nature to anyone working in Albert. And, my mask apart, my hair was now up under my cap, instead of floating round my shoulders as on the occasions when Andrew Lairg had seen me without a headscarf—and he was not expecting to see me. One fourth-year nurse in uniform looks very like another, particularly in the night lights. I thanked the guardian angel of all night nurses, and breathed out, 'Yes, Dr Lairg. Good evening.'

'This oxygen for the Professor? Is the special nurse with him?' He tilted the stand on its back wheels. 'Any urgency for this?'

I explained the position.

'And how is he?'

I gave the latest details, added Mr Franks had been in and that we had not yet had the latest clotting-time from the Path. Lab.

He had seen Fatso. 'His condition has not changed since you came on duty?' He looked at and through me as he spoke. I found that reassuringly correct. Every doctor had to acquire that technique of looking through nurses. Bridie swore they practised with mirrors.

'No, Doctor.'

'Good.' He smiled. I had not seen him smile before. It took about ten years off his age and transformed his face. It was such an incredibly gay smile. 'If he's not worse he has to be better. Good.' He gave me a brief but friendly nod. 'I'll take this along to him. I expect you're busy, Nurse.' He moved into the ward, pushing the cylinder.

'Nursie—here——' whispered Tiny. Beside him Hubert and Kevin raised their heads. 'Who's that gone to see the Prof? Isn't that the heart specialist Sister called in this afternoon?' I nodded. 'Then why is he wearing a white coat? And what's he doing shoving oxygen round? Doesn't he know his union rules?'

'Don't ask me.' The telephone was ringing. 'I must answer that. Try and sleep, there's a good boy.'

It was the pathologist with the clotting-time. I made a note, took it behind the curtains, and handed it to Mary. Our pundit had his back to me and was listening to the Professor's heart. The old man slept on undisturbed.

At midnight Bridie took over Albert for an hour while I stayed with the Professor during Mary's meal, then went down for my own. The Professor woke briefly when I was there, mistook me for his daughter, then his wife who had died a quarter of a century ago, before sliding back into a sleep that was very close to coma.

A shadow fell over the bed as I was making another blood-pressure check. I glanced round, still wearing my stethoscope. Andrew Lairg had returned with the S.M.O. Dr Barnes nodded at me. Andrew Lairg held out his hand for the chart. They studied it together, then looked at the old man in silence.

Dr Barnes said, 'He's hanging on, sir.'

Andrew said very softly, 'He's got a good heart. It's too early to say how much damage he's done to his myocardium, but he's got a very good heart. You listen.'

I unbuttoned the Professor's pyjama jacket. The S.M.O. bent over him, then straightened, and removed his stethoscope thoughtfully.

'Well?' asked Dr Lairg.

The S.M.O. looked long at the Professor before turning to his colleague, and nodding agreement. They did not exchange another word, or express any opinion to me, neither of which surprised me. Good physicians seldom said or did very much at a patient's bedside. They merely stood around and watched. Yet when one was used to physicians one could learn how to interpret from their particular silence what was going on in their minds. I had not seen Andrew Lairg in a ward in what—for a physician—was action before, but the S.M.O. I knew well. I could see now Dr Barnes was puzzled, but pleasantly puzzled.

Dr Lairg suddenly turned to me. 'Are you the regular night senior here, Nurse? You've nursed him since his admission? Then how do you find him now?'

His questions were not as odd as they might have seemed to anyone unused to Sir Joshua's methods. Old Josh had always asked the ward nurses for their opinions on their—and his—patients. He was the only pundit I had worked for, or heard of, to do that. Andrew Lairg was one of his old boys. I answered as I would have done his predecessor. 'More ill than I've seen him previously, Doctor, but'—I hesitated, then stuck my neck out—'he looks to me as if he can get over this.'

'From his pulse?'

I had to be honest. 'No, Doctor. Just his look.'

The two men exchanged another glance. 'Thank you, Nurse.' They took themselves off.

When I returned from my meal Bridie was breathless. 'I thought Albert was meant to be light! Do your boys never sleep? I've not been off my feet once!'

The quiet of the small hours settled over the hospital. The lights went out in the theatre block. The night rounds were over. Only an occasional white-coated figure went by the lighted windows of the tiered corridors connecting the blocks.

In Albert the quiet was uneasy. The men were unusually restless, and there was always some one awake watching the comings and goings of the pathologist. He grew wearier at each visit. 'Wish I had the old boy's strength. This is killing me.'

Between 1 and 4 A.M. every man but the Professor woke and needed attention. At half-past two from the balcony end I saw Andrew Lairg leaving the Professor's curtains. Mary told me he had gone to bed. 'He wants to be rung if necessary.'

Twenty minutes later she beckoned me urgently. 'I can't get his pulse at all. But he's still breathing.'

I had my hand on the old man's wrist when the beat picked up again. The rhythm had altered. Mary, beside me, murmured, 'Will you ring Dr Lairg?'

'Not yet.' I touched the Professor's forehead. It was cold, but no colder than it had been all night. I turned the oxygen higher, added two more blankets to the pile already over him. 'We'll wait a little longer. I think he's settling again.'

After that I went back to look at the old man every ten minutes. I was actually taking his pulse when his heart seemed to stop for the second time, but again it picked up.

At five even the pathologist was growing hopeful. 'If his heart is fighting its last battle it's fighting a bloody good fight. It must be tough as leather.'

I leant against the corridor wall. 'I wish we had used the heart-rest machine.'

'That would have finished him, if we had,' he retorted, and produced a stream of pathological reasons to explain why. 'Lairg said it wouldn't do for the old boy, and that his heart would probably manage best alone. Looks as if he's going to be right. Oh, well—back to the old drawing-board. I'll ring down the result.'

The November dawn was late that morning and the men drinking tea when the first grey light crept in through the ward windows. Our extra junior had at last arrived and was attending to the early routine work while Mary and I very carefully

59

washed the old man and remade his bed. He was awake, but too weak to talk. He looked asleep again when we heard Sims' sepulchral whisper, 'Has the old Prof. gone yet, Jock? Shame he's packing it in. Ever such a decent old basket, he was.'

The Professor opened his eyes, and his eyes were smiling. 'A pleasing obituary,' he mumbled, 'if—somewhat—premature.'

CHAPTER FIVE

ALBERT IS NOT SO QUIET

SOMEWHERE a bell was ringing. It had to be the duty-room telephone—but it was making too much noise. Eccles must have forgotten to put on the night switch—it was going to waken the Professor—and I leapt out of bed and found it was eleven o'clock in the morning and I had only been asleep an hour. The bell was on my front door, and it was still ringing.

I grabbed my dressing-gown, cursing. On the doorstep a florist's delivery man handed me a large bunch of red out-of-season roses. 'Having a lie-in, miss? Sorry to wake you. Sign, please.'

I signed in a daze; and in the same daze noticed the roses were from Charles. I'll think about them when I'm awake, I thought, and, putting them in water, went back to bed. I was nearly asleep when the bell rang again. I put a pillow over my head. I was deaf, gone away, dead. The ringing went on. I had to stop it or go mad, so I got up.

'About time!' My twin brother removed his finger from the bell. 'Why the hold up, Cathy? Were you in the bath?'

'Trying to sleep. I work nights, remember?' But I was very pleased to see him. 'Come on in. What are you doing in London?'

Luke had a new girl-friend who worked in the same bank in the same county town as himself, and her parents lived in Chelsea. She was home for the week-end, they both had Saturday morning free, he was taking her out to lunch and a party that night, and wanted a bed for two nights.

He was intrigued by the flat, which he had not seen, as he and Francine detested each other. 'Is all this stuff insured, Cathy?'

'I hope so. Should I ask Charles?'

'Does he see to her affairs? Then it'll be all right. Charlie-boy knows his stuff where money is concerned.' He noticed the card on the roses. 'Why the floral tribute?'

I smiled smugly. 'To thank me for dining with him last night.'

'He dating you?' He grinned. 'Why? Are you going to bed with him? Or hasn't he asked you yet and the tribute is to soften you up?'

'That's what. But I'm going to hold out for diamonds. And mink, of course.'

'Mutation, I hope?'

'Naturally.'

He laughed. 'Poor old mum's in a fine old state. She's convinced that smoothie must have the worst possible intentions towards her darling daughter. I've been trying to get her to believe your virtue's in no danger from Charlie-boy.'

'And why not?' I protested immediately.

'He's such an obvious lecher, love. Wolf is written all over him. You don't like wolves—unless they are ill and consequently harmless. You dig lame dogs. Which reminds me, how's old George?'

I smiled reluctantly. 'Still borrowing my shoulder when the mood takes him.'

That night was my last before nights off. I was very sad but not surprised to find the Professor had been moved to William, the acute male cardiac ward. He needed absolute quiet for the next few weeks. Albert had done its best for him last night, but it would not have been fair, or possible, to keep Albert silent indefinitely. We admitted a new man to the Professor's old bed shortly after we took over.

Two more night nurses had flu; Bridie had to relieve in Matilda; at midnight Night Sister rang to say Eccles and I could relieve each other, as there was no one 'ill' in Albert.

Mary was perturbed. 'What if something happens when you're away?'

I looked all round. 'With luck, it shouldn't. The new man's fine, the others are whacked after being so restless last night. You'll manage. Night Sister wouldn't be leaving you in charge if she thought you couldn't. She doesn't make mistakes—and anyway on your next spell of nights you'll be a senior relief. But if anyone worries you, Night Sister said you must ring the Office at once. And do that. She means it.'

Albert was very quiet when I returned, and Mary writing a letter at the table. She did not hear me until I was beside her. She looked up embarrassed. 'Oh—sorry——' She thrust an addressed envelope into her apron bib and closed her pad.

'Don't look so worried. Night Sister doesn't object to letter-writing when we are quiet. It's only knitting and sewing that infuriate her. All well?'

'Yes, thanks. None of them have woken at all.' She moved out of my chair. 'Dr Lairg came in.'

'He did? Why? We've no medical patient now.'

'He thought he had left his pen here. He had. It was in

Sister's drawer. And he said the Prof. was doing quite well. His daughter is flying home.'

'She is? That's splendid! I wonder why Sister Albert didn't tell us?'

'Dr Lairg only talked to Mrs Gunning at ten to-night.'

'She rang the hospital? From Melbourne? What a pity she couldn't talk to the Prof.! He'd have loved it.'

She said, 'He did talk to her. William was expecting the call; the Prof. had been warned. Dr Lairg said he was very pleased and not at all over-excited after.'

I was delighted. 'This'll do the old sweetie more good than all the drugs in the British Pharmacopoeia!'

I missed the Professor badly all that night, and kept looking at his old bed and getting a slight shock because it contained the wrong man. We were always transferring or discharging patients, yet I had never grown accustomed to the constant need to say good-bye. When a patient like the Prof. left us, for some time after I felt as if I had lost a little part of myself. The feeling was stronger now, as the old man was still on the D.I.L. I was grateful Andrew Lairg had had to come in for his pen. Neither Bridie nor the William night senior had been at the same meal as myself, and with Meg sick my main source of inside Office information had dried up. I was also grateful for Mary's lovely face. It was not surprising that even a pundit with a reputation for saying little should linger and say a good deal to her about a mutual patient.

At breakfast the William night senior said the Professor was making a gentle progress and had sent me his compliments.

'Give him my love to-night, Rosemary, and tell him Albert isn't Albert without him, and that I'm thrilled he spoke to his daughter.'

'You've heard about that? My dear, the riot that call has started!'

'Why? It can't have hurt him. Presumably, our Dr Lairg gave permission first?'

'Permission!' She smiled. 'It was his idea. He booked the call, spoke to Mrs Gunning to put her right in the picture first, then had it transferred to us. We fixed up the portable. I held the receiver.'

'What's wrong with that?'

'Ask the Accounts Department. They are all having nervous breakdowns over the cost. Dr Lairg insists as it was his idea the bill mustn't go to the Professor or his daughter, and if the hospital won't settle it he will. But he says before he does he wants to know why the Accounts Department are querying what amounts to his treatment of a patient, and whether they consider drugs the only means open to him? You know what pundits are when they think some lay person is trying to tell them how to treat a patient! And all the other pundits'll back him. There's no question but that call was of therapeutic value. Your old boy-friend took a new lease afterwards.'

I said, 'This Lairg seems good. How do you get on with him?'

'All right—I think. He was in and out a lot last night and the night before. He was polite, and clearly allergic to chaperons, and as William's male I left him to it. Night Sister would have had a coronary had she seen a pundit going round alone, but what could I do when he said pointedly, "You must be busy, Nurse; don't let me detain you"? What's more, I was busy.' She was quiet. Then, 'The men seem to like him. They feel safe with him, and his not talking doesn't worry them. Most of them are so ill and so do get fed up with all those constant "How are you to-days?" '

I had to finish moving out of my room. I met George in the park on my way over. He was out for air after an all-night session on Cas. call. 'The usual Saturday-night roads, with a few busted heads and knife-wounds from dock fights as light relief. Why did no one tell me taking up medicine meant giving up sleep?'

I sympathised, swopped my news about the Prof. and Luke. 'Any chance of your getting over to the flat?'

'Wish I could. Not a hope, as I'm on.' He rubbed his eyes. 'Why can't I get flu and retire to Jenner?'

'You probably will, but will end up in the Private Wing, as Jenner's full. There are still three empty beds in Nightingale. Maybe they'll let you join Meg.'

'Meg Harper? She's in Nightingale? I wondered where—I mean—why—I hadn't seen her. Why didn't you tell me she's sick? What's wrong? Have you seen her?'

'I forgot. Flu. Not badly. And no one can see her as Nightingale is closed to visitors on Matron's orders. The bug must not spread. Official.'

'Oh! I see. That's too bad. I—I thought I ought to thank Meg for being so decent that night in Matilda. I needed that brandy.'

'She dosed you with the stock brandy?'

'Didn't I tell you?' He was far too casual. 'Yes. She was very decent.'

I suddenly guessed why he had chosen to take air in that particular spot. It was the short cut any night nurse living in the Home was bound to take. 'Why don't you send her some flowers to cheer her sick-bed?'

'Me?' He flushed deeply. 'Why would I do that?'

'Why not? It would be a nice gesture. Most girls like flowers, particularly when sick. It was just an idea. If you don't like it, forget it.'

He ignored that. 'She'd send 'em back, stat.'

'So it was a bad idea. Sorry.' I walked on, alone.

He caught me up. 'You must have had some motive for making it.'

'Sure. I hold shares in flowers.'

'Don't be a moron, Cath!' I said nothing. 'Anyway, what kind of flowers? And where would I get some on Sunday morning when I can't go out?'

'Chrysanthemums. Red, yellow, or bronze. Meg loves them. Henry'll get them. Henry can get anything for anyone at any time. And as it's Sunday he'll be in the Cas. porters' lodge until nine. You've got fifteen minutes.'

'So he will.' He smiled sheepishly. 'Can't do any harm, I suppose?'

'Might even do some good. But, George——'

'What now?'

'This was your idea, not mine, remember?'

'What——? God, yes! Right. Thanks.' He shot back towards Cas. No one would have guessed from his speed that he had been working all night. Well, well, I thought. As he would say, here's a turn-up for the book. George and Meg. Could it be serious? I had a hunch he was. If only he could have the same effect on her they might be a good pair. Meg was a few months older, but that should not matter, as George loved being told what to do and would be far happier leaning on, as opposed to mentally supporting, his wife. Personally, I had no objection to mothering him mildly as a friend, but the only people I ever seriously wanted to mother were my future children. Meg loved making her own and other people's decisions, she was very strong-minded, and, whether she knew it or not, just about ready to fall in love again. If not, she would not have kept insisting to me that she enjoyed the single life. Could George break through to her? He was a simple soul, but that might be in his favour, since from what she had said I had gathered her ex-fiancé had been a Charles type. That reminded me of his roses. I forgot Meg and George and thought of that dinner, then found the thought led me straight to the Prof. and all that had happened later. It was a strange thought that Andrew Lairg and myself had been in a minority of two that night, and that he had seen so clearly exactly what the Prof. needed to boost his will to live. Only a pundit could have arranged that telephone-call, and not every pundit would have taken the trouble for just one patient among the many. It was the kind of thing Joshua Billings would have done. Old Josh must have known what he was doing when he pulled those strings to get Andrew Lairg back. I was very glad he had. I loved our old Prof.

I finished packing and took a taxi back to the flat. Luke, in pyjamas, was cooking himself a late breakfast. I had a second with him, and while we ate told him about the new neighbour. I had been too sleepy for that yesterday.

He echoed Charles's remark on Francine, and then my own reaction. 'She's always been peeved that you have stuck nursing when she couldn't. I don't know why you put up with her, Cathy. She's a complete bitch. Not that this isn't a very handy flat.'

'She's not all bitch. And I'm very sorry for her.'

'Don't tell me she's down to her last hundred thousand!' He jerked a thumb to the right. 'So that bloke didn't recognise you? That would nark her.'

'I don't think he did.'

'Didn't he know your name?'

'Doubt it. If he did, it isn't all that uncommon. There's a Michael Newenden in the final student year. He's no relation to us.'

He looked at me. 'Even if you weren't wearing a mask, if you looked as you do now, he wouldn't connect you with Francine. She wouldn't be seen dead without eye-stuff, and with that tight hair-do. You look hideous, love,' he added reassuringly. 'That the 'phone? It'll be June. Shove on some more toast for me.'

It was not June. It was Charles for me. He was flying to Paris for two days and wanted to know my taste in scent. He had not realised I was having nights off, but, having seen Luke when he came to get something from his car earlier this morning, had guessed I would be late going to bed. 'How infuriating to think I've got to be away while you are free!'

Luke's ear was pressed to the other side of the receiver. 'Tell him life's a rugged business,' he murmured.

I pushed him away, thanked Charles for the roses.

'I hoped you'd like them, darling. They reminded me of you.'

That might have had me walking on air had I been alone, but not with my twin giving a boxer's double hand-clasp two inches from my face. 'It's nice of you to say so. I hope you have fun in Paris.'

'Just a business trip. It'll be deadly dull. Take care of your-self. And give my regards to Luke.'

Luke shook his head sadly as I replaced the receiver. 'I'm sorry I've spoilt your trip to Paris, Cathy.'

'You don't think he intended asking me?'

'Not once he saw I was around. What's that smell?'

The toast was on fire. I dealt with it, then said, 'He wouldn't want to take me to Paris. He doesn't even know I've got a passport.'

'He knew you had one last year. Mum had lunch with him when she was up here shopping one day while we were in Italy.'

'So she did. But, Luke—that Paris routine—it's so corny, it must be true. People can do business on Sunday. I think he was telling the truth.'

His retort would have deeply shocked Albert. I had heard the word before. 'You can't be swallowing that smoothie's smooth talk! He's as much a phoney as Francine.'

'In some ways. Not all.'

Luke took after our mother. He was only slightly taller than myself and nearly as dark as Andrew Lairg. His chin was blue, as he had not yet shaved. He scratched his beard impatiently. 'You wouldn't be doing anything bloody crazy like imagining you are falling in love with him, would you?'

I thought before answering. We were as close as most twins, so there was no point in pretence. 'I don't think so. I do think he's very attractive, and I was a bit worked up about him after that dinner. It was such a wonderful evening.'

'I'll bet. He's got the lolly—and enough experience.'

I said drily, 'Then he must have seen I was worked up. He only kissed my hand—and he didn't make a meal of it.'

'Crafty. Dead crafty.'

'Maybe. It certainly made a good impression on me. I thought him a honey and went on duty in a glorious dream with my morale boosted way up. It didn't last, as once in Albert I had to wake up smartly, as we had a bad night.'

'Because that old man had a heart attack?'

I nodded. 'We're not meant to get too fond of patients, but every so often, of course, we do. I really love that old man. Seeing him so ill'—I hesitated, trying to find the right words—'well—Charles and dreamy evenings just didn't belong. Not that I don't find Charles a lot of fun. I do. He just doesn't seem quite real.'

'He isn't. Scratch him, and he won't bleed blood. He'll bleed after-shave lotion. And, talking of shaving, I must get this beard off. June'll be here soon. I thought we'd all go out to lunch. You want the bathroom first? Then I'll put something over these and go out and buy some more papers. I've read all yours already.'

67

He was away some time. I had a quick bath, and after his comment on my appearance left my hair down and made up with more than usual care. Then I leant out of the front window to see if there was any sign of Luke. From what had become a habit in the last week I looked at Andrew Lairg's flat, even though I was certain he was in Martha's. The windows were now open; they had been closed when I got back in the taxi. At that moment he came out of his front door, glanced up, and our eyes met.

'Morning, Miss Newenden,' he said briefly.

He wore a thick blue sweater over a shirt and slacks and looked as unlike his professional self as my floating hair, shadowed eyes, and scarlet sweater were unlike my uniformed self. There was no trace of any 'so it was you' in his expression. I was both amused and slightly piqued. I would have enjoyed watching him eat his own words. But perhaps it was as well to keep up the act.

'Good morning to you!' I smiled a Francine-type smile. 'Lovely day.'

He looked at the low sky. 'It's not raining yet.' He turned, as Luke came slowly up the mews reading his favourite Sunday paper. 'You found a pitch?' he asked him.

'Yes, thanks. There was one where you said, but he'd sold out of this one, so I had to walk a couple of miles.' Luke looked up. 'Cathy, love, open up for me. I'm come out without my key.'

Dr Lairg gave him a cool look, glanced again my way, then walked off down the mews. I opened the front door. 'You seem to have been fraternising all round this morning. First Charles, now him.' Luke was grinning. 'You did tell him you were my brother.'

'Didn't have a chance. He was putting away his car when I came out, and told me where to find some papers. Why?' Then he saw what I was getting at. 'No wonder he gave me such a queer once-over. I should have used my nut. Does it matter?'

I looked at his unshaven face and the pyjama collar sticking up over his jacket. 'I hope not. No. Why should it? He certainly hasn't recognised me. He's always thought me another Francine. This'll just prove it.' He was silent. 'If he does get hold of the wrong impression again it'll be his own fault for jumping to the wrong conclusion. Why should I worry?' Luke was still silent. 'I now think he's a very good doctor, but as a man, I can't be doing with him.'

Luke said quietly, 'He's a bit old for you, isn't he, Cathy?'

'Old? Don't be so damned silly! Of course he is! What's that got to do with it?' I went on upstairs, feeling very annoyed. 'As I've just told you,' I flung over my shoulder, 'I don't like him.'

'You did.' He followed me up. 'One thing, he doesn't look a smoothie. He got a wife?'

'He's been a widower ten years. So what?'

'So I just thought I'd ask. Mum'll be interested. She's been anxious about your neighbours.'

'She doesn't have to be anxious about this one!' I was surprised by my own annoyance. It was years since I had lost my temper with Luke. I was obviously overworked, overtired, underpaid, and generally hard done by. I blamed it all on night duty and drifted back into the sitting-room. 'Hey, Luke! Is this June?'

'God, I hope not! I can't find my razor!'

'Come and see, then I'll look.'

The young woman below was hovering by our front door. She was not very young, attractive rather than pretty. She had auburn hair the same colour as her tweed suit. Luke said, 'Not June, but quite a doll. She coming here?'

'Doubt it, as she hasn't rung. No—look——' We backed as Andrew Lairg returned to the mews. The girl went to meet him smiling. She linked an arm in his.

Luke said, 'Now you've seen the strength of the opposition, suppose you find me my razor. I know I packed it.'

'Then it's bound to be in your suitcase.'

It was. I handed it to him in silence.

He said, 'Whose throat are you going to cut first? Yours or mine?' He was not talking about my finding the thing, and we both knew it. I did not answer, as I had no answer. He did not mention Andrew Lairg again for the rest of his visit. As we understood each other so well, I found that rather disturbing.

When I got back on duty Albert was back on accident take-in. Hubert and Kevin were the first to disappear to make room for the new patients, then Sims, Chalmers, Dawson, and Dick Yates. Donovan was transferred to Roehampton to have his artificial limb fitted. When the week ended we still had a line of emergency beds down the middle of the ward, and over half the men the Professor had known had gone.

From Bridie, who was still taking Meg's place, I heard my old friend was getting along nicely in William. His daughter had arrived and was at present staying in one of the hospital rooms reserved for close relatives of D.I.L. patients. 'A decent woman,' said Bridie, 'but you should see her skin! The poor old bag looks as old as her father. There's a lot to be said for the weeping grey skies of England. We may all suffer from the rheumatics and the bronchitis, but our skins stay good.'

It was rather odd to hear all this at second hand after the

Prof. had been so much a part of my life. I wished it had been possible for us to continue nursing him in Albert. I still missed him dreadfully, despite the rush of take-in week. During that week, as always on take-in, I was so tired in the mornings that I fell into bed directly I returned to the flat, and slept undisturbed until my two alarms went off. I did not hear the cars coming or going below, the door-bell, or telephone, if either rang. On one of those mornings towards the end of the week I found another note from Charles again asking me to ring him so that we could fix up another dinner date. I had not even the energy to talk to him. I wrote a brief letter explaining Albert was busy and I would not be able to think straight about any dates until I surfaced for nights off on Sunday. I posted it on my way back to work that night.

I saw nothing of Andrew Lairg in the mews that week, but once caught sight of him talking to Chesty Hartigan, our thoracic specialist, at the far end of the ground corridor on my way to my meal. He had his back to me, but I was too worried about Tiny that night to have bothered had Andrew and myself met face to face.

Tiny was now our oldest inhabitant and, to the new patients, the official Albert oracle. 'That Tiny,' they said, 'he's a sharp lad. Knows all the answers.'

That was the trouble. Tiny was far too bright for his own comfort. He knew the condition of his leg was deteriorating, why he was still in a bed close to the table, why he was back on four-hourly temperature-taking, and visited so persistently by pathologists as well as orthopaedic surgeons. He winced at the sight of a thermometer, and his pulse took well over a minute to settle before he could be properly checked. He insisted, often obviously untruthfully, that his leg gave him no pain, and unless forced to by a straight question, refused to discuss it at all. But the subject was so much on his mind that he regularly talked about it in his sleep, and lately had started having bad nightmares. He had just finished one of these before I went to my meal. Bridie had relieved me now we were heavy again, and I had left Player sitting by Tiny while he drank hot milk, and wished Mary Eccles was on. Her presence soothed him better than anything else.

George was in Albert when I got back. His round had been delayed by a late theatre case. He warned me Fatso was still in the hospital and might be in.

'He's not doing Joe Briggs' round?' I groaned. 'All these pundits around at night are beginning to get me down!'

Joe Briggs had flu. 'No. The S.S.O. is doubling as Joe again to-night. But Fatso may stay on, as we are so pushed. You should worry, Cath, You only see the chaps at night. Our House is now so full of them the ruddy place looks like a Medical Convention. The conversation at meals is so flaming erudite I can never understand what it's about. All the same'—he went on illustrating some operation notes—'must hand it to the old men. They're long past their prime. All this walking the wards by night as well as teaching by day can't be easy for them. And it must be playing hell with their private practices.'

'They're not all past their prime!' I heard myself object a little too quickly.

'Hell, Cath! There's not one under thirty-five.' He added an arrowed note to his drawing. 'By the way, what happened when Lairg walked in here that night? He put two and two together?'

'No. Oh—blast!' The telephone was ringing. 'That can't be another admission. We haven't an emergency bed left to put up.'

He said placidly, 'Then you'll have to shift some one out. Matthew have got room.'

Player had answered the telephone. 'That was the S.S.O. from Cas., Nurse Newenden. He asked how Hodd was sleeping. I said not very well, and he had just had a drink. The S.S.O. said that was good, as we must move him, bed and all, to Matthew. He's just admitted a new man for us.' She turned up her apron hem and read the note she had written on the reverse side. 'His name is Stanley Alan Gould. He is thirty-four, C. of E., his next of kin is now being informed by the police and should be up shortly. He has three fractured right ribs, a chipped sternum, nine fractures in his two legs, extensive soft-tissue damage—and he's shocked.'

George and I looked at each other. I said, 'He was driving.' George said, 'Typical rapid deceleration injuries. He was driving something big with good brakes. Lorry?'

Player gaped. 'Yes. How did you know?'

George said, 'We've seen 'em all, Nurse, we've seen 'em all. It won't be all that long before you have too.'

Hodd was in One. He was upset about moving until Tiny sat up. 'You're in luck, chum,' he whispered over the sleeping man in Two. 'This means they'll be chucking you right out soon.'

'How do you make that out then?' asked Hodd suspiciously.

Tiny said, 'When they have to shift out some one in a hurry they always pick the chap doing the best.'

Hodd looked at me, 'Is he right, then?' I nodded. 'But I only been in a few days. That lad Tiny, he's been here weeks.'

'Months,' corrected Tiny. 'Two and a half something months, chum. They can't do without me. You come back next year, and I'll still be here—right, Nursie?'

'I dropped my crystal ball this evening.' I drew the curtain that shut out Tiny and the rest of the ward. 'I'm really sorry about having to disturb you, Mr Hodd.'

'Oh, aye.' He helped me stack his belongings on his bed. 'You got your job to do.' He glanced at the curtain. 'Might be worse. What's this Matthew Ward like then?'

I had already rung Matthew and for a porter. Ten minutes later his bed-space was clear. It was another three hours before Stanley Gould came up from Casualty. During those three hours he had to have ten pints of blood in the Accident Cleansing theatre attached to Cas. before the first emergency treatment to his injuries could be started. He was conscious when the S.S.O. came in shortly afterwards. Conscious, free from pain, and perfectly coherent.

'Honest, guv! I still don't feel nothing, like as I said downstairs.' He had a thin grey face and the kind of light brown hair that looked grey in the night lights. 'It were the same when it happened. I saw the bloke in the van in front go over. I drew up, see—must have been a good two feet from him—me brakes is fine, see—and then the bloke coming up behind bashes me van up the—bashes into me, see. Me cab just folded up. I thought— hello, hello, I've caught it! But I didn't feel nothing.' He smiled at me. 'All right, eh, Nurse?'

I smiled back, 'Splendid, Mr Gould.'

The S.S.O. looked him over, then wrote up another injection. 'You'll have a little sleep, and in the morning we'll see about patching you up properly.'

'Suits me, guv! You on the night shift?'

The S.S.O. caught my eye. It was after three, his eyes were red-rimmed, and he looked deathly tired. 'You could say that.'

He told me he would take himself round while I gave that injection. Player witnessed for me. He was at the table checking George's notes when we had left Gould settled.

'Where's that man's wife, Nurse? I only had time for a couple of words with her in Cas. and said I'd see her up here. She in the duty-room?'

'No, Mr Simmonds. She's left the hospital.'

'Left? Who was the fool who let her go? Her husband's a dangerously injured man and far too with us for my liking! Or did she have to fix up about their kids?'

'They haven't children. They aren't married.' I was going on to repeat the long conversation I had had with the Cas. staff nurse, but he was in his Big Doctor mood, probably as he was so tired.

'What the hell does that matter? I'm not interested in his morals, Nurse, merely saving his life! He gave her as his next of

72

kin, the cops brought her up—and she was bloody upset, because I saw her—and I want her back. When this shock wears off that man is going to do one of two things. He'll either collapse and die, or live and start feeling the pain. We can knock some of that out for him, but in his condition we can't knock it all out without pushing him over the edge. I daren't touch him for hours. When I first saw him I thought he was a B.I.D. [Brought in dead]. He needs his wife or mistress or whatever she is by him. Ring Night Sister; tell her I want a car sent for her at once!'

'Mr Simmonds, she is coming back. She had to go. She works in the cloakroom of some night-club, and she told Staff Nurse Wilson in Casualty that her husband was going to be furious with her leaving the job before the club closed. He owns or runs it or something.'

'Her husband? Then she doesn't live with Gould?'

'She does. She just works for her husband.'

'Won't he object to her coming back?'

'Apparently not, so long as she gets back to work to-morrow night. She said she'd be back here by four.'

'Good God!' He allowed himself a weary smile. 'I was convinced she was his wife. This'll teach me to spot diagnose.'

Momentarily I thought of Andrew Lairg. 'Do you want me to let you know when she arrives?'

'Yes. I'll still be up. I must talk to her.' He yawned. 'You wouldn't have any nice stewed tea going?'

'Of course, Mr Simmonds.' I went quickly to the kitchen, then took his tea back into the ward. I did not add a cup for myself. He had mellowed slightly, but not enough for that.

'Heaven will reward you, Nurse, even if I don't. Now, tell me about the rest—and what's all this talk about Tiny's nightmares?'

CHAPTER SIX

CHARLES TURNS KING COPHETUA

LUKE came up for another week-end. He had borrowed a car and drove June up, then planned to park the car on the other side of the mews during the nights. On Saturday evening he met Charles, who offered him the loan of his garage over the week-end, as he was away until Monday. I thought of driving back home with Luke and June on Sunday evening, but when the time came decided to sleep instead and go home on my next nights off, when I should not be so tired, as we would be off take-in.

June was unused to night nurses. When I fell asleep at tea as well as during lunch she was convinced I was ill and wanted to call in the doctor next door. 'Of course he won't mind! He's a doctor, isn't he? We must do something, Luke! This can't be normal.'

I said good-bye and took myself to bed after tea, leaving Luke to reassure her. I slept until eleven the next morning. I had been up only a short time when my door-bell rang.

I recognised the plump, youngish woman in the floral apron as Mrs Shaw. I had often seen her arrive next door on her moped and returned her friendly wave, even though this was the first time we had met. She was holding a tissue-wrapped sheath of carnations. 'These come for you early, miss. I guessed you was having a lie-in from your curtains, and took them in for you. Lovely, aren't they? Ever such a nice way to start a Monday morning, eh, dear?'

They were from Charles, and reminded me of the scent that had not yet materialised. 'Thank you very much.'

'No trouble, miss. Like as I said to the doctor, you're only young once, and I expect you had another of your parties last night, and why not? If you can't enjoy yourself when you're young, when can——' She sneezed twice. 'Ever so sorry! I been trying to keep this cold at bay! But you know how it is when you got kiddies at school—sneeze all over each other they will—and I got my two youngest home with the sniffles to-day. I told the doctor as I was ever so sorry, but I'd have to leave off dinner-time, and he's ever so good.' She beamed. ' "You go back home now, Mrs Shaw," he says straight. "I can manage." But I

74

couldn't do that! I mean, it's not right, is it? A gentleman like the doctor working all day and half the night up that hospital of his—you'd not credit the hours, miss! One week-end a month, that's all he should do up the hospital, but every Monday morning it's the same. He had to go in all Saturday and Sunday morning like as not! And then he has to come home and see to hisself.'

I agreed life was tough for single men, and did not add the remedy, in most cases, lay in their own hands. 'Dr Lairg is lucky to have you to look after him so well.'

She looked pleased. 'That's just what his young lady said when she came in one afternoon last week. You met Miss MacDonald, miss? Ever such a nice young lady, she seems. And how's the other young lady getting on? The one as has gone on her holidays. Your sister, won't she be?'

'Cousin. Didn't the doctor tell you?'

'Oh, no, miss! He's not one of the talkers, is the doctor. He's a lovely quiet gentleman. Did you say the other Miss Newenden was your cousin? I'd not credit it! You could be twins!' From the glance she now gave my carnations, she had read Charles's card. 'So Mr Newenden—he'll be your cousin too?'

'That's right.' She was a pleasant soul, and I thought it would amuse her, so I told her about our fathers being twins, and then my being half of one. 'I don't suppose you've seen my twin brother. He was here for the week-end. He looks quite different from me.'

'You don't say! I never did! One of my neighbours, she's got two girls, identical-like, they are. Talk about two peas in a pod. I can't never tell which one's Marilyn and which one's Linda! Lovely little kiddies, they are! But this won't buy the baby a new frock! I got to finish off upstairs—take the doctor's supper out the oven for him to heat up when he gets in from work— and what time that'll be I'd not like to say, I'm sure!' She sneezed again. 'Then I got to get home to get my husband his dinner. My neighbour's seeing to my two kiddies, but she'll have to get back to see to her own man. All rush, isn't it?' Then she answered herself. 'But you wouldn't know that yet, would you, miss? And why should you, eh?'

I smiled weakly, thanked her again. 'Take care of that cold. There's a lot of flu about.'

'That's what the doctor was saying! I dunno. If it's not the one thing it's another!'

She had something there, I thought, on reading Charles's card. He wanted me to dine and go to a theatre with him that evening, expected to be back in London at his office by twelve and asked me to ring there if my answer was no. 'May I take no news as good news?'

I put the carnations in the sitting-room, then sat on the gold satin sofa and looked at them. They made the room look even more Francine-ish than the roses had done, but if Francine came in now the prospect would not please her. She would promptly assume I had enticed them from Charles as part of some dark scheme to entrap him in her absence. Her mother would ring her psychiatrist, solicitor, and my parents, in that order, and when the audience was large enough she would have hysterics. My aunt was superb at having hysterics. Nothing would persuade her, or Francine, that while those roses had enchanted me, the carnations were now making me vaguely uncomfortable. And instead of being thrilled by the thought of this evening, I was seriously wondering if to invent a previous engagement. Yet I had enjoyed that last evening with him so much, and I did love the theatre.

I did not back out of it. During dinner I came close to wishing I had. Charles, having already given me the massive bottle of expensive French scent he had been keeping to give me in person, suddenly announced he had come to the conclusion nurses must make excellent wives. 'I'm beginning to feel it's time I settled down, Cathy. Do you think I'm right?'

'You're the only person who can answer that.'

He gave me a very strange look. 'It takes two to make a marriage.'

I did not want to talk marriage. I said something trite about marriage being a situation one should not rush into, and asked what time the theatre started.

He cut through that. 'You don't believe I'm serious, my sweet. I'm sorry, but not surprised. We must talk about this again.' There, to my relief, he let it drop.

He took me straight home after the theatre. 'Is it too late? Or can I ask myself in for a coffee?'

He had given me a very pleasant evening, if not as wildly exciting as the last time, the scent, those carnations, and I was living free in that flat.

'Sure. Come on up. I'll make some.'

In the kitchen I took my time fixing the coffee, and thought, Here it comes.

Nothing came. We sat in the sitting-room as decorously as if we had been in my parents' house with them present. He talked about my family, how glad he was Luke was visiting me at the week-ends and seemed to be so enjoying life. 'That's a very pretty girl-friend he has. Are they engaged?'

'Not yet. Luke's rather young.'

He smiled. 'As I recollect—ten minutes younger than your-self!'

I asked about Francine. He had not heard anything of her since he rang New York the morning they arrived. 'My mother is no great letter-writer. My father has not written a non-pro-fessional letter for years. I have heard indirectly that his first lecture was a success.' He went on to talk hospital.

I generally kept off hospital 'shop' with non-hospital people. I tried changing the subject, but Charles took it firmly back to Martha's and seemed genuinely interested. 'Tell me about this ward of yours. Why is it called Albert?'

'After the Prince Consort. He came to Martha's once, so they altered a ward name smartly.'

He was amused. 'A sound reason. You always work there? What happens when you are off?'

'A regular senior relief takes my job. The two juniors alternate.'

'Nice girls?'

'Very. And very different. Player, the most junior, is a chubby, chatty little thing, who's inclined to knock things over and wake the patients up asking them if they are asleep, but she doesn't do so much of either now, and is very willing.'

'And the other?' He lit a cigarette. 'She willing?'

'She's very good—much better than Player. Her name is Mary Eccles. She never talks at all, is very good with the men. She has got the most wonderful face. I'm not kidding, Charles. She ought to be a model or a movie star. She's absolutely beauti-ful.'

He said with sudden warmth, 'My sweet, you are very generous.'

'No. Just honest.'

'Possibly, but still generous. I would like——' But he could not finish as the telephone was ringing. 'You expecting a call?'

'No.' I got up to answer it. 'Probably a wrong number at this hour.'

A feminine voice I did not recognise asked if I was Miss Catherine Newenden, and then apologised for disturbing me.

'Not at all. I've not been in long.' I shrugged at Charles, who had followed me into the hall. 'Something I can do for you?'

'My name is Ann MacDonald. Yes, please, if you would help me I would be grateful. Have you noticed if your neighbour Dr Lairg is home?'

'His lights were on when we came in.' I was now very in-trigued. 'Do you want his number?'

'No, I have that, thanks. I've been ringing him all evening. I hope you don't mind—I rang you twice. I can't get out myself,

77

but I must speak to him, and now I've discovered his phone is out of order. Would you object to my talking to him on your phone?'

There was only one answer. 'Of course not. Would you hold on?' I covered the receiver, and explained to Charles.

'This his woman?' he asked.

'According to his cleaning lady, she is his young lady as seems nice. But the doctor is ever such a lovely gentleman.'

'Point taken. Shall I get him?'

'Charles,' I said gratefully, 'thank you.'

I handed this on to Ann MacDonald, left the receiver on the hall table, and went back to the sitting-room, leaving the door open. The two men returned almost immediately. Charles joined me and closed the door. 'He hadn't been in long either.'

The closed door was thin. We had to overhear most of Andrew's conversation. It concerned some house. After a long pause he said, 'Ann, my dear, if you really like it, then the hunt's over. Yes. I've read the lease. It's a pity it's not freehold, but ninety-nine years should see us all out. He has to know at once? My dear girl, that's what they always say! What?' Another pause. 'Yes. If you like. And tell him I'll confirm it in writing to-morrow.'

A minute or so later he called, 'Miss Newenden.'

Charles opened the door. 'All well?'

'Yes, thanks.' He looked at me. 'This is kind of you. I am sorry to have intruded.'

I said I was glad I happened to be in, and seeing him glance at the coffee-tray had to ask if he cared to join us. As I expected, he refused politely.

Charles saw him out, then came back. 'It would seem you might be having a new neighbour shortly.'

'Yes.' I felt that should please me. It did not. 'But why bother to get fixed up next door if he's house-hunting?'

'He has to live somewhere now his job at Martha's has started. It's typical of life that they should find the right house directly after he settles for a flat.'

'I guess so.' I poured more coffee for us both. 'She must be his fiancée.'

'Presumably.' He took his cup.

'I would have thought obviously.' He was frowning into his cup. 'Would you like milk this time?'

'No, thank you. This is perfect.' He looked up. 'I was merely thinking of your remark.'

'You don't believe from that conversation that they are obviously engaged?'

'Darling,' he drawled, 'there are few things in which I believe,

78

and one thing I always suspect, and that is the obvious. If I may give you some not wholly disinterested advice, don't judge everything and every one by appearances. They can be deceptive.' He finished his coffee and stood up. 'I must let you catch up on some more of all that lost sleep. Thank you for a very happy evening. I'll be in touch very soon.'

Next morning I was in the bath when his gladioli arrived. Mrs Shaw had again taken them in. 'No, miss! As if the doctor would mind! Ever so pretty he thought they were! Your young man spoils you, he does—and why not, like as I said to the doctor?'

The mews was very quiet that morning, but my personal quiet was shaken by the crashing of all the fine castle in the air I had built round a man I had fitted with Charles's face and name, but who had never existed outside of my imagination. All that day I felt very much as I sometimes did at home when I came across some old, now forgotten, but once-cherished toy. Amused, mildly astonished, and saddened that anything that could once have been so important had now become unimportant.

Yet there was more in it than that. From vaguely, I was becoming very, uncomfortable. The flat was beginning to worry me. I did not mind living for a while on Francine, since I had done quite a lot for her in the past, and she had often made long visits to my home. Charles was different. I had never done a thing for him; I could not remember when he last drove down to see my parents, and then for no more than a meal. I was having a disturbing notion that he was in all probability paying the flat expenses while Francine was away. The fact that he could well afford it did not come into it. But surely he was going to expect some return some time? He was not a philanthropic institution. He had never bothered about me in the past, but was now falling over backwards to get in good with me. I supposed I ought to be wild with joy. Instead I only wondered wildly what Cinderella would have done when the glass slipper fitted if she had suddenly discovered that though she liked the Prince, as a prospective husband he left her cold.

My stand-in in Albert was Valerie Gower. She was a pretty brunette eight months junior to myself. My set was now the most senior in training, which made Albert officially mine. On the odd nights when Val and myself were on she took over some other ward. We met going into the dining-room on my first night back. Tiny had woken the entire ward twice the previous night. 'He screamed and screamed. Sister Albert blames his sleeping-tablets. She's getting them changed.'

'That won't stop his nightmares unless they give him real

knock-outs. Wasn't Eccles back last night?'

'Yes. Didn't make any difference. He's lost interest in her. Some idiot day junior told him she's getting engaged.'

'I didn't know that. Not that I'm surprised, with her face. I hope Tiny isn't too upset?'

She smiled rather self-consciously. 'I don't believe he was too serious about her. But he's terrified of having that leg off. He says it'll kill him.'

'He tell you that? I haven't been able to get him to discuss it.'

'Nor me. This was in his sleep. I told Sister. I had the impression she thought I was fussing. She reminded me how well Don had adjusted himself.'

'Every one always thinks night nurses are fussing!' I exclaimed annoyed. 'I'm with you, Val. I think that boy's going to crack. I know Don was splendid. He was a splendid, tough type. And his leg was off before he knew anything about it. Even if it hadn't been he'd probably have taken it well. Don was the Bader type. If he had lost both legs he would probably invent a fast motor for a wheel-chair and start a new form of racing. I adore Tiny, but he hasn't got Don's guts. He may put up a good show in the day of being tough, but it all comes off at night, as you and I know.' I told her I had discussed the nightmares with the S.S.O. 'He said he'd get another psychiatric report.'

'That's come. It was quite good.'

'Trust Tiny to get the answers right. He's not a three A-level honours type for nothing.'

'That's what I thought. Snag is, he never has nightmares when the men are there. I don't mind telling you, Cathy, that, much as I like Albert, I'm only too happy to hand it back to you to-night. What with Tiny's nightmares, Mrs Stan's matrimonial problems, the S.S.O. being thoroughly bloody-minded, and Mary Eccles' constant silence, I've had a surfeit of the place.'

I had to wait until after grace.

'Mrs Stan? Is that what we are calling "Mrs Gould"?'

'At her request.' She smiled not unkindly. 'Hubby's name is Binns. But she says she just doesn't care for Binns—never did—and will we think of her as Mrs Stan. Binns, incidentally, is her third.'

My eyes widened. 'Is he divorcing her?'

'She says she doesn't want a divorce, as her Stan isn't the marrying kind. He's cute—and doing very well.'

'Thank God for that. What ails the S.S.O.?' I helped us to the tea that was served us at supper as well as breakfast. 'Overwork?'

'Expect so. It always makes him foul. And he is upset about Tiny.'

'He's a good surgeon. All good surgeons get in a state at the prospect of an amputation. And how about Eccles?' I looked across the dining-room. 'She's very pale. She getting flu?'

'Don't ask me. She nearly bit my head off when I suggested that last night. She didn't open her mouth once!'

'My poor Val! You have suffered!' I noticed Bridie had not come in. 'Is Sullivan on nights off?'

'No. She's skipped supper to go to some art gallery with Hugh Devine.'

Bridie arrived as Night Sister called her name for the second time. 'So sorry, Sister—here, Sister.'

Night Sister gave her a long look, and then read on. After the register she produced her change list, and as usual started with the senior changes: 'Nurse Ashbye from Matthew Ward to the Office, please. Nurse Sullivan, from the Office to Christian Ward until further notice.'

Christian was our infants' ward. Bridie was very good at nursing small children. Her face lit up. 'Yes, Sister. Thank you.'

Sister looked at Val and myself. 'Nurse Gower, back to Albert Ward for to-night. Nurse Newenden, much as I dislike moving permanent night seniors, I am going to move you to Casualty, as Staff Nurse Wilson is unwell, and I must have a senior nurse in that department with previous night Casualty experience. Sister Albert has been informed.'

For different reasons Val and I were outraged. We glared at Sister until she dismissed us all, then exploded at each other. 'What do they think I am?' I demanded. 'A flaming senior relief? Albert's my ward!'

'And don't I wish you were having it!' retorted Val. 'If I have another night like last night I shall start screaming myself.'

Christian and Casualty lay in the same direction from the dining-room. Bridie was waiting for me. She was in revoltingly good form, insisted on telling me about her date. 'Do you not remember my telling you Paddy MacAndrew was at art school with me?'

'Who's he? I thought you went with Hugh Devine.'

'It was Paddy's first one-man show. Girl, it was good! I must take you along.' She beamed at me. 'And how's life with you?'

I used Luke's favourite expression of annoyance.

She laughed. 'Albert'll be there to-morrow night. A change'll do you good. You're getting too possessive about your men. I was as bad until they pitched me out of Robert. But I wonder now, why do they want me in Christian? The babes were fine last night.'

81

'Who should be on there to-night? Forbes-Smythe?'

'It's her night off. But Davids is on. Ah!' She snapped her fingers. 'I have it! That poor little boyo must have arrived from India—or was it Hongkong?'

'What boyo?'

'David Stone.'

I stopped in the corridor. 'And who the hell is David Stone?'

'Didn't I tell you myself at breakfast this morning? Oh, no, you were off. It was Val Gower.'

David Stone was the baby son of an old Martha's man who now worked for some oil company. The baby had a valvular leak. 'And what else would any Martha's man do but fly him back to us?' she demanded. 'He was expected this morning. No doubt at all they want me for him.' She waved at a porter walking by. 'Henry, my old friend, can you tell me if that little fellow has been flown in from Ceylon?'

The elderly porter was used to Bridie. 'That blue baby from Singapore? Our Dr Stone's nipper? Yes. He come in an ambulance from the airport not an hour back. Not too good neither, he wasn't. They say as Dr Lairg had him in a tent soon as look at him. Cruel shame.' He tugged his ear sadly. 'Not right to see a little nipper that bad. And to think as I mind his dad when he was no more than a lad hisself. In the same lot of lads as Dr Lairg, he was. Great pals, they used to be.'

Bridie asked, 'Both parents here?'

'Still up in Christian with Dr Lairg, Nurse. You up there to-night? You're in for a night. Sister Cas. was saying as we sent up three youngsters with pneumonia since tea—and not one more than a twelvemonth.'

Bridie on the job was a very different girl from Bridie off duty, apart from her brogue. 'Is that a fact, Henry? I've four for sure in tents? I'll get my skates on.' She hurried off so quickly that the starch in her skirts crackled.

Henry looked after her. 'She's a one, is that Nurse Sullivan. Mind you, I'd not mind having her to look after one of my nippers, if one was poorly. She's got a real way with the nippers has Nurse Sullivan. I'd not be surprised if we wasn't to see her as Sister Christian afore long—if that Mr Devine don't talk her out of it.' He then realised I was walking in the wrong direction. 'What they doing to you, Nurse Newenden?'

I explained a little less peevishly than I might have done a few minutes earlier. I was thinking of that baby's parents. 'Henry, was Mrs Stone a nurse?'

'Not as I recollect, Nurse. Wealthy young lady, she was, and a great friend of that poor young lady as Dr Lairg married. They was always driving up, the pair of them, when the four of

82

them was courting, in one of them long red sports cars. Real gay pair of young ladies they were. I dunno.' He sighed deeply. 'No telling, is there? There's that other poor lady gone these past ten years, and now poor Mrs Stone is having all this trouble with her nipper.'

'Is he their only child?'

'That's right, Nurse.'

I said, 'It's a pity Mrs Lairg had no children.'

Henry's face turned wooden. 'Maybe it is, Nurse. Maybe it isn't.'

I glanced at him curiously. 'Because it would be hard on the child to be motherless?' He did not answer. 'Dr Lairg might have married again much sooner.'

'Sooner? He's not got hisself spliced again, has he?'

'Er—no. At least, not as far as I know.' I was annoyed with my own thoughtlessness. 'I expect he will one day. Most people do.'

'There's some,' said Henry cryptically, 'as never learn. I'd not have said that Dr Lairg was one of 'em. Real sharp gentleman he's always struck me. And mind you, though he never was a one to say much, you could see as he took that carry-on about his missus cruel hard.'

I had a sudden mental picture of those two girls driving up to Cas. in their red sports car. 'It was a terrible thing to happen.'

'Aye,' agreed Henry sadly. 'Could have been worse. She killed herself and her—' he hesitated—'her passenger. She might have killed some one else, state she was in. They was leaving some party. Streuth! There was that much alcohol content in both of them it's a wonder she got that car moving at all. But there. We all got to do these things when we're youngsters—and there's a lot as don't grow any older because of it.' He opened the side door to Casualty. 'Here we are. Quite like old times, eh?'

'Exactly,' I agreed absently and untruthfully. Last year when I worked in Casualty I had been living in the Home, running around with George in my off duty, and my only problems had been our fast-approaching State and Hospital Finals. Charles had been no more than a golden creature of my imagination. Pundits had been just pundits, not human beings. I would never then have believed the day would arrive when I would find myself thinking of one by his Christian name, and wondering how much he could still be hurt by meeting people like the Stones. Even if he had long got over his wife's death, seeing them again must bring back the past. It was only then I fully appreciated what hell it must have been for him to come back to us. Of course, his job was too good to be refused, and, as George had said, he had to be a mental tough to have got it. But being mentally tough did not make a person invulnerable; it merely helped one to give the appearance of being so. I thought of Don's attitude to his phantom leg, and then of other patients, women and men, who had also seemed to carry their personal disasters lightly, because they had the courage to carry the full weight themselves. The lightness only really came in the demands they made on other people's sympathy.

I looked round Casualty Hall. Last year was a long time ago.

CHAPTER SEVEN

EVERYTHING HAPPENS IN CASUALTY

THE clock in Casualty yard chimed eleven as Bert, the youngest Cas. night porter, put his head round the open duty-room door. 'You seen the Senior Casualty Officer, Nurse Newenden?'

'He's in Eyes dark-room looking at that man with the query corneal ulcer.' I blotted the entry I had just completed in the log-book on the standing desk. 'Why? What's coming in now?'

'Not another customer!' Nurse Potter, the senior of the two night juniors, emerged from the stock lotion-cupboard. 'My poor little cupboard! I shall never get you tidied!'

Bert said there was no call for her to take on so as he only wanted the S.C.O. because Henry had the S.C.O.'s missus on an outside line. 'She said not to fetch him if he was busy. Henry reckons she's wanting a bit of company. They not been married long.'

'Bert,' I said, 'you, Henry, and Carmelo are nothing but a trio of Cupids behind glass!'

He grinned. 'I'd not say that, Nurse Newenden! Not that there's much we misses from our lodge of a night.'

'Not much,' echoed Potter as he disappeared. 'Not one small thing!'

Potter was in the same set as Mary Eccles, and her greatest friend. She was a large, good-natured girl with curly red-gold hair and a high-pitched, squeaky voice. She talked as much as Bridie. We had not worked together before, but in the last two hours I had learnt more about Mary than in all the nights she and I had worked together in Albert. Mary had never mentioned her boy-friend to me. According to Potter, the romance was enthralling her set. 'You should see his car! It can hardly get through the main gates.'

I smiled. 'From that I gather he's not a resident?'

'Lord, no! Something in the City. Don't ask me what!'

'And they are engaged?'

'Not yet. I guess she can't make up her mind. She's crazy about him, and he's just gone on her! He never seems to stop giving her presents—a watch—bracelet—flowers—chocolates— and that's the trouble! He's loaded with lolly, madly generous, but gets annoyed when she tries to refuse anything—which she does. Then they have awful rows, make up, and it all starts again. She worries, as he has sown more than the odd wild oat. She's afraid he may be just playing around again.'

I thought of Charles and could see her problem. 'Poor Eccles! She's a nice girl. I hope things work out for her.'

'Yes.' She looked as if she was going to say more, then changed her mind and returned to her cupboard. A little later she remarked, 'I wonder where Sister Cas. got the notion Wednesday night is the quietest and we'd perish of boredom if we didn't have the extra mid-week cleaning to get on with? This is our first breather. How many have we had so far?'

'Fourteen, counting the man in Eyes.' I glanced through the log. 'Five roads, one coronary, one bronchitis, one lobar pneumonia, one acute indigestion, one migraine, one baby with pyloric stenosis, the boy with the severed right radial artery, and one splinter in thumb.' I walked to the door to look round the empty hall. 'No customers now for fifteen minutes. Sister Cas'll wonder why we haven't turned out the splint- and linen-rooms with all that spare time.'

The duty-room door was never closed. It overlooked the whole hall, the main doors to the ground-floor corridor on the far left, the glass-fronted porter's lodge on the far right. The angle of the lodge hid the main entrance to the department from the yard, and the great double-glass swing doors through which an ambulance could—and on one occasion which I had seen actually did—drive through. In Martha's, unlike some hospitals, every patient coming into the hospital for the first time with anything from a splintered finger to acute heart failure had first to be seen in Casualty and not the Out Patients Department. Our O.P.D. was the other side of the hospital, concerned exclusively with clinics, and closed at night. Consequently every patient to the hospital came in through those glass swing doors. They creaked when swung. By day that creak had Sister Casualty out of her duty-room like a jack-in-the-box. It had the same effect on her night staff. It was accepted, if unproven in Martha's, that those door hinges could only be oiled over Sister Cas.'s dead body. Sister Cas. was a very lively lady. The creak remained, a splendid warning system.

The hall was lined with many varying-sized dressing and examination rooms, all now in darkness. The Ophthalmic Department lay beyond the hall, at the end opposite to the main entrance. It had an independent existence by day, but at night turned into part of Casualty. The department at night was permanently staffed by three nurses (one of whom had to be State Registered), three porters, six resident dressers, and the Senior Casualty Officer, an F.R.C.S. who held Senior Registrar standing. The housemen doubled as Junior Casualty Officers in the daytime, and one houseman from each firm was on Casualty call every night. The same applied to the Registrars at night. During the day they were called to Cas. at the S.C.O.'s discretion. The present S.C.O., Mr Laughton, a phlegmatic Yorkshireman, had endeared himself to his colleagues by keeping his requests for help to a minimum, and to the Cas. nurses by his competence and speed, and the fact that he was too much in love with his wife to be aware there were any other women in the world. We found that attitude reassuring, since in all probability one day most of us would marry doctors. It was also—from a nurses'-eye view—rather rare.

Casualty occupied the ground floor of the fifth of the nine blocks that made up Martha's. The surgical blocks lay on the left, the medical on the right. The administrative offices were directly overhead. But, as parts of the hospital were very old, the many specialised departments that make up any modern general hospital were strung out all round us, above and below.

Owing to the pathologists' passion and need for peace and light, there was a laboratory of sorts on the top floor of nearly every block. In much the same way, to meet their specific requirements, the various radio-therapy units were scattered along our vast, pipe-lined basements. Casualty X-ray was under our hall. In Patients' X-ray under the medical blocks; the Deep Ray Unit under the theatres; the Cobalt Unit under the first surgical block. Spaced between these in the basements were the dispensary stores, general surgical stores, the laundry, the repairs and works shop, our blood bank, the Isotope Lab., all of which maintained a skeleton staff at night.

Nine times out of ten the quickest route from anywhere to anywhere was through the hall. Sister Cas objected strongly to this, and by day dealt firmly with all short-cutters. But she was not on at night, and ever since we took over a stream of men in white coats, porters' blue boiler-suits, students' assorted garb, and the occasional dark jacket of a pundit had gone to and fro past the open duty-room door.

My head jerked round as another dark jacket went by. It was Dr Hartigan walking from the medical side to the side-door to the car-parks. Potter noticed my reaction. 'I expect you've got out of the habit of ignoring all men at night unless they actually come into this room.' She watched a little posse of dressers arrange themselves in the wheel-chairs lined up by the lodge. 'The place is just like a railway station. People drift in, sit, or stand around chatting, exactly as if waiting for a train.'

'Yes—hey—the creak!' I went into the hall. 'Henry, with one lady in one wheel-chair.'

The lady was a Mrs Flora Dorothy Bates. She was fifty-four and looked ten years older.

'It's this pain in me back, see, duck. Catches me across the shoulders. I wanted to leave it until morning,' she apologised in the husky, slightly breathless voice of a chronic cardiac, 'but when I got to bed it caught me cruel. I only lives over the road. So I said to my friend—I'll just pop across the hospital and ask the doctor to give me something.'

I asked, and only because I had to, since I guessed the answer, 'You haven't called your own doctor, Mrs Bates?'

'Bless you, duck! I wasn't going to bother with him! I knew I could just pop back in here.'

The Health Service might be sixteen years old. The habit of popping back to Martha's was older. The people living round us had been doing that for the past six centuries. 'Of course you can, Mrs Bates.' I took her pulse. 'You have been in to us before?'

Her tired face relaxed in a wide smile. 'I been in and out of old Martha's since long before you was born, duck! I wouldn't like to say the times I been in that Florence Ward. They all know Mother Bates up in Florence! Been under Sir Joshua for years, I have. Gave me a real turn when I heard as he was too poorly and had to leave off. Ever such a lovely doctor he was, and a proper gentleman. But my friend Mrs Gaskin as I live with now we both lost our husbands and got our girls married' —she stopped for breath—'my friend, she just come out of Florence again last week. That's why I couldn't let her come up with me. And my friend says as this new doctor's got a real touch of the old Sir Joshua about him. A Dr Lairg, ain't he, duck?'

'Yes.' I shook down a thermometer, asked Potter to collect her old notes from the massive file that filled the entire room next door, and Henry to buzz Dr Johnson, the junior cardiac registrar on Cas. call for that night. 'Let the S.C.O. know, Henry,' I added to him aside, 'but as she's obviously medical and belongs to the cardiac firm, we may as well get straight through to them.'

Potter returned with the notes, then wheeled Mrs Bates to a couch in one of the examination rooms. Dr Johnson arrived almost immediately. He had been talking in the main ground-floor corridor only a few yards from the department when Henry buzzed his specific code signal on the lodge transceiver. All our residents wore pocket receivers in the breast pockets of their white coats.

'Sorry to get you back again, Doctor.' I gave him the notes. 'An old friend.'

'Old Mother Bates, eh! Not that I'm surprised. Where is she?'

'Getting ready in Seven. She'll need a few more minutes.' I added the new name and time to the log. 'How's Dr Norton?'

'Away on sick-leave, the lucky sod. How did you know he was sick? You've not been on the medical side for ages.'

I reminded him I had nursed Professor Brown. 'I hear he's sitting out of bed.'

'He is. Incredible old chap. You also heard he's still determined to fly to Australia? He says his house is let from the first week in January, and why shouldn't he fly back with his daughter? She's staying on another month.'

'Bless him! He is wonderful! But he can't fly now, surely? Would any airline risk it?'

'It'll be dicey. He'd need to be fitted with oxygen all the flight. My boss was just discussing him. He thinks he may be able to persuade some airline to take him, and if he can the old chap should make it, as he is so determined. There's nothing like a white-hot reason for living to keep the aged alive.'

'That's true, and the Prof. so hates the sea. Your boss still in the hospital? This late?'

'He's waiting to run the Stones to their hotel. You know we've Bill Stone's kid in Christian?'

'Yes. How is he?'

'Not too good. Lairg hasn't given an opinion yet, which isn't a healthy sign. Stone's very upset. He knows too much, poor sod, and what his wife doesn't know she can guess from his attitude. They waited years for this kid—and he has to have a bloody great leak! She wanted to stay with him for the night, but she's whacked, he's asleep in a tent, and there's nothing anyone can do to-night but let him rest after the journey. Maybe he'll tolerate surgery later. It'll be his only hope from the look of him now. If he can, thank God I won't have to give that anaesthetic. Lairg'll do it.'

'Does he give many?'

'All the dicey jobs. For which the Lord be praised. I may be only a small cog in the Health Service, I may work an average fifteen-hour day six days a week and sometimes seven for the kind of salary that would bring most unskilled workers smartly out on strike, but I have my compensation. A boss who actually does his own dirty work.'

Mrs Bates was readmitted. Henry got a message to her friend. Bert and Nurse Soames, the junior junior, wheeled her to Florence. Potter and I returned to the duty-room. The six dressers followed us in. 'All quiet now. All right if we go to bed, Nurses?'

Potter and I exchanged glances. The dressers worked on a weekly rota. Tuesday being the first day of their week, this was only their second night. 'Go along to your rest-room if you like,' I said. 'It's a bit early for going back to the House.'

'But we were up until three this morning!' protested a fair boy.

'Aye. And you'll like as not be up until three to-night,' remarked the S.C.O. from behind them. 'Sleepy, are you?'

'Yes, sir!' they chorused hopefully.

'Then get back to your rest-room and make yourselves some nice strong black coffee. The night is young, and so are you.' He waited until they disappeared. 'So Mother Bates is back?'

'Yes, Mr Laughton. I hope you didn't object to my buzzing Dr Johnson straight?'

'Why should I? I'm no physician. I don't like wasting time either.' He looked over his shoulder to the hall. 'I didn't hear the door. Who's that with Carmelo?'

Carmelo was Maltese. After nine years in Martha's his always fluent English had acquired a perfect East London accent. He still used his hands constantly while speaking. They were now waving all round a very scared-looking young coloured man. 'All right, all right, mister! So you want to see the doctor? Then you ought to come in by the big door, see, mate? Not creep in the side. That's not for patients.'

I went up. 'Can I help, Carmelo?'

The man with him looked more scared than ever and backed away. 'I have to talk with the doc., lady. Just the doc. Not you.'

Mr Laughton was at my elbow. He caught my eye. 'I'll see to this, Nurse Newenden. We'll be along in Eighteen.'

Eighteen was the room reserved for patients suffering from what Martha's euphemistically termed 'The Specific Disease.' We had a large 'Specific' Department. It was in a building by itself the other side of the Medical School and closed at night.

Three minutes later Mr Laughton appeared briefly in the duty-room. He was smiling slightly. 'The poor lad's only got acute retention and didn't like to mention it in front of ladies. I'll deal with him in Eleven.'

'Shall I ring for a dresser, Mr Laughton?'

He hesitated, then nodded. 'Get them all back. If there is one thing they are going to meet, this is it!'

The dressers reappeared and vanished into Eleven. The quiet was becoming unnatural. Potter finished her cupboard. 'How about the splint- and linen-rooms?'

'Start on the splints. They are chaotic. The linen is quite tidy.' I was now polishing instruments. 'Leave the door open, in case I have to call you. And where's Soames? She ought to go to the first meal.'

'Finishing the plaster-room. Shall I tell her?'

Potter had been gone about ten mintues when I found I had somehow splashed metal polish on Sister Casualty's special hand-towel. I rinsed it out, had another look round the hall before going along to the small alcove between Casualty proper and Eyes in which the splint- and linen-rooms lived side by side. The S.C.O., dressers, and now beaming young man came out of Eleven.

'Nothing else for me?' asked the S.C.O.

'Nothing, Mr Laughton.'

He told the dressers they could go back to their room, reminded the young man to return in the morning. 'Got it straight, lad? You come in through those glass doors, then knock on that door there and ask the young lady you'll find there for this card. Then you ask her to tell you the way to the Urological Out Patient Clinic. Right. Fine.'

'Thanks, Doc. You done a great job there, Doc. You done a great job.' The patient shook his hand warmly and took himself off.

Mr Laughton handed me the Casualty card. 'Nice lad. He'll have to have something done about his stricture. And it's time I did something about my thirst. While we're still quiet I'm going to grab some coffee.' He tapped his pocket. 'I'm tuned in if you want me.'

'Thank you.' I returned to the duty-room to enter the card's details in the log, then file it, then went along to the linen-room.

This was divided from the splint-room by a hardboard partition reaching almost to the ceiling. The gap at the top let me hear Potter's urgent whisper clearly, without the double advantage of her half-open door.

'Mary, honestly! You're crazy! I know it's your meal-time, but you are still on duty! Night Sister would raise all hell if she saw——' She broke off abruptly because I had banged on the partition.

'Just getting a clean hand-towel, Potter,' I called. 'Must get back. Night Sister'll be in at any minute.' I hurried off without looking round the splint-room door. Mary's calling on her friend in her meal break was not a crime in my book, but Night Sister would certainly take another view. Casualty at night was strictly out of bounds to all but the official Casualty night nurses. The department had so many small darkened rooms, so many side-doors, and so many stray students sitting around quite legitimately, that authority promptly assumed any nurse loitering in the place was loitering with the darkest intent. If Night Sister had seen Mary she would not hesitate to report her to Matron.

I retreated to the duty-room and worked on my instruments with my back intentionally to the open door. I heard the side-door to the car-park being opened carefully and was relieved Potter had had the sense to get rid of Mary that way and not risk her using the hall, or main corridor. Night Sister was long overdue. That corridor was long, straight, and by now likely to be empty.

The swing doors creaked, so I had to go into the hall. I could not see who had come in, as no one had appeared round the lodge. As I neared it I heard Henry say apologetically, 'I'm not sure as I should, sir. The Night Superintendent wouldn't like it. But if you say it's just for one minute——'

I was round the lodge. 'Charles!' I stopped, astonished. 'What are you doing here?' I looked at Henry. His face was expressionless. In the lodge Bert was suddenly fascinated by the switchboard and Carmelo by the transceiver. Charles was smiling. 'Are you ill?' I asked shortly.

'No.' Henry vanished, just like that. 'I was driving by here, and as I had something for you in the car thought I'd hand it in. I never guessed I'd any chance of seeing you until the porter told me you were working here to-night.' He produced a flat packet. 'This is the book on which that play was based. You said you hadn't read it. I thought it might interest you.' He held it out. 'Have I committed a hideous crime? I honestly hope not.'

I had to smile. 'I daren't think how many rules we are breaking. If you see anyone in dark blue, for God's sake start to limp or something. You didn't call to see me.'

'Perish the thought! I'm forgiven?'

'Nothing to forgive. You didn't expect to find me here. It's sweet of you to get me that book. But, please, don't ever walk into Martha's at night and ask for me again.'

'If you say not. I have to say I'm so glad I did, sweetie. Night.' The door creaked as he turned to go. My head froze over my shoulder. Andrew was holding the door for Charles.

Charles had the sense to reply to Andrew's 'Evening,' with equal brevity and vanish into the darkness of Casualty yard. The three porters were suddenly busier than ever. They had not a spare moment for noticing anything outside their lodge. I could not run away, so I waited, holding the book as if it were hot.

Andrew let the door swing to, and walked up to the lodge as if I was invisible. 'Henry, would you please let Dr Johnson know I'm back and am going up to Christian for another look before going home?'

I watched him cross the hall, then looked at the lodge. The three porters shook their heads at me in unison. I shrugged, smiled feebly, and went back to the duty-room.

Potter was there. 'I'm sorry about that business in the splint-room, Nurse Newenden.'

'What? Oh! I suppose it was Mary Eccles.' I spoke absently. 'Never mind. But do warn her never to risk coming here again.'

'I did, my dear! It's not really like her to be so crazy, but—oh —the door!' She looked out. 'Can't see the customers. Sounds like more than one, and they don't seem to be coming this way! Here's Henry.'

Henry looked grim. 'Lad with a cut face, Nurse. Fight. I've told young Bert to take him along to Twenty.'

Twenty was the male surgical dressing-room we used first at night. On occasions—I remembered several—every dressing-room in the hall could be in use at the same time. 'Thanks, Henry. Bad?' I washed my hands. 'Police involved?'

'Nah. And he's not too bad. He's got a mate with him. Dodgy pair of layabouts. I've told that young Bert to stay along of you until the S.C.O. and the dressers get back. Want me to buzz Mr Laughton sharpish?'

I had to stop feeling feeble and act like an efficient night senior. 'I had better have a look at him first, Henry. This is the first break Mr Laughton has taken to-night. And don't look so worried. Nurse Potter and I should be able to handle them.'

Potter crossed the hall with me. 'I was just telling Mary something like that,' she said cheerfully. 'Nursing's wonderful for teaching one to handle men of all types, isn't it?'

I said, 'Just so long as they are patients, patients' relatives, or wear white coats. I'm not sure it's much help with the gaps.'

'I never thought of that! Is that our uniform?'

'Probably. Remember Sister P.T.S. saying when we put it on we put on our professional armour?' I walked into Twenty and had to push the last ten minutes out of my mind. 'Good evening.' I smiled politely.

A tall, very plump youth with a long fringed haircut, draped coat, and narrow trousers stood by the other youth on the couch. He wolf-whistled at us, but did not return my greeting, smile, or so much as take the trouble to step aside.

'Hello.' I smiled at the patient. 'May I see your face?' I bent over him. 'You have got a couple of nasty cuts. How did you get them?'

'And what's it to you, doll?' demanded his friend belliger-ently.

93

Bert stiffened. Potter kept on smiling. 'Dressing-tray, Nurse Newenden?'

'I'll manage, thanks. Could you ask Henry to buzz Mr Laughton?'

An emergency setting, as ever, was ready. 'I'll just get your face cleaned up before the doctor gets here,' I explained to the hurt man, then faced the other. 'Would you like to sit on one of those benches in the hall while we attend to your friend? And I'm sorry, but I'm afraid you can't smoke in here.'

'And who's going to stop me, eh?' He stuck a cigarette between his lips.

Bert was growing purple. I caught his eye soothingly, as I pulled up my mask. 'Probably those bottles on the shelf over there. Yes—them. They are full of ether. I am going to have to use some now. Ether's very inflammable stuff. If one bottle goes up the lot'll go up. But you can smoke in the hall if you wish.'

He put the cigarette in his top pocket. 'I'm staying with me mate.'

'By all means. May I just have a little more room? Thank you.' I covered the man on the couch with another blanket, adjusted the head to a more comfortable position, cleaned up his face. 'May I now have your name, age, and address, please?'

He said he was John Bull, and he was eighteen. He refused to give an address. I did not press him for it. He was trying to act tough, but his face had to be hurting, and he was shocked. 'I only asked in case you had been in before and we had your Casualty card, or old notes, in our files.'

His mate grunted, 'He don't have no card, doll. We don't come from round here, see. And we don't like people trying to keep tabs on us neither, we don't. You'd best remember that, doll.' He flicked a finger up his face. 'Or you might be in real trouble, darlin'.'

'And why is Nurse going to be in real trouble?' asked a very quiet voice.

We all looked round. Andrew had come in. His expression told us nothing. His presence told Bert and myself that Henry had briefed him. Old Henry always brooded over his night nurses like an anxious mother hen. He had to stay in his lodge, but when he scented trouble for one of his young ladies—as he invariably referred to us—he would never hesitate to ask for help from even the Dean himself. Nor would it have been refused. Henry was one of Martha's most cherished institutions.

I said, 'A little difficulty over an address, Dr Lairg. I expect we'll sort it out soon.'

'Good.' He came to the couch. 'Let's have a look at your face, laddie. H'mmm!' He altered the angled lamp. 'You've a couple of good scratches there, but luckily they are not very deep. You should not have any trouble with scars. And how did you get them? Cleanish knife? Rusty razor? Or dirty broken bottle? I'd say, knife. Am I right?'

'Why don't you lot just get on with your something job and mind your own something business, Doc?' put in the mate.

'That's right,' muttered John Bull, taking his cue. 'You ain't something cops.'

Andrew glanced round. 'When I want you to answer a question, laddie, I'll ask you one. Just you sit down and keep quiet.' He might have been speaking to a tiresome small boy. 'And try and remember you are in a hospital, and not acting in some ham movie. I'm talking to your friend. I want to know how he was hurt, because that will affect how we treat him. No more interruptions, or you'll have to wait outside.'

'Yea? And who's going to make me?' He sat on the edge of the couch. 'Carry on, Kildare. Don't mind me.'

Bert was longing to explode. Andrew smiled slightly, then tapped the youth on his shoulder. 'Out, laddie!' His voice was soft. 'Out! Now!'

The youth looked at him. Andrew stood still. His stillness was suddenly dangerous. The plump youth mumbled, 'If I'm in your road why didn't you say so?' and swaggered self-consciously into the hall as the S.C.O. came in with his posse of dressers.

'I'm sorry you've been involved, sir. My receiver's got a short. I didn't know that until Henry rang me.'

Andrew said, 'I haven't done anything, Mr Laughton. I'll leave you to it. Good night, Nurse—Bert.' He disappeared as quietly as he had arrived.

The S.C.O. murmured to me, 'Wouldn't the damn thing have to short in my one coffee-break,' then moved to the couch. 'You've been keeping rough company, lad. What caused this?'

John Bull stopped acting tough without his ally. 'Knife. Don't know if it was clean.'

'We'll cover that. Been in this hospital before? Any hospital? Ever had an anti-tetanus injection? Any injection after a road accident? Any accident?'

His name turned out to be Trevor Frank Townly. He was sixteen, not eighteen. He did not like giving us his father's address, but he did give it.

The fat youth vanished when Mr Townly appeared. He was a huge man with a red face and very black hair. 'What's all this, eh? What they been doing to you, Trevor boy?' He turned on the S.C.O. 'Who done it? Eh?'

Mr Laughton came up to his shoulder. 'How would I know the lad's friends? Would you sign this form, please? It's time we patched him up. We have to have your consent. Then if you'll wait outside we'll fix him up for you to take home.'

The father scowled at the consent form. 'You reporting this, eh?'

Mr Laughton sighed. 'Sir, this is a hospital, not the nick. So your lad's in luck—this time—isn't he?'

Later Mr Townly shook all our hands. 'Much obliged, Doctor.' He produced a full wallet. 'We don't belong round here. How much?'

The S.C.O. reminded him the Health Service had been in action for sixteen years.

Mr Townly flushed. 'My money's not good enough for you, eh?'

'It's not that,' said the S.C.O. 'It's just that we are a little strange here. We like our jobs, and we like to keep them. We'd not do that five minutes if we took your or anybody else's money. No offence.'

Mr Townly considered this, shook his head as he put away his wallet. 'You'll never make your pile this way, Doctor.' He shook our hands again. 'Much obliged, all. I'll not forget this.' He turned to go, turned back. 'You run a car, Doctor? Or the young lady? Any time you wants a new one—you let me know.' He thrust business cards on us. 'And don't you forget. I'll fix you up good. Joe Townly don't forget.'

The S.C.O. waited until we were alone. 'When are you going to trade in your Rolls, Nurse Newenden?' He went on to say he had been surprised Trevor had only squealed like a stuck pig while being stitched. 'From Henry's build-up I expected to find a dozen Mods and Rockers taking the department apart and raping you girls.'

I explained what had happened before he arrived.

He laughed. 'That lad with the obesity problem was wise not to push Lairg too far. You knew he was once inter-hospital heavyweight champion?'

'No!' Potter was as surprised as myself. 'He doesn't look like a fighter. He's the wrong build. He's so thin—and so quiet and polite.'

'This was some years ago, Nurse. But I wouldn't want to walk into his left yet.' He glanced at me. 'Wakey, wakey, Nurse Newenden. You can't drop off into a daze now. Here we have one ambulance—as you were—two ambulances! We may have some real work to do at last. Where are those lazy louts, my dressers? Not gone again! Get 'em back! We'll show 'em what a quiet week-day night can be like in the Casualty Department of St Martha's Hospital, London!'

CHAPTER EIGHT

MRS SHAW ASKS FOR HELP

IT was five before the dressers got to bed, and then they were in such a hilarious wide-awake state that we had almost to push them bodily out of the department. The guardian angel of all night nurses was on the job again. Two minutes after I broke up the boys' wheel-chair race and got rid of them Night Sister walked into the hall.

'Quiet at last, Nurse Newenden? Good. I want one word with you.'

I took one look at her serious expression and thought, God help me! He's told her about seeing me entertaining Charles! I followed Night Sister into the duty-room and held my hands behind my back, the correct position for a Martha's nurse when being addressed by a senior.

Night Sister said, 'I have just reached a decision which I am afraid you will not like, Nurse, but I have no alternative.' She then explained I would have to stay in Casualty until Staff Nurse Carr, one of the five Cas. day staff nurses, returned from her holiday and took over Wilson's job from next Tuesday night. 'I am sorry to remove you temporarily from Albert Ward and to postpone your nights off. I trust this will not upset any special private plans? I do so dislike having to alter my nurses' off-duty.' She looked round. 'You have managed quite nicely to-night. Good girl.'

Praise from Night Sister was rare. I would have enjoyed it even more had my conscience not nagged. It was not so much the fact that Charles had turned up that caused it as the thought that, having seen us together in the flat and around the mews, our Dr Lairg had to have recognised me as his neighbour, Charles's cousin, and had by now probably added deceitfulness to my other unpleasant characteristics. I could talk myself out of feeling guilty over Charles, as that genuinely had not been my fault, but I had been acting with Andrew in the mews, and I did not now care for the memory of that at all.

I returned to the flat feeling very apprehensive that morning. There was no need. He had left before I got in, and I did not hear his car in the evening. From the pundits IN and OUT board on the lodge wall, he was in the hospital until ten that night and on two other of my Cas. nights. He did not come near the department. I was sure of that, as I was looking out for him.

Charles sent me more roses and a very apologetic letter. He seemed so sincerely upset about causing me trouble that I rang him to say thank you and explain there appeared to have been no repercussions. 'Charles,' I added, 'I am grateful, but you mustn't send me any more flowers.'

'My sweet, why not? Short of vases?' He sounded as if he was smiling. 'Or do roses give you hay-fever?'

'Of course not! But—oh, hell! Charles—you know very well what I mean! I am living more or less on Francine.'

'I wouldn't let that bother you.'

'But it does.' I decided to get the truth. 'Or are you paying my rent and electricity bills?'

He said slowly, 'Would you object very much if I was? That would make me very sad. I would love to explain why. Do you have to go home for your next nights off? It's high time we had another dinner together.'

'I must go home—I've promised the parents.'

'Then home you must go. But I must see you as soon after as you can manage it. I'm serious, Cathy.'

I had to discuss him with some one. I wrote to Meg. She wrote back by return. She was well, but had given her parents flu and had written to ask Matron for an extension of her sick-leave. She advised me to do some hard thinking about Charles. 'Are you sure you are not frightened of admitting you love him to yourself? Be sensible, my dear. You will be crazy to let a man like that slip through your fingers just because he is a first cousin.'

I took her advice. It did not change my mind, or make me feel any better about being so much in his debt.

George was on Casualty call that night. He told me Matron had given Meg that extension. 'I—er—rang her this evening.'

'How did you know her address?'

He looked as embarrassed as if I had caught him inhaling the stock ether. 'Asked the Office. I thought of going down her way this week-end. Somewhere to go on the scooter. I asked if I could look her up. She said that would be all right with her.'

We had our first smog that night. It was a blanket by the week-end and kept Luke at home. Charles went down to Devon by train. He sent me a huge box of hand-made chocolates and a card. 'These won't need vases.'

I shared them with the Cas. night staff, which eased my conscience and saved my waist-line. Potter was intrigued. 'Mary had a box just like this! You are lucky girls!'

The smog cut down our normal quota of week-end road-accident cases, but sent soaring the number of medical admissions. The pundits' board showed me it was Andrew's week-end off, but he was still in the hospital on Saturday night. Dr Johnson and his opposite number in the thoracic firm, Dr Osborne, were more or less fixtures in Casualty the whole week-end, as ambulance after ambulance crawled to the entrance and dislodged seriously ill cardiac and bronchial patients.

The Senior Medical Officer bustled in on Saturday night. 'The general "yellow" warning to all London hospitals has now turned "red." We can now only admit urgent medical cases.'

'What does that mean?' asked a dresser after the S.M.O. had gone. 'If the customers weren't urgent they wouldn't come in.'

I said, 'Roughly, it means we can't take any chronics, and the medical wards have got to discharge every one who can be sent home to make room. The pressure must be up in all the other hospitals, and if we all went on admitting at random soon there'd be no beds left.'

'Can that happen? Then what if a D.I.L. comes in?'

'Here, we wouldn't turn one away, even if it meant stacking them in rows in the Private Wing. I'm not sure that's allowed officially, but that's what we do.'

That happened the next night. There was not one bed, emergency or otherwise, left in the medical blocks, and an ambulance arrived with two very old sisters who lived alone and had been found by a fortunately inquisitive neighbour in a near comatose condition. The ambulance men, though accustomed to shocks, were very distressed. 'You never saw any room in such a state, Nurse! I wouldn't have kept a dog in the place! Not their fault, mind! They both been in bed all week and were too weak to fend for themselves. But it fair turned me up, eh, Frank?'

Frank removed his cap and mopped his forehead. 'I'll say, Tone.' He looked at me unhappily. 'Think you'll be able to take 'em, Nurse?'

The S.M.O. had been examining the old sisters with Potter as chaperon. He came out to us, holding a letter from their G.P. 'They oughtn't to come to us. They should be in a geriatric ward. This is a general hospital.' He frowned at the letter. 'I'm not allowed to admit chronics.'

Tone asked bluntly, 'Then where do we take 'em, Doctor? No one's got any room. We tried three other hospitals before you. And their doctor rang all round. He said if they had another night alone he'd not answer for the consequences.'

'Nor will I,' said the S.M.O., 'if they don't have proper treatment and food swiftly. They are both chronic arthritics, but one's got pneumonia and the other bronchitis. We'll take 'em. They'll have to share a Private Wing room. Its booked for to-morrow, so may the Good Lord have mercy on me when I have to tell Mr Franks his private patient is going to have to wait.' He signed the admission forms I had ready. 'Ring the Wing and say I'm sending them two G.W.E.'s [general ward emergencies], Nurse Newenden. I expect they'll be very rude to you, but take heart! Think what Mr Franks is going to say to me to-morrow!'

The temperature dropped sharply while I was asleep next day. The fog had gone when I went on duty, and London was having its first snow of the winter.

The dressers were now old hands. They said they had forgotten what sleep was, and were not all that clear on minor details like eating regular meals. 'You wouldn't have any more chocolates, Nurse Newenden? We are suffering from acute malnutrition.'

Mr Laughton was less phlegmatic that night. He had just heard his wife was expecting a baby, and as she was a healthy young woman he was convinced she must suffer every complication in the book. 'Everything always goes wrong for doctors' wives. Remember Joe Frasling's wife had eclampsia last year? Nearly killed her. And Mrs Hartigan's third was a breech in a transverse lie. She had fifteen stitches.'

Not having done midwifery, I could only make soothing noises. He refused to be soothed and remembered hearing I was a twin. 'My God! It might be twins! I'm sure my wife's internal measurements are too small.'

I said my mother was very slight, but had had no trouble.

'Ah—but how large is your father?'

'Very tall. Like my uncle. Or weren't you here with him?'

He had not realised I was Tropical Medicine Newenden's niece, and as it kept his mind off his wife, I plugged Uncle Tom for the next five minutes, then added that I was living temporarily in his daughter's flat.

He smiled. 'Hers is it? George Martin was talking about your classy flat. I hear you cook a good breakfast—and have a very high-powered neighbour.'

Sooner or later that had been bound to get back to Martha's. After the other night's episode I doubted it mattered, but could have done without the barrage of questions I had from my friends at our midnight meal. Bridie said I was a dark horse no less. 'Living next door to that dreamboat and saying not one word.'

'Sorry. I forgot.'

'And have you seen this woman he's engaged to? Hugh's met her. He says she has fine red hair and is a sister in that heart place across the river. A Miss MacKay—or it could be Mackenzie.'

'MacDonald,' I corrected. 'I've seen her. I didn't know she was a nurse.' I noticed the time with some relief. 'Girls, I must love you and leave you.'

The snow left off in the night, but Casualty yard was still white when Mary Eccles waited outside for Potter next morning. I pushed open the swing doors. 'Eccles! The very girl I want to see.'

She looked round slowly. 'Me, Nurse Newenden? Why?' Her voice was colder than the air.

'I want some Albert news. Nurse Gower is never at the same meal as myself, and as she will skip breakfast and hates talking at supper, I'm out of touch.'

'Oh, Albert!' She relaxed. 'Sorry. I was miles away.'

She had good news of all my old patients but Tiny. He was running a slight but constant temperature. 'Sister Albert hopes it's only a nervous reaction, but is afraid it may be the final pointer.'

'Could be. Poor little Tiny!'

His nightmares were continuing, but he was now writing sonnets to Gower.

'That boy leads a full life!' I was delighted he had recovered so quickly from hearing about her private life. 'Isn't she his third in Albert?'

'Fourth. The first was that student-physio.'

'So she was! Keeping tags on his love-life is a full-time job. The strange thing is the way each time he seems to kid himself it's the real thing.'

She said, 'Perhaps it is—while it lasts. Some men are like that.' The way her whole manner stiffened reminded me of what Potter had said about her own affair. 'Only a fool would take them seriously.'

I thought of Charles. 'Unless one happened to be in love with a man like that. Then it might not be so easy to be sensible.'

She looked at me hard, but said no more, and as I knew how much she disliked any personal conversation I went back into the hall.

At breakfast Sister Dining-room came out of her office and over to our table. Bridie murmured, 'And which of us has not done what?'

My mother was on the telephone. Sister said I could take the call in her office. It was only a few yards, but before I raised the receiver I was sure my father and Luke were dangerously ill, or dead, and the house had burnt down.

Robert, my father's bachelor curate, had chicken-pox. Our

G.P. had just diagnosed him before his morning surgery. Mother was nursing him in our house, and as I had not had it thought I ought to keep away.

She was right, but I was disappointed. I had been looking forward to getting right away from Martha's, Charles, the flat, and, as I now realised, from Andrew Lairg. He had been on my mind too constantly during the past nights in Casualty, but I had been too busy to work out why. I would have time for that in the flat, and for listening for his car, watching his windows, wondering how much longer he was going to be next door, and why I found the thought of Ann MacDonald vaguely annoying. I knew he was beginning to fascinate me, and I did not want to be fascinated. I was happy the way I was.

Bridie was alone at the table when I returned. She was not due off for two nights and was then visiting a married sister in Liverpool. She looked very tired and was worried by her babies in Christian. She told me to stop moaning and thank heaven fasting I was not the mother of one of them. 'Think of that poor Mrs Stone with her one and only pale blue and gasping even in a tent.'

That cut my own problems down to size. 'Are they going to be able to operate?'

'It's in the air. The parents are so keen—they know it's the only hope. Hope! Honest to God! It'll be more like a miracle if the poor little scrap survives the first whiff of anaesthetic.'

'We can't just let him die.'

She rounded on me, her eyes blazing. 'And would he be alive at all if he was not getting all we have to give him? Do you think we enjoy having to watch him, the way he is? When it's hell on earth for his parents? His mother hasn't left the ward for days. She was sitting up all night by his cot. But she wants to save her son—not finish him off! That'll happen for sure, if they operate too soon! I was there when Lairg said so to his father only last night!'

The Stone baby was very much on my mind when I left the Home. I saw George across the road, but we only waved and went our separate ways. By mutual consent, and without either of us having to say anything, our friendship had suddenly fallen apart. I knew he had seen Meg on his week-end off, as he had given me her love, but he had not enlarged on that, and I had asked no questions. While I waited for my bus I wondered if my move to the flat had speeded our break-up, or whether that night in Matilda had been the catalyst. I decided it was the latter mainly, but the flat had helped by removing me physically. In the Home I had been so handy when he wanted a shoulder, but he had not wanted mine enough to make him

102

cross the river. Meg was different. He had driven eighty freezing miles on his scooter to see her. I was pleased for Meg, even if that did nothing for my morale.

Mrs Shaw arrived in the mews on her moped a little after I let myself into the flat. I heard Andrew go out some minutes later, and then, almost immediately, the sound of Charles opening his garage.

I did not go down. I knew I should let him know I was not going home, but I did not yet feel strong enough for dealing with him. To-morrow perhaps, after a night's sleep. I told myself I was very sleepy until his car disappeared round the mews, and then I turned too restless to think of going to bed. I had a bath, washed my hair, spring-cleaned the flat, and it was still only eleven.

I was delighted to be interrupted by the door-bell. It was Mrs Shaw, in outdoor clothes. 'I'm glad I caught you before you went out, miss.'

'Something wrong?'

'I tell you dear, there's times when it's hard to know what to do for the best. I got my man in bed to-day, and you know what men are when they are poorly! Well, no'—she corrected herself —'you won't yet! You wait until you're married! Have a man in bed with a sniffler, and he'll play you up worse than six kiddies!'

I sympathised. 'And how are you? That's a nasty cough you've got.'

'I'm none too good, miss. The doctor, he spotted it soon as I come. I had to ask again if he'd mind me leaving off dinner-time. He wanted me to go straight back. I couldn't do that— what with no warning—I mean it wouldn't be right, would it? So then he said as he'd be real cross if I wasn't away by eleven and so much as showed my face round here for the rest of the week. "You keep on like this, Mrs Shaw," he says, "and you'll be real ill. You go home by eleven and look after yourself as well as your family. And no coming back here," he says, "until you got rid of that cough!"'

'He's right, Mrs Shaw. Is your cough hurting?'

'It catches me, miss. I've had it worse. That smog didn't do it no good, and I can't say as I'd mind a day or two quiet. But I don't like leaving the doctor to hisself.' She looked over her shoulder, then lowered her voice, conspiratorily, even though the mews was deserted, apart from the inevitable mechanic working under a car by the garage at the far end. 'The doctor shouldn't never have gone to work this morning. Real poorly, he looked. I told him straight. "Doctor," I says, "you ought to be in bed yourself and not going out in this cold. Feels like more

103

snow." But he said he was all right, and he must know.'

Being more accustomed to doctors, I had my own views on that. Tom Orme had not been an exception. Off-hand, I could remember a row of equally well-qualified men who had ignored their health as he had done his. Doctors when ill came in one of two classes—those who took to their beds and screamed for antibiotics and D.I.L. labels with a temperature of ninety-nine, and those who refused to admit an illness to their colleagues, and dosed themselves on the quiet until they cured themselves or collapsed.

I asked, 'Has he got a cold?'

'If you ask me, miss, it's the flu. He looked just now as if he didn't know how to lift his own weight. I was hoping as his young lady might be able to stop by, and his mum phoned from Scotland not five minutes after he gone and asked me to leave a note to say as Miss MacDonald arrived safe early this morning. Seems as she's spending her holidays with his mum, and the doctor was worried as she might have missed some connection last night. I didn't like to worry the old lady with his being poorly,' she added confidingly, 'what with her being so far off, and—well—she can't be young, can she? Shame, though, his young lady being away! And she a nurse.'

'So I've heard. It is a pity.'

She put a hand on my arm. 'Then you'll not mind if I ask you to keep an eye on things for me, dear? Just see as he fetches in his milk and the papers. And if you need me'—she handed me a slip of paper—'that's the address. I'll come back any time and give the place a lick and a promise and see to his dinners. You'll let me know? And you'll not say nothing of this to him? He'd not like that at all.'

She was an exceedingly kind, thoughtful woman. There was nothing I could do but agree with all her suggestions. I watched her *putt-putt* away, thinking how nice she was, and feeling slightly perturbed as well as amused at being left holding this specific baby. I could well imagine Andrew's reaction could he have overheard our conversation. I guessed he had flu, but had chosen to walk round with it, as the hospital was too full of germs for his to make any difference, and being so busy he felt he ought to put in an appearance. That would not do his flu any good, and of course he would never allow one of his flu patients to behave like that, but as he seemed to belong in the Tom Orme class, the thought of applying those rules to himself would not occur to him.

I was quite sanguine about him during that morning, but in the afternoon I went to sleep in the sitting-room and had a long, involved, nightmarish dream in which I was nursing him

104

with pneumonia in Albert and he kept thrashing about the way Tiny did in his nightmares, and then lay very still as the Professor had done, and while I was taking his pulse it stopped and did not start again.

The sound of a car below woke me with a start. I found I was shaking and very cold. I heaved myself over to the window to see if it was Charles, and longing with an urgency that surprised me for it to be Andrew. That dream had been far too vivid, and it was still too close.

It was Andrew. It was raining, not snowing, and as on that first evening the rain slanted through the wide beam of light from his open garage. Again his hat was turned down and coat-collar up, and I could not see his face, but even when the light went out I recognised the outline as his own. When he disappeared I stayed a while watching the rain, remembering that other occasion and how thrilled I had been when I thought him Charles. In time it was a few weeks back. It seemed to belong in another century.

A few minutes later the paper-boy pushed my evening paper into the letter-box. I went down for it at once, but the bit that had stuck out was already soaked.

I read the paper over my tea-cum-supper without taking any of it in. My mind kept drifting back to that dream, and then to Tom Orme. Hell—I stared at the dividing wall—the man is a physician! He's a lot older than Tom. He can't be that crazy about his health. If he is ill he'll know what to do and do it.

I was firm with myself. I had to think of something else. I rang my home. Luke answered. He had had chicken-pox at school, but did not want to come up for the week-end, as June was staying down and he was taking her to some dance. 'Mum wants to know if you'll be seeing a lot of Charlie-boy in your nights off?'

'Nothing's fixed yet. He still thinks I'm going home.'

My mother took over and gave me a 'Darling, I know you are twenty-one and have your own life to live, but . . .' lecture. I insisted she could stop worrying. 'Charles is only being very nice to me.'

'Darling,' said my mother, 'that is what worries me. He may look like his father, but he is very like his mother. You know how I feel about your Aunt Frances. I am sorry, but I do not care for that young man. And he is far too sophisticated for you!'

Luke was on the line. 'Dear old mum! If that doesn't make you leap into Charlie-boy's arms nothing will! Those the pips—right. See you, love!'

I felt more normal after talking to them, so rang one of my

105

set who was now married and lived in Hampstead. As I hoped, she was hungry for hospital news and asked me to spend to-morrow with her. 'I love being married, and the infant is heaven, but how I miss it all! Come early, Cathy! Or do you want a long lie-in?'

'Not if I go to bed now, which is what I'm about to do.'

I had forgotten to put out my milk bottles. I took them down. It was still raining. Andrew's lights were on behind drawn curtains, and his limp evening paper was hanging from the letter-box. That reminded me not only of Mrs Shaw and my dream, but the odd fact that I had never met another man who could resist reading an evening paper the moment it arrived. Probably he had not heard the boy. I reached out, pushed the paper right through, making the box clatter intentionally, then closed my door and sat on the stairs. I had frequently heard him on his own stairs from down there. I heard nothing now.

So he did not feel like reading the news? Why should he? He might be in the bath, on the telephone, watching television. I was letting myself get obsessed with the man. It was all very well to keep brooding on Tom Orme collapsing in the Doctors' House, but Tom had had a strong motive for wanting to keep going. Andrew was now free for the night. He could dose himself and retire to bed. His front lights could be on because he had forgotten to turn them off. And if he really needed help he had a telephone.

That gave me an idea. I looked up the number of the last tenant right in Francine's list, and rang the number, intending to put down the receiver directly I heard his voice. That would show he was up and about, which would stop my bones niggling because of that paper.

He did not answer his phone. Maybe he was asleep? Or it was out of order again? To keep myself quiet, I checked with the exchange. There was nothing wrong with his line. The girl said helpfully, 'Perhaps the gentleman doesn't feel like taking any calls to-night? He doesn't have to.'

'No,' I said, 'thanks.' I did not explain he was a physician on the staff of a busy hospital, and that while he might well detest the telephone, if he heard it ring he would have to answer it.

I was now seriously perturbed. It was not only my imagina-tion. Something very odd had to be going on next door. Why on earth did his wretched young woman have to choose this time to take a holiday in Scotland? But would it have helped had she been in London? Bridie said she worked in a heart hospital, but, knowing Bridie, that could be any hospital anywhere in London with a cardiac department. And if I had the right hospital, could I have rung her out of the blue?

The telephone gave me a second inspiration. I could say some one had called to ask if his phone was out of order, as Ann MacDonald had done. Some man, and he was holding on. Could I help it if the caller had rung off when I got back? It might have been some one playing the fool, or a would-be burglar checking to find who was at home before raiding the mews.

I took my receiver off the hook, to lend colour to my story, grabbed a jacket and my front-door key before I lost my nerve. It nearly failed me at his front door. I told myself I was crazy. He did not like me. He had been very decent about ignoring that Cas. episode, but from the way we now never met in the mews I suspected he was as keen to avoid me as I was him. A pundit no more wanted one of his own nurses on his doorstep than vice versa. If he really had flu, with its inevitable depression, I might now set the cat among the pigeons.

Nervously, I touched the bell. I heard the ring. Nothing happened. I rang again, more loudly. Again, nothing. Obviously he had forgotten to turn off the front lights and had gone to bed. I stood back, looked up, then pushed open his letter-box to see if the light was on in his hall. I could not see into it without stooping, so that was what I did. That was how I immediately smelt the unmistakable scent of leaking gas.

CHAPTER NINE

ANDREW FORGETS HIS MEDICINE

THE door was unlocked. I shouted, 'Dr Lairg! You about?' then took a deep breath of fresh air, clamped a hand over my nose and mouth, and, leaving the door wide, tore up the stairs and straight into the kitchen. I remembered Francine telling me the three flats had been redesigned ten years ago by the same architect. Her gas-mains tap was in a cupboard under one of the kitchen sinks. The hissing was coming from the kitchen. I found a similar cupboard and tap. When I turned it off the hissing stopped.

My heard was bursting. I threw up the kitchen window, stuck out my head, and gasped in clean air. Then I saw the lidless saucepan of hot water on a ring of the gas cooker. The tap was open, and the cooker old-fashioned, unlike Francine's, with its many safety attachments. I flicked the tap shut on my way back to the hall in case there was any gas left in the pipe.

The flat geography was identical to Francine's. The bedroom doors were open and in darkness. The sitting-room door was shut. I dived in and straight for the windows, before looking closely at the figure stretched on the leather sofa. The room was very warm. The heat was coming from a powerful electric fan-convector. I switched it off, looked quickly for anything that might spark off an explosion, and seeing nothing had to hang out of a window again. I was getting too giddy even to dial 999.

The rain hitting my hot face was as gentle as a caress. The wind was quite strong and swept into the room to join the draught from the open doors and kitchen window. I inhaled deeply, and in a few seconds my head cleared. Suddenly, I was very frightened. I had seen the effects of gas-poisoning in Cas. He could be dead. I turned to face what had to be faced and stood staring, transfixed with relief.

He was sitting up. Languidly, he swung his legs to the floor, stretched his shoulders, and blinked as if waking from normal sleep. 'The place on fire?' he asked calmly.

I was more than relieved. I was struck dumb by an astonishing and totally unexpected joy. I grinned foolishly, shaking my head.

'Then might I ask what you are doing here?' His voice was polite, but it had an edge. 'Why the open windows?' He stood up. 'I hope this is not another wee joke.'

'No! And don't get up! It could be dangerous. You left——'

'Dangerous?' he echoed, coming towards me. 'You are sure this isn't another joke?'

I was too anxious to get him back on that sofa to remember tact. I had a very good reason. 'Of course not!' I snapped. 'Would I risk bursting in here like this unless I was forced to? Can't you smell the gas? There wasn't much in here, but I can still smell it.'

'Gas? That saucepan——' and he vanished.

I hurried after him. 'I've turned off your mains and the cooker. Don't go into the kitchen—you'll only inhale more. I'm sorry about the howling gale, but it was essential. The atmosphere up here was grim when I arrived.'

He was now looking a little dazed. 'How long have you been here?'

'A few minutes. Maybe less. Your front door wasn't locked. I did call, but you didn't hear, so I came in.'

He put his hands in his pockets. 'Thank you. You smelt it from your flat?'

'The front door.' I did not specify which one. 'Dr Lairg, please sit down—or better still—lie down. You may have inhaled more than you know.'

'I'm all right, thanks.'

He did not look all right. His face was a yellow-grey. The shadows beneath his eyes were as dark as his hair. He opened the bedroom windows, then followed me into the sitting-room, closed the door, and examined the fit. 'This is quite good. Not much can have got in under it, or I'd not have woken up so easily. And the fan kept the air moving, but it couldn't filter it. If you had not come in, as I was asleep, eventually enough would have got in to keep me under.' He faced me. 'I woke as you switched off the heater. I couldn't think what was going on. I was feeling rather hazy, as I've a touch of malaria and took some quinine when I came in. That was why I didn't smell it. For some reason quinine always inhibits my olfactory nerve. It was singularly lucky for me that you happened——' and his voice stopped. He went down as if I had hit him on the head with something very heavy.

'No!' I muttered. 'I knew it!' For the second time that evening fear had me by the throat. I knelt by him, reached for his pulse with one hand, put the other on his chest. He was breathing. His heart-rhythm was typical of an ordinary faint. Thank God! I thought. Thank God! I took off his tie, loosened his collar, and was about to leap for the telephone when he came round.

He shifted himself on to his back and stretched out his legs. He smiled up at me, and I was reminded of that night in Albert. In a way, I was back in Albert. From the moment he went down I had mentally snapped into uniform. He said, 'Being a well-trained St Martha's nurse, of course you won't say "I told you so." '

I smiled back, still holding his pulse. 'No, Doctor.'

'How long was I out?'

'Around a minute. No'—I held his shoulder down—'don't try and sit up yet. You'll be very giddy and may pass out again.' I pulled a flattish leather cushion from the nearest chair and put it under his head. 'That more comfortable?'

'Fine, thanks.' He met my eyes. 'It could be said I am well and truly hoist with my own petard.'

Momentarily I thought of that first night. I guessed it was in his mind too. 'Have you fainted before?'

'I've been knocked out. I've never fainted. It's an interesting experience, seeing the other side of the picture. I've always given patients the advice you've just given me about not moving too soon. I never realised the aftermath left one quite so giddy. I haven't had a head like this since the morning after I qualified. Must be middle age.'

I sat back on my heels. 'Couldn't it be carbon monoxide?' He raised an eyebrow. 'I remember Dr Barnes saying a very little could have the same effect as a few double whiskies on an empty stomach.'

'That could be a contributory cause. You seem well acquainted with gas-poisoning. From Casualty?' I nodded. 'Did you wonder if I had gone into acute failure?'

'Yes. I've seen that happen.'

'You have? When? I've only seen it once.'

I did not answer immediately. I was suddenly feeling as if I was sitting on my own shoulder watching us both. I had a splendid imagination, but never ever could I have imagined us both on his floor, with him in his pundit's suiting and myself in sweater, jacket, and slacks, swopping hospital 'shop.' 'It was in Casualty last winter. A man walked in saying he had suddenly felt very queer when driving himself home from his office. He had been working late. He had no pain, no dramatic or even definite symptoms. Then he collapsed. We couldn't bring him round.'

'Faulty car heater? And the car windows closed?'

'Yes. He'd been inhaling the exhaust fumes.'

He said, 'Carbon monoxide can do that if there is too much

110

exertion too soon. The heart goes into acute failure and that's that. As I should have remembered, when you tried to persuade me to sit down. I forgot.' His smile was self-derisive. 'As Sir Joshua used to say, even Homer sometimes nods.'

I nodded absently, thinking now of the original anxiety that had been driven out of my head by the gas. 'Doctor, I think you should see some one. Can I ring Martha's for you?'

'Martha's?' He raised himself on an elbow. 'Whatever for? I don't need hospitalisation.'

'But you should see a physician.'

'Because I fainted? I'm over that. There's nothing wrong with me now that can't be put right with some more quinine and a night's sleep. If necessary, I'll take to-morrow off. I very much doubt it will be necessary.'

I felt a strong fellow-feeling with the Jenner nurses. 'You don't look well, Doctor.'

'In what way?'

I gave him the truth. 'Your colour's wrong. Your pulse is now too fast. And your skin feels as if your temperature is up.'

'I know I've got a temperature.' He dismissed that one. 'And under the circumstances it would be odd if my pulse wasn't behaving oddly. Now, my colour. Yellowish or reddish?'

'Yellowish-grey.'

His mouth twitched. 'You have my sympathy—and nothing to worry about. If there was any carbon monoxide hanging around in my lungs I'd have a red face. The yellow is just malaria cum quinine.'

'Do you often have these bouts?'

'Most winters since I picked it up when I was in the Army in Malaya. They aren't serious, merely a nuisance. They never last more than four days, and quinine works better on me than the new anti-malarial drugs.' He sat up and leant against the back of the sofa. 'You needn't look at me like that. I may have my weak moments, but in general I do know what I'm talking about.'

That would have slapped me down had he not still looked so wretched. I said, 'I am sure you do, Dr Lairg. But you can't listen to your own chest. Nor can you take a picture of your own skull. You did fall. You are a tall man. You may have hit your head.'

'I doubt it would have hurt it if it did, on this carpet. Being unconscious, I fell soft. If it'll ease your mind'—he felt his head—'no sign of any damage.'

'Isn't it possible to have a hair-line fracture without any outward signs or immediate symptoms?'

111

'It is.' His voice was grave, but suddenly his eyes were alight with laughter. 'It's also possible to fracture a femur by fainting on a floor with a carpet even thicker than this one. And to crack half a dozen ribs, with a perforation of one or both lungs. I have known all those things happen, but the patients were slightly older than myself. Over eighty. I have a little way to go before I reach that age, though that may well surprise you. Please,' he went on, 'don't think me ungrateful for your concern, but I think I'll take my chance on a query fractured skull, pneumonia, a lung abscess, cerebral anaemia, general cardiac deterioration, and—what have I left out?'

I had to smile. 'A cold in the head? It's freezing in here now.'

'Of course! Thank you.' He stood up. 'It's a bit early to close the windows. We need something to deal with this cold.'

I opened my mouth for another protest, closed it without uttering one. I did not like giving in, but could see I had no alternative. I got on my feet and found I was shivering. 'Have you an electric kettle? Shall I make some tea?'

'The kettle's fused; that's why I put on the saucepan. I was going to make tea first and fix the fuse later. I think this'll be the better answer.' He produced a bottle of whisky and two glasses from a cupboard then handed me a drink. 'That suit you?'

'May I get some water? I don't like the taste of whisky.'

He took a soda siphon from the cupboard. 'Since you have in all probability saved my life this evening, I'll overlook that remark. No Scotsman could do more. Say when.'

'Thank you.' I shivered violently and dropped the glass. 'I'm so sorry!'

'Don't worry—it won't hurt the carpet.' He looked at me keenly, then gave me his own untouched drink. 'You have that straight whether you like the taste or not. And sit down. You've had an exhausting evening.'

'I'm only cold.' I drank the whisky fast, as I was also feeling suddenly very peculiar. 'One is always cold on night duty.'

'That's because night nurses never have enough sleep.' He closed one window and left the other only a little open. 'Have you had any to-day?'

I looked at his back and thought what a relief it was that all pretence was over. 'All afternoon.'

'Good.' He sat on the arm of the chair next to mine. 'You complained about my colour. You should now see your own.' He pushed forward one end of the sofa. 'Get your feet up on that.'

'I'm all right. Honestly.'

He said, 'I have a kind of feeling that this is where we came in. Now, be a sensible girl. Do as I say, if not as I do. That's better.' He got up to pour us more drinks, adding soda to mine. 'Take this more slowly. It won't go to your head.' He felt his neck. 'Where's my tie? You take it off?'

'Yes. It's on the floor somewhere.'

'Don't move. It'll turn up. I'll get another and close'—he opened the door—'Oh! Good evening.'

I saw who was behind him, and nearly dropped a second glass. 'Charles! What are you doing here?'

Charles came in smiling apologetically, but otherwise unembarrassed at having walked into a casual acquaintance's flat. 'Looking for you, my sweet. Your lights are all on next door, but answer came there none when I rang.' He turned to Andrew. 'Your door was open. I did knock, but no one seemed to hear, so I came up. I was going to ask if I could borrow your phone to ring my cousin. I hope you've no objections?'

'Not at all.' He offered Charles a whisky, then noticed his tie sticking out from under the sofa, and put it on while he explained why I was there with a lack of embarrassment that equalled Charles's.

Charles sat on the arm of my chair. 'What a good thing you changed your mind about going home, darling!'

'It was changed for me. Robert's got chicken-pox.'

'Robert?' echoed Charles in a drawl as affected as Francine at her worst. 'For God's sake, darling, which one is Robert? The scooter-owner? But isn't that George?' He sighed. 'Cathy, my love, you are getting an even larger collection of scalps than my cherished sister.'

Suddenly I caught on. Andrew had said nothing about my being a nurse in his explanation, and Charles was merely backing up my old Francine routine. I glanced at Andrew and wished I had not. He was looking like a pundit again.

'Robert is Father's curate; he's got chicken-pox and Mother's nursing him. As I've not had it she told me to stay away. I don't think Matron would like me to add chicken-pox to the flu that's circulating round Martha's.'

Charles caught my eye. I nodded slightly. He smiled, but did not alter his manner as he turned to Andrew. 'I wonder if Robert knows how wise he is to take to his sickbed? My cousin has a sad weakness which I prised out of her twin brother after a vast quantity of beer. To gain her interest one has to be sick or maimed.'

Andrew said drily, 'Then she would seem to be in the right profession,' and changed the subject to chance and the way people tended to underestimate the part it played in all our lives. 'If a curate unknown to me had not developed chicken-pox this morning I should now be a dead man.'

Charles was dubious. 'You said the door was shut and fits well. Could enough have got in?'

'Unquestionably. It takes only a half to one per cent concentration in the air breathed to be very quickly fatal.'

I watched them, comparing them mentally. Charles was by far the better-looking and the younger by five years. He could have been younger by double that. For once, instead of seeing the one man among the boys as at Francine's parties, he looked immature. There was charm, humour, and intelligence in his face, but I saw now what was lacking. Character. He was far more like Francine than I had thought, if not in the way my mother and Luke assumed. He knew how to give a girl a good time, cope with waiters, attend board meetings; he was an expert at living it up; but he did not yet know as much about life in general as George. That was in his face. I should have seen it before, but I had not been looking. I looked again at Andrew, and then away quickly as he was watching me. That did not matter. I now knew the lines of his face very, very well.

He noticed me stifle another yawn and suggested I must be very tired. I took the hint. In a few minutes we were all down in the mews. The rain had stopped, and the wind was drying the cobbles.

Andrew thanked me again, said good night to us both, and went in, closing his door.

I disentangled my arm from Charles's and unlocked my front door. 'I hope you don't mind, but I'm not going to ask you in. I'm whacked.'

'Can't you stay up a little while longer? It's not really late.'

'It is if you haven't been to bed for twenty-four hours.' The lights went out in Andrew's sitting-room. 'And it's been quite an evening.'

'But a very profitable one.'

I stiffened. 'In what way?'

'Darling! You've now got him eating out of your hand! No matter what you do at Martha's, he can't make any trouble for you.' He put his hands on my shoulders. 'I have always thought you a very clever girl.'

I said coldly, 'I didn't turn that gas on, Charles.'

'No. But you saw your opportunity and used it. I must say I was a little, shall we say—surprised—when I walked in and saw you lying on his sofa. I did wonder what his woman would have said.'

'As I presume his fiancée would rather have him alive than

114

dead, I imagine she would have said thank you.'

'So he's engaged to this ward sister?'

'Yes.' I was surprised. 'How did you know she's a nurse? Did I tell you?'

'I expect so, darling. Or he may have done. I forget. And I'm nearly forgetting something else. I'm very cross with you.' He shook me gently. 'Why didn't you let me know you were staying in town?'

'I was going to do that to-morrow. I'm always so sleepy on my first night off.'

'Was that really why?' he asked and kissed me. He kissed very well. I noticed that academically. His kiss left my emotions untouched.

He moved away. 'A very clever girl, darling.' He walked off quickly, leaving me gaping after him in the mews. I waited until he disappeared round the corner, then looked up at the darkened windows and knew exactly how George had felt after that night in Matilda. I'll think about it all when I've slept, I thought. Not now.

I woke earlier than usual after a first night off. I heard both cars being taken out while I was still in bed. When I left to visit Beth in Hampstead there was a note in one of Andrew's empty milk bottles asking the milkman to stop delivering temporarily. That could mean his malaria was worse and he had taken himself to Martha's, but it seemed more probable that, as Mrs Shaw was away, he had decided to move into some club of the Doctors' House to save the bother of having to fend for himself. It also saved us both from having to meet again too soon. Once I would have been very glad about that. Now the sight of his closed windows had me feeling quite hideously lonely, and longing to get back on duty, not because of my precious Albert, but to work in the same building as himself.

I enjoyed seeing Beth, her husband, and baby son, and was delighted when, on realising I had so much free time, they asked me to spend the rest of my nights off with them. Beth drove me back to the flat to collect a suitcase that evening, leaving her husband to baby-sit. The flat impressed her vastly. 'Cathy! It's not true! Won't you hate going back to the Home after this?'

Twenty-four hours ago I would have denied that firmly. I now found myself looking at the dividing wall. 'It'll be a wrench.'

She wanted to know about the neighbours. I explained not having yet seen the absent Americans, and Andrew.

'Next door? A pundit? Oh, you poor dear! How ghastly for you! Do you have to see much of him?'

'Hardly anything.'

115

She said kindly, 'That's a break! Of course, there was bound to be one snag. There always is.'

It was the time of evening Charles often put his car away. We did not hear it come in while we were there, nor did the telephone ring. I was a little surprised and very relieved. It was clear that Charles was working up for some sort of a show-down with me, and I had expected to find the telephone ringing as we walked in, or at least a note on the letter-box. That only contained another letter from Meg giving me a much fuller account of George's last week-end. She still had another ten days at home, and he had promised to borrow Hugh Devine's car and drive down to fetch her on his next free week-end. 'George,' wrote Meg, 'is really rather sweet. He is so thoughtful.'

Beth had been reading my evening paper while I read Meg's letter. 'Cathy, is this your cousin?'

In the gossip column was a rather bad photo of Charles talking to an elderly American oil man at London Airport that morning. 'Yes. That's Charles. He's better than that, and that old man must be tall, as he looks the larger, and Charles is nearly six two.'

Her eyes widened. 'Why did no one ever tell me Little Miss Money had a brother like this? I used to wonder how you put up with her, Cathy! Now I know! You are so lucky! All that lovely money—and good looks!'

'He's only my cousin, dear. Remember?'

She was not listening. She was gazing at me dreamily. 'Johnny hasn't been christened yet. You must be a godmother! We haven't one rich relation for him between us.'

I laughed. 'And what if Charles doesn't ask me to marry him?'

'You must make him! Does he date you? Duckie, you're as good as up the aisle! He must like you—all you have to do is nail him down.'

'How?' I was intrigued. She used to be a shy girl, and when she had announced her engagement to an equally shy school-master, how they ever reached even that point had been a favourite speculation in our set.

'Oh—the usual! Make a fuss of him, tell him he's wonderful and you can't live without him. All men'll swallow that! He won't have a hope if you really make up your mind. And you must have brains, Cathy. You always did very well in our exams. Think of your advantages! You are a blonde with brains, and you don't look as if you've got anything between your ears. You can't lose! And it'll be so lovely for Johnny.'

'One small snag, Beth. I don't want to marry him.'

She waved that aside. 'Don't tell me money isn't everything! Believe me, it means the hell of a lot when one's married. The only rows Jack and I ever have are about cash. Everything seems to go on food and rent. I can't remember when I last bought any new clothes. Jack has to be respectable for school, but he looks like a tramp at home. And babies cost the earth. We want more—we can't think how we'll afford them. But if you marry your cousin you will never ever have to worry about the grocer, new shoes, finishing up revolting little messes of baby food, as it's too precious to throw away, or pretending a maternity dress you hate is a shift and quite fashionable because you've nothing else to wear! Think of all that!'

'I am.' I glanced again at the dividing wall. 'I hope Johnny won't be too mad at me. No dice.'

'Then you are either a nut case—or in love with some one else!'

'Could be. Beth, shouldn't we go? You said we'd be back by eight.'

She had a final disappointed look at that newspaper photo. 'My poor little Johnny! Yes. Let's go.'

CHAPTER TEN

ANDREW TURNS NEIGHBOURLY

'NURSE!' Stan Gould hissed the length of Albert. 'He's off!'

I reached Tiny as his muttered jumble of words turned into semi-coherent sentences. His voice rose. If not woken at that point he started shouting.

A few minutes later I put my head round the kitchen door. 'Sorry, Player. We've got to change Tiny again.'

She dried her hands. 'Bottom sheet as well as the draw?'

'Yes. He's drenched.'

'I didn't hear him.'

'Our Stan was on the job.'

'Bully for Stan,' she said wearily. It was her last night before nights off, and we were back on take-in.

Albert had had another general post during my absence. Tiny was now in Twenty-five, Stan in Twenty-six. Sister Albert had told them she was putting them together as they had become great friends. There was some truth in that, but it did not blind Albert to her fundamental reason. Tiny, as always one step ahead, collected thirty bob from his fellow-patients on the night following the move. He was now offering odds-on that he would be in Twenty-four before the New Year.

Barry Cuthbert, the present man in that bed, had both hands crushed. He was a maintenance mechanic in a local factory. He had thought the machine he wanted to check was switched off. It was not. When he was admitted it seemed impossible that his hands would ever be any use to him again. The operation on both had taken six hours. There was now a good chance that his left hand would get back to normal. The right could never be that, as he had lost the tips of all four fingers. He was very pleased with the set of plastic tips Mr Franks left with him. 'I'll not have to bother clipping me nails, eh, Nurse? And you can't say as I'm not in luck, me being left-handed and all!'

Tiny's move had worried me a lot, but I was very glad to have him between Cuthbert and Stan. Tiny was looking ill. He was visibly thinner, his eyes were too bright, and he was either unnaturally gay or black with depression. Neither Cuthbert nor Stan knew the meaning of that last word. Cuthbert I liked and admired, but Stan Gould, in a different way, was filling the gap left by Professor Brown. His behaviour on his first night had not been, as we thought, a touch of euphoria induced by severe shock. It was simply great courage, though he would have been shocked all over again had anyone told him so. He now had one steel pin through his left knee, another through his right ankle; both his legs were immobilised and strung up on pulleys; his ribs were strapped, and he had only recently had the full use of both lungs. The strapping bothered him, as it would itch, but not so much as his own weakness at forgetting to remove the four-letter words when speaking to us. He was also very distressed by the loss of his van. His boss had promised his job back as soon as he was fit. 'I'll never get another —— van like that lovely —— job what was crushed by that —— —— what come crashing into me —— behind! Never played me up once, she —— didn't! Engines,' said Stan, 'is like women. You get 'em —— good and you get 'em —— bad. Don't matter how you treat 'em. The —— good never give you no trouble, and the —— bad never give you nothing —— else. What's that, mate? The nurse? Streuth! I —— forgot!'

Albert was constantly being upset by Stan's language. There was no need, since we seldom understood any of Stan's assorted swear words. I asked George the meaning of a couple. He told me to ask Luke.

Player came up to the table as I added the latest record to Tiny's four-hourly chart. The graph was now showing a clear swing, and each rise and fall was increasing. He had just dropped four degrees. She said, 'Many more of these sweats, and he'll melt away.' She tapped with her scissors the long list of antibiotics in red ink above the graph. 'We can't plug him more. Why don't they control this?'

'No one knows. Obviously, he's either worked up a resistance to them, or he's cooking some new bug they can't touch—or can't touch on him. Can work like that.'

'How long can they let this go on?'

'I asked the men that on their rounds. I couldn't pin anyone down, but I had the impression not much longer.'

'Week?'

I shook my head.

'Less? Then thank heaven I'm off from to-morrow. I'll warn Eccles—no—I can't! She's not flying back from Edinburgh until lunch-time. I want to get the nine-fifteen.'

'Eccles live in Edinburgh?'

'No. Devon. She's visiting friends. They wanted her to fly to save time.'

'Good idea.'

'If you can afford it.'

I guessed Mary Eccles' young man was paying. 'Player, are the theatres working?'

She went over to a window, then came back. 'There are a few lights on in the general theatre. They must be clearing up.'

'Hell! I wish our Unit was working. I don't want to get Mr Briggs out of bed just to make him take another look at this chart now, but I'd feel happier if he did.'

'How about Mr Martin? Housemen expect to be called up.'

'I don't want a houseman,' I told her honestly. 'A houseman can't tell me any more than I see for myself from this chart. Mr Martin'll only quote the books at me. Mr Briggs knows his stuff too much for that. Perhaps he's up. Look after the men. I'll ask old Henry.'

'Mr Briggs, Nurse Newenden?' echoed Henry. 'It's not his Cas.-call, but he was down here not a half-hour back. Hang on. I'll take a look.' I hung on. 'You there, Nurse?' He was back on the line. 'The S.S.O. wants to know why Albert wants Mr Briggs?'

'So-help-me, Henry! Is he standing by you? I didn't realise he was in Cas.'

'He's not the only one! We got a real do going on round the corner. S.S.O., S.M.O., Dr Norton, Dr Phillips [the Paediatric Registrar], Mr Orme, Dr Hartigan, Dr Lairg, *and*'—Henry played his ace—'Sir Ivor!'

The latter was our Senior Consultant Surgeon and a world expert on repairing holes in the human heart. 'Whose heart have they been mending?' I asked curiously. 'Or are they fixing up a job?'

Henry said there was no telling, as he had not been able to hear what they were saying, but he reckoned he would be surprised if that Dr Stone's little lad wasn't along the theatre to-morrow morning. 'I'd best get over. The S.S.O.'s looking this way. Why did you want Mr Briggs?'

'Only to have a word with him about Ellis in Twenty-five.'

'Hang on again.'

I had to wait some time. I spent a lot of it wishing myself back in Cas. at that moment. I had not seen Andrew since the night he left that saucepan on. Through Bridie I had heard he had spent the rest of that week in one of the rooms reserved for pundits in the Doctors' House. Bridie got it from Hugh Devine, and for once had her facts right. 'It's no wonder at all the man had to move in. Who would expect him to cook his own meals and do his own chores after the hours he puts in here? The sooner he marries again and doesn't have to depend on his home help, the better for him.'

'Has Hugh heard when the wedding is going to be?'

'He has not. He's a notion it'll be soon, now his boss has got settled in the job. And why wouldn't it be? When there's no reason at all for hanging about?'

Andrew was now back in the mews, but since his return his lights had not once been on when I left for the hospital at night. He was leaving for work earlier. Previously, I had heard his car going out around half an hour after I returned. Now he left directly after I got in.

As my attitude towards him had so completely altered, I very much wanted to meet him, particularly in the mews when I was out of uniform. I would have been glad to see him in the hospital, having already reached the stage when just to see him would be enough to make my day, or night. But in Martha's the habit of regarding pundits as a-human creatures, to be treated with the same circumspection as Matron, was so ingrained in me by training that I doubted I would have the nerve to do more than say, 'Good evening, Doctor.' I had rehearsed a row of conversational remarks about his malaria for our first meeting in the mews. It did not look as if I was going to get the opportunity to use them. We were seeing even less of each other as neighbours than we had done in the past—and that had been little enough.

I wondered again if he was avoiding me on purpose. That seemed probable. His hostility had vanished during that evening in his flat, but he might well now dislike me still more for putting him so overwhelmingly in my debt. My father said it was much harder to be a generous taker than a generous giver, and that while the expectation of gratitude gave great pleasure to the giver, in nine cases out of ten it was the only return the giver could expect. 'There are few things more irritating to the human spirit,' said my father, 'than the knowledge that one should feel grateful. Genuine gratitude like genuine love has no concern with knowledge. It's a rare gift.'

I remembered that when Charles ignored my request and some more flowers arrived. Carnations again. The card was written by his secretary. He had asked her to send them as he had had to leave on an unexpected business trip. The card did not say for how long, or where he had gone. Mrs Shaw had been so enthusiastic about the carnations when she called to tell me she was back that I had given her half. They had so annoyed me I nearly gave them all away, but I knew that would make me feel guiltier than ever, so they were still in my sitting-room and kept nagging me on my ungenerous spirit.

The flat itself was beginning to irk me in much the same way, but I now could not bear to think of leaving it as long as Andrew remained next door. Had what had happened not happened to me, I would never have believed anyone could have changed their mind about a man, as I had about him. On occasions I had thought myself in love before, but I had never felt then as I did now. I had been able to forget those other men, exactly as I had Charles, directly I walked on duty, and then picked up the thoughts of them when I was off and had nothing better to do, just as I would have picked up a bit of knitting.

I could not get Andrew out of my mind, on or off duty. I knew I was being absurd. I had not forgotten he was engaged. Yet just looking at the medical blocks or seeing his name on the pundit's board gave me a kick. And though I was at this moment genuinely anxious about Tiny, the knowledge that Andrew was standing in Cas. a few yards from the switchboard had my hand holding the silent receiver shaking.

'Well?' the S.S.O.'s voice demanded. 'What about Tiny, Nurse Newenden?' When I explained he asked what else I expected on present showing.

I apologised for bothering him.

'Don't be so bloody silly, Nurse!' he snapped. 'What in hell am I here for? I'll look in later.' He slammed down the receiver.

I went back into Albert. Player was giving Cuthbert a drink. I helped her re-do his pillows, then lift him higher in bed. Tiny mumbled in his sleep. Cuthbert whispered, 'Thought he was too quiet.'

In Martha's the beds had a senior and junior side. The senior worked with her back to the ward door, the junior facing in.

Player suddenly looked over my shoulder. 'Nurse! Look who is coming in!' she murmured aghast. 'Mr Franks, the S.S.O., the S.M.O.—and it looks like another pundit!'

'Gawd!' Cuthbert was intrigued. 'Top brass!' And in the next bed the mumbles were growing louder.

'I'll have to go to them. Player, see to Tiny'—I shot down to escort the high-powered round. The men were waiting in the doorway. I collected Tiny's chart on my way and glanced again at Andrew, wondering if he was a mirage. He was standing between Fatso and the S.M.O.

Albert belonged to Fatso. I looked at him. 'Good evening, Mr Franks.'

'More like morning than evening. Well? Got that boy Ellis's chart? Let's have it.'

I waited, my hands behind my back, while they studied the chart. Behind me Player was doing her best, but Tiny was still deeply asleep. He was now framing sentences. 'All wet—swimming in the sea—not the sea—all wet—soaking wet—I can't swim——' he gasped, '—my legs—too heavy for swimming——'

122

'Tiny! Wake up, dear!' Player whispered urgently. 'It's only a dream.'

She was not getting through to him. I looked quickly at the S.S.O., but he was watching Tiny. Andrew said quietly, 'Mr Franks, I think Nurse wishes you to excuse her while she helps her junior.'

Fatso grunted. I took that as approval and shot over to Player. 'I'll cope. Stay with the round.'

She looked horrified yet relieved as she vanished. Tiny was gasping, 'Can't swim—can't swim——'

I took his shoulder, shook him gently and kept on. 'Tiny, stop it! Wake up! You are all right—understand, dear? You—are—all—right. This is Nurse Newenden. There'—his eyes had opened—'see? Just a dream.' He had grabbed my arms. I got one free to stroke back his hair. 'Poor old thing! That was a bad one. Have a little drink.' I reached behind me for his glass and felt it put in my hand. 'Have a little drink, dear.'

'I don't want a drink!' His voice broke. 'Leave me alone! I don't want——' Suddenly he saw the men around his bed. He took the glass from me and hurled it straight at the S.S.O.'s white figure. 'Get away from me, you bloody butchers! That's all you are! Bloody something awful butchers!' The glass had sailed over the S.S.O.'s shoulder and crashed on the floor. The noise jolted Tiny fully awake. 'Christ! I'm sorry—sorry. Please go away. Oh—Nurse——' His voice was strangled by an uncontrollable sob. He reached for my hand as he tried to hide his face in the pillow on the side away from Fatso. The physicians were there. They stepped back, but he had seen them. He turned, sat up as much as he could, and threw himself against me. I held him in my arms.

He had not broken down before. He did not now weep easily. It was anything but easy to watch and hear. The men round his bed were silent, and Albert was suddenly unnaturally still. The other patients had to have woken. They did not sound as if they were even breathing.

Fatso moved at last. He patted Tiny's shaking shoulders. 'Poor laddie! Poor laddie! We are not going to disturb you more to-night. Nurse'll look after you.' He nodded at me, walked quietly out, followed by the others, with Player trailing after. The S.S.O. said something to her. She went back to the table for the rest of Tiny's notes, and then his stack of X-rays from the X-ray cupboard.

The S.S.O. returned them all when he came in alone later. 'You couldn't have timed that better if you tried, Nurse Newenden.'

I was on edge too. 'No, Mr Simmonds. But as he's had so

123

many of these nightmares, I'm glad that for once some one apart from night nurses was here to see one.'

He said sharply. 'Don't spit at me, young woman, or I shall certainly spit back!' He opened Tiny's ticket at the prescription sheet. 'I've written up his premedication. Mr Franks wants it given at 1.15 to-morrow afternoon, but will you tell Sister Albert that nothing, I repeat, nothing, is to be said about this to Tiny until Mr Franks speaks to him himself to-morrow morning. He'll be in about ten.'

There was something like lead in the pit of my stomach. 'I'm sorry.'

'So am I. I don't enjoy the prospect of butchering a patient.' He looked over to Tiny's sleeping figure. 'Trust the subconscious to come out with the truth.'

I was sorry for him as well. 'You are doing it to save his life.'

'I hope so. The physicians agree that we've no alternative. I also hope we can get his consent—which I would not bet on at all. Oh, well! Just have to keep on hoping, as the bishop said to the actress.' He went over and stood looking down at Tiny, then walked out of the ward without another word.

George was coming up the block stairs as I went down next morning. 'I hear you had quite a party in the small hours?'

'We did.'

'How's Tiny this morning?'

'Bright as a button. And I feel like Judas.'

He said kindly, 'Know something, Cath? You take these chaps too seriously. You shouldn't let yourself get so involved. It doesn't do any good.' He misunderstood my silence. 'He'll be better off without that leg. And it's not as if he'll be the only chap in Martha's to-night with one short. Happens all the time. Face it—he's lucky to have got away with his life.'

'What makes you so sure he has?' I retorted furiously. 'I'm not, even without Fatso's popping up in the night with Andrew Lairg and the S.M.O. in tow.'

'You don't have to read too much into that! They were all up late because Ivor Carter only just got back from his holiday last evening and wanted to look at Bill Stone's kid. Fatso happened to be dining with the Dean, and they all got talking. You know what pundits are like! Nothing they enjoy more than looking at each other's patients.'

I was in too bad a temper to eat much breakfast. Bridie had left already, as she had an early hairdresser's appointment. I did not feel like chatting with the other girls, and as the need was now long past, for once could not be bothered to change out of uniform. My outdoor hat and coat were in Bridie's cupboard.

They made me look like an overgrown schoolgirl of my mother's generation, but I was in no mood to care about that either. I was later than usual. Andrew must have left for the hospital long ago, and I did not give a damn if Charles was back and saw my dowdy get-up.

'Excuse me, Nurse,' said a woman beside me in the bus queue, 'but would that gentleman be wanting you?'

I looked about vaguely. Andrew's car had stopped at the lights some yards off. He was driving away from the hospital. He caught my eye and gestured to a point beyond the stop. When the lights were green he moved into the left lane, stopped the car, and opened the front passenger-seat door. 'I presume we are going in the same direction. Quick—or I'll have every cop in London after me!'

'Thank you very much.' I closed the door as he drove off.

He handed me the right half of my seat's safety-belt. 'Manage the clip?'

'Yes. Thank you very much,' I said again.

He was going back to his flat for some notes he had forgotten and needed for his first teaching round. Every set of lights turned red as we arrived.

He smiled slightly. 'Fate is not with us this morning.'

I agreed with him, untruthfully. That hideous coat and hat had probably helped him spot me in the bus queue, and I had never been so delighted by all those red lights. Being with him like this was more wonderful than anything I could have antici-pated. I watched his profile while he concentrated on the traffic, and knew with a certainty that astonished me, despite the amount of thinking I had done about him lately, what I wanted in life. I wanted to marry him.

That astonished me because, though I had always thought that one day I would fall seriously in love and marry, I had not been in any hurry. I had girl-friends who longed for a husband and home. I had not even been looking for a serious boy-friend. I had wanted to finish training, do midder, perhaps return to Martha's for a year to get experience as a senior staff nurse, and then to travel. I had had vague ideas about working in Aus-tralia, then maybe the States or Canada. An English S.R.N. who had done midwifery and held a Martha's certificate could get a job just about anywhere in the world our side of the Iron and Bamboo Curtains, and even they could be penetrated. One of Meg's set was now doing some sort of a course in Moscow, and another girl in the same year had somehow managed to get to Peking.

I had wanted to see some of the world before I settled down. I had not wanted a husband, yet. But suddenly all those nebulous ideas faded as completely as my old infatuation for Charles. Those far-away places could stay far away; I wanted to stay right where I was; alone with Andrew.

Then we reached the mews. My hand was on the door-handle when he asked about Tiny. 'Mr Franks told me he was going to have to amputate to-day. I believe he's talking to the boy this morning.'

'Yes.' I repeated my words to George about feeling like a Judas.

He said, 'One does, when one has to lie to a patient. There is often no way round that, but that has very little effect on one's peace of mind.' He looked at me in silence for a few seconds. 'Are you afraid he won't consent?'

I thought before answering. 'I think he will. He trusts Mr Simmonds—and, of course, Mr Franks. But he knows Mr Simmonds so well.'

'Then he should be all right. An amputation at his age is tragic, but once over the physical and mental shock, he should be very well. Or'—he paused again—'does he want to die?'

I was startled by his putting into words a thought that had hovered at the back of my mind for some time, but which I had lacked the courage to bring out. 'I'm not sure.'

'Doesn't that mean you are afraid of being sure?' he asked gently.

'Yes,' I said, 'yes. But, Doctor, he's got so much to live for. His parents are well off, he's their only child, they are devoted to him, he's keen on his work—he'll have a good job once he's qualified—even without a leg, he'll have that job—and though he's had a bad time, we've had dozens—hundreds—of men in worse conditions who have done wonderfully. Look at Professor Brown! I know he wasn't as badly injured as Tiny, but remembering his age and then that coronary, and he's doing fine, isn't he?'

'Very well indeed. He'll be with us over Christmas, but on present showing, not much longer.' We were both silent. Then he added, 'I'm not saying your instincts are wrong, though I sincerely hope they are. Unfortunately, instincts have an uncomfortable habit of being right. But do remember you are on night duty. It's very easy to get things out of proportion the morning after a long night.' He leaned forward and opened the door for me. 'I hope you will feel better after a good sleep, and when you return to Albert to-night find you have sound reason for optimism.'

'I hope so. Thanks for giving me a lift.'

'I'm glad I happened to be going your way.' He got out of the car as Mrs Shaw opened his door.

126

'Not something wrong, Doctor? Ah!' She gasped at me. 'It's Miss Newenden! You been doing a little nursing too, miss? There! Isn't that nice!'

I said it was splendid, and let myself in. I did not know how I was going to feel about Tiny to-night. I did know one thing; I was not going to alter my mind about Andrew Lairg. His being sixteen years older than myself, and a Martha's pundit, did not matter at all. It would have made no difference had he been the Dean, or Matron's brother. I loved that man so much it hurt.

Then I remembered Ann MacDonald. She mattered. I thought I'll think about her and Tiny when I've had some sleep. I went to bed and to sleep at once. I woke some time during the afternoon and heard a car engine below and then the sound of my letter-box clattering. I blinked at the time. It was cardiac clinic afternoon in O.P.'s, so it could not be Andrew below. I did not bother to get up. On my way out later I collected Charles's letter and pushed it in my coat pocket, to read during the night. At supper I heard Tiny had had his operation and everything had gone well. 'And no more shop now, Cathy,' insisted Bridie, 'as the old bag'll soon be in to read the register, and I must hear the rest of this story about Mary Eccles. Is it true she's been two days on the road hitching her way down from Glasgow—or would it be Inverness?'

'Edinburgh,' corrected Carr from Casualty.

I said, 'Bridie, this time you are way off. She was flying back. And anyway, she couldn't have hitched in this weather. I heard a forecast. The whole of the north is deep in snow.'

'She did hitch,' said Carr. 'I know. I've just been talking to my relief, Potter. Eccles was in her room when she got off this morning. Because of the snow it took her until last night to reach Manchester. A lorry brought her down the M1 early this morning and dropped her at Covent Garden. She walked the rest.' Carr smiled thinly. 'After walking out on her boy-friend.'

'And why would she do that?' asked Bridie. 'When they tell me he's loaded!'

'According to Potter, he had told Eccles he was taking her to visit great friends who lived outside Edinburgh. Only when they got there—guess what—the friends just happened to be away. Eccles said that was too bad and moved off. She hadn't enough cash for the train, so she hitched. Not that she'd have had any difficulty, with her looks.'

Bridie said, 'The girl also has guts, no less.'

I asked, 'What was her boy-friend doing while she was on the road?'

Carr shrugged. 'She refused to discuss him with Potter. I expect she feels an utter fool to have fallen for that corny routine. I must say, it wouldn't have fooled me.'

Bridie looked thoughtfully at Carr's plain, bespectacled face. 'It's too bad she'd not your insight, Nurse Carr.'

Mary was in Albert changing-room when I arrived. She looked so tired that even Sister Albert remarked on it before starting her report. That was unusual, as every one expected night nurses to look tired, and they generally did. 'What time did you get to bed, Nurse Eccles?'

'Twelve, Sister. I was back early from my nights off.'

Sister recollected Mary was nearing the end of her night duty, and dismissed the subject. 'You may have quite a busy night, Nurses. We have now five men on the Danger List. Three of them are accident admissions who came in to-day, plus Blakelock from last night, and, of course, Tiny Ellis. We have also another accident coming in at any moment. Is that the lift?'

I said, 'Going down, Sister.'

'No doubt to bring him up. I'll give you his details quickly, as you'll have to admit him, Nurse Eccles. He's an Edward Thomas Curtis, age thirty-six, Church of England, next of kin' —she consulted a note—'his father. He was knocked down by a taxi just outside here. He has a fractured left os calcis, with some bruising and lacerations of the left leg. Degree of shock, mild. He is to go in Fourteen, and is for theatre to-night. Manson has been sent to Arthur Ward to make room.'

The lift had returned and stopped at our floor. Sister waited while Mary ushered in Bert and Carmelo with their stretcher-trolley. 'Well, Nurse Newenden, let us get down to it!'

Tiny's leg had been removed at mid-thigh. He had taken the news with a wholly unexpected and wholly admirable calm, and signed his consent form on request. 'His reaction,' said Sister, 'has been a great comfort to us all. I am afraid we have much underestimated that boy's courage.'

'Yes, Sister.' I felt very ashamed. It was some consolation to know she felt the same. 'Are his parents very upset? I suppose they've been up?'

Her mouth tightened at the corners. 'When I talked to Mr Ellis on the telephone this morning he said this was a great shock and disappointment to them both. His wife was too distressed to speak to me.'

'But, Sister—they were warned?'

'Of course. I spoke to them in the duty-room last Sunday. Mr Simmonds had had a long talk with them before that. Unfortunately, as they did not want to believe us—which is understandable—they assumed we were painting an unnecessarily gloomy picture. Tiny was so cheerful on their visits.' She

128

paused. 'I am beginning to wonder if they know their son any better than we do.'

I was puzzled as well as upset for Tiny. 'Sister, when he first came in—I know they weren't here during the nights—but you said they were very good.'

'His father was excellent. The mother was somewhat over-emotional, but under the circumstances that semed reasonable. They have visited him regularly, been most generous in their gifts to him, but they do live very near London and are very comfortably off.'

We exchanged glances. I asked, 'Are they coming up to-morrow, Sister?'

She shook her head. 'Mr Ellis assured me they would come at once at any time, should we send for them. Unless we have to do that he considers it best if they keep away for a few days, as there is nothing they can do, their son is in safe hands, and it will only distress him to see his mother's distress. She does seem to have gone to pieces.'

'Sister,' I said tersely, 'it isn't her leg that's come off.'

'He's her son, Nurse. Maternal love is a very strange as well as very strong emotion. In fact, it is more than emotion. It's one of the most deep-rooted instincts. Possibly only self-preservation goes deeper, and not always, as anyone who reads a newspaper learns almost daily from the number of mothers who give their lives to save their children's. I have noticed that some mothers identify themselves with their children, and refuse to cut the umbilical cord even when the children reach maturity. Then, when anything happens to the child, the mother reacts as if she herself is the greatest sufferer.'

'Is that really mother love? Or self-love?'

'My dear Nurse,' she replied drily, 'I'm not a mother, so I am not qualified to answer that. Possibly one day you will find out the answer for yourself.'

CHAPTER ELEVEN

HOSPITALS CANNOT WORK MIRACLES

TINY'S curtains were half drawn at the sides to prevent the light from his shaded bedside lamp disturbing the other men. All our shade-covers were red. His bed was illuminated in a soft crimson glow, and the white metal transfusion stand looked pink. When I turned off the main ward lights the five pools of crimson gave Albert a queerly festive look. When the S.S.O. came in later he said it was as if we had our Christmas decorations up already.

I went first to the five D.I.L.'s. They were all deeply sedated, all 'satisfactory.' Tiny's bed was raised right up at the foot, and because of his height his head was pressing against the pillow tied across the head bedrail. I turned his face to one side. He did not wake. He was breathing well beneath his oxygen-mask. He looked much younger. Then I had to check his stump dressing.

I had seen so many stumps. I never got used to them. I had to fight down the wave of pity and nausea with a conscious effort. It was intact, but one of the sandbags needed readjusting. My hands were steady as I corrected its position. I did not know how.

Stan beckoned me when I had finished. 'Having a good kip, is he, Nurse?'

'Yes.' I had to smile. 'Doing very nicely. How are you?' Night Sister rang a little later to ask for Tiny's condition and say she was lending us a junior to take Mr Curtis to the theatre.

I expected Mary to be pleased by this. She loathed the theatre, and despite her disclaimer to Sister Albert was looking very strained and tired. If she was pleased she showed no sign. 'What time is Curtis going down? Should I dress him? I've put a theatre pack by him.'

'I'll see to him. It's early for the men, and I've nearly finished my first round. You finish the drinks, and help yourself to some strong tea. You look a little weary.'

'Thank you,' she said politely, 'but I don't need tea.' She removed herself to the kitchen.

Had I not had a ward to look after, I would have liked to follow her and suggest it might help to talk about it, even though we had never been on matey terms. It was not so much her looking tired that worried me; that could be put right by a long sleep. She was so tense. She looked as buttoned up as Andrew had seemed until that night he passed out on me. My mind, having shot to him, stayed with him until I realised what it was doing and that it just was not safe to think about him now. Tiny apart, there were some very ill men in Albert. I finished my round and went behind Mr Curtis's curtains.

He was a solicitor. He had brown hair and a rather ugly face that was somehow attractive. His voice made me like him at once. It was as deep as Andrew's. He had never been in hospital before and was fascinated to find himself a patient.

'Are there only you two nurses here all night? With all these patients?'

'Yes.' I helped him into his theatre gown. 'A third will arrive shortly just to escort you to the theatre—ah—no! That's back to front. This gown ties at the back—so.'

'What an extraordinary garment!' He had a nice smile. 'Very draughty. Or won't I worry about that?'

'I doubt it. How's the leg?'

'I can't feel it at all after that shot they gave me downstairs. I feel splendid. How are all my fellow-sufferers? All asleep?'

'Not all. They will be soon.'

He raised a corner of one side-curtain to look into the ward. Holland, in the next bed, raised his head. 'Evening, mate! So you copped yours from a cab? Which way would it be going?'

Holland was a plumber. His pelvis had been fractured when he was knocked off his push-bike by a motor-cyclist. The motor-cyclist, Fenner, was in Sixteen with a hair-line fracture of the base of his skull and two broken collar-bones. The two men were now great friends.

When Mr Curtis dropped his curtain after swopping injuries he asked very quietly, 'How did that man know I walked into a taxi?'

I told him ward patients always knew everything. 'I'm surprised Mr Holland hasn't given you the taxi number, the driver's name, and how many children he has. He'll probably let you know to-morrow.'

He was amused. 'I had heard this hospital had an efficient grape-vine. I say'—he noticed the operation stocking—'isn't that on the large side?'

I held it up. 'These are knitted to fit all sizes. No heels.'

'Very crafty. That for my bad foot?'

'No. To keep the good warm. The bad one stays all wrapped up as it is now until you get to the theatre. You'll find a plaster bandage on it when you wake up.'

131

He wanted to know about his anaesthetic and whether his having had dinner mattered.

'It won't by the time you get to the theatre. It is why you are having this little wait. Not much longer.'

'How long will I be out? And when I come round I suppose you'll hear all my darkest secrets?'

I smiled. 'I've always read about people telling all while coming round. I've been here nearly four years. I've never heard one dark secret. All most people mutter is, "Can I have my teeth, please!" Which reminds me, if you have any false teeth, would you mind taking them out and putting them in this mug here.'

'All my own, I'm happy to say! Anything else that has to come off?'

'Your signet-ring, please. I'll lock it away.' I safety-pinned it inside my bib pocket. 'You'll need this cap, but you don't have to put it on yet.'

He examined the cap. 'I shall feel like my future brother-in-law. He wears these things when he gives anaesthetics.'

'A Martha's man?' I remembered that remark about our grape-vine. 'Were you coming to see him when you were knocked down?'

'I had been dining with him. He was lucky——' He paused as Mary's head appeared. 'Now what's going to happen?'

Mary wanted me. 'Mr Franks is here with the S.S.O., Nurse Newenden.'

As I slipped away I heard Mr Curtis ask, 'That's Nurse Newenden? And may I ask your name, Nurse?'

One of the Night Assistants did Night Sister's first round. She was still with us when Mr Curtis's injection was due and helped me give it.

He asked, 'This the knock-out?'

I explained it was merely his premedication before operation and would make him a little sleepy and very dry. When we left him settled and returned to sign the Dangerous Drug Book at the table the Night Ass. advised me to watch my step with him. 'He has friends in high places. The Dean has already been into the Office to ask after him.'

'My God, Nurse! That's too much on top of everything else to-night!'

'Everything? I know you've five D.I.L.'s, but they couldn't be quieter. You're lucky to be in Albert, Newenden. Albert's a lucky ward—we all know that! You should see Robert. They've already had one death to-night, and they'll probably have two more before morning. And as for Christian—did you know they tried to operate on the Stone baby this afternoon?'

'No! I thought Dr Lairg was against it?'

'He was. The parents went on insisting, so he insisted they called in a second opinion from outside.' She named the cardiologist who had come in from one of the other London teaching hospitals. 'He said he would risk operating. Sir Ivor was reluctant, but agreed to do what he could. He couldn't do anything. That baby's heart is completely misformed. They couldn't even put on the machines. Sir Ivor had to stitch up the chest wall and send him back to the ward.'

'He's still alive?'

She nodded. 'Night Sister's in Christian now, with Dr Lairg and the parents. Not that there's anything anyone can do.' She paused. 'I'm sorry for Sullivan.'

For a few seconds after she had gone I stood by one of the ward windows overlooking the park. The general surgical block directly ahead hid the children's block, three blocks on. I did not have to see the building to see Christian in my mind. It was one of our most modern wards, circular, with the cots divided by glass partitions. The walls were decorated with a frieze of fairy-tale figures. There was a small town of dolls' houses in the play area, a great glass-fronted cupboard stacked with washable teddy-bears, and other fluffy cuddly toys, and above the cupboard a row of blank-faced dolls. The children's cots were pink and blue. The colours were gay, but one did not notice the colour when a cot was enveloped by an oxygen tent. A child in a tent looked just like a doll in a transparent plastic box. But if there was any sadder sight in life than a small child trying to cling to life under an oxygen tent I had not seen it.

Mr Curtis was dozing when the theatre trolley and spare junior arrived. I gave her his notes, the wet X-ray plates that had been sent up from Casualty, his anaesthetic bowl, instruments, and towel. 'Do see we get our own gag and tongue forceps back,' I told her aside. 'Sister Albert has strong views on our instruments being left in the theatre.'

Our telephone rang as Mary and I were making up his empty bed. I took the call, expecting it to be an inquiry about one of our D.I.L.'s.

'That you, Nurse Newenden?' asked Henry. 'I got a gentleman on an outside line as says he must speak to you special. I tried to put him off, but he says as it's urgent. Your cousin, he says he is. Mr Charles Newenden.'

'Henry! I can't—or is it bad news about my family?'

'Couldn't say, Nurse. I'll put him through.'

'Cathy, dear—Charles,' said Charles's voice apologetically. 'I'm sorry to intrude like this, but I expect you have guessed the reason after reading my letter.'

'Letter? Oh, Lor!' I now remembered it was still unread and in my outdoor coat pocket. 'I'm sorry, Charles, I've not had time to read it. Something wrong? My parents? Luke? Your family?'

'Darling—relax! They are all fine. But I need your advice——'

I stopped him. 'Have you rung me to ask me for advice? Now? Are you crazy? Don't you realise I'm on duty? And if you don't, just let me tell you I've got thirty-two injured men to look after, and five of them are dangerously ill. One of the five is quite liable to have a sudden haemorrhage, and if he does he can easily bleed to death inside a couple of minutes! I cannot and will not waste any more time like this!' I slammed down the receiver really violently, then picked it up and jiggled for Henry. 'Henry? Nurse Newenden. If any more urgent calls come from outside for me to-night or any other night put them straight through to Night Sister's Office. Thanks.' I shot back to the ward in a white fury.

Eccles was at the table. My expression startled her out of frozen politeness. 'What's up?'

I swallowed. 'As Stan would say—my —— cousin wasting my —— time on a —— night like this!' I picked up the ward stethoscope, and my torch. 'I must do the D.I.'s blood-pressures again, and it's just as well no one is going to take mine, or I'd find myself warded with acute hypertension!'

Another Night Assistant relieved our meals, because of our five D.I.L.'s. Bridie was not at the same meal as myself. The girls at my table had heard about the Stone baby, but no one had any more recent news than my own. Some one mentioned Meg Harper. It gave me quite a shock to discover how completely I had forgotten her now she had temporarily dropped out of my life, and then I realised that was always happening in hospital. One worked with or nursed a person, got to know them far better than one knew one's close friends, and then suddenly they moved to another ward or were discharged, and one often never saw them again. I thought of the Professor, Hubert and Kevin, and Don. I had liked the last three so much, but this was the first time I had remembered them in weeks. The old man I had loved. Yet even he had nearly faded from my thoughts. Then, as it was safe, I thought about Andrew, how little I had really seen or knew him, and yet what a hold he now had over my mind! Would he fade too? On past showing that seemed inevitable, even if now incredible. I would have to make him fade, particularly once he married again. Falling in love with a pundit was crazy enough. I knew my friends—and his—would say I had only some sort of a schoolgirl crush on

134

him. They would say it would not survive his marriage any longer than the average fan's crush survived a pop-singer's marriage. I almost wished they were right. Loving a married pundit would just about rate me a bed in one of our psychiatric wards. I would have to do something about him, but I had no idea what, and as it was time to go back to Albert I could not work on it now. I did not remember Charles until I had reached our floor and let myself into the flat. Again I thought of him in Stan's terms, and again forgot him.

Tiny had woken in my absence. The Night Ass. had given him another injection, changed the final pint of blood for the first of glucose-saline, and he was asleep again. 'His dressing's not through,' she said; 'his pulse is a nice steady sixty-eight. His blood-pressure is creeping gently back to normal. The S.S.O. looked in again. He was quite pleased.' She handed me the tourniquet she had in her pocket. 'You'll want to hang on to this, I suppose but I'm sure you won't need it. Mr Franks' patients don't have reactionary haemorrhages.'

'Nurse! Please!' I begged. 'Don't tempt Providence.'

She was a girl without much sense of humour and very conscious of her own seniority. 'I'm only stating a fact, Newenden. Perhaps you should remember we have doctors here, not witch-doctors.'

Mr Curtis was back from the theatre. He came round, spat out his anaesthetic tube, and slid immediately into a deep normal sleep. Mary came up to see me as I felt the toes of his injured foot, and tested the fit of his wet plaster to see if it was being tightened by new swelling. 'Can I vanish for my routine, Nurse?'

'Sure.'

The night junior had a great many jobs that had to be done outside the main ward. These included setting the kitchen for early teas and breakfasts; emptying, cleaning, refilling, and resterilising the sterilisers, and setting the sterilising-room for any dressings or skin preparations that had to be done before breakfast; setting the sluice for the washing, shaving, and mouth-wash round; collecting and putting out all empty dressing-tins for the surgical stores porter who arrived at half-past six each morning; checking the stock lotion cupboard for any empty or near-empty bottles, listing them in the dispensary book and leaving them and the book in the dispensary basket in the clinical room for the junior day staff nurse to deal with when she came on at 7.30. Apart from the sterilisers, the only cleaning done in Martha's at night was the cleaning of the clinical room—another job for the junior. This was a narrow slit of a room just inside the door connecting Albert corridor with the main corridor. It was a little room with many uses. The flowers lived there at night, all the specimen glasses, with or without contents, the ward microscope under a glass dome, the acid cupboard, the ward's stock of textbooks all heavily stamped 'Albert Ward, DO NOT REMOVE.' And during the whole day and a large part of the early night there was generally at least one student permanently in there, borrowing the microscope or books. The clinical rooms were the only parts of any Martha's ward into which the students could walk at will up to midnight. The door was officially forbidden to be closed, and was in fact only nearly closed at night while the junior was cleaning the acid cupboard, for the good reason that that cupboard was so fixed on the wall that it was impossible to open its door when the room door was open.

I looked at all the men, caught up on the four-hourly pulse charting that had got behind before my meal, wrote a long and belated midnight report for Night Sister, and had only just finished it when she walked in to do her own second round.

As it was her first visit of the night, she wanted all the details on our D.I.L.'s verbally as well as having them in my written report. Then she went very slowly round. It was gone three before she left us. I took my torch, shielding the light with my hand, and did yet another round. Martha's night seniors were expected to go round at least every twenty minutes all night, more frequently if the ward had any D.I.L.'s. I must have walked miles during my time in Albert. That night I only sat down to write my reports. Yet though we were heavy on paper, as could happen when we had very ill patients in the immediate post-op. stage, the ward was far quieter than usual. The ill men were too heavily drugged to do more than stir occasionally, sip a drink, need their pillows turned, or faces wiped. They had to be watched constantly in case anything went wrong, but when as now all was going well there was little I could do for them beyond taking pulse after pulse, blood-pressure after blood-pressure, giving injections when necessary, watching their wounds, the four drips we had going in addition to Tiny's infusion, the gauges on their oxygen cylinders, the speed of the bubbles in the flow-meters, the fit of their oxygen-masks, the colour of the faces under the masks.

It was typical of Albert that the other less ill men were keeping their own requests to a minimum. That kept the ward quieter and helped them all to sleep better. They were all asleep on that round.

I stopped by the piano at the balcony end listening to the assortment of snores, grunts, slow and heavy, light and quick, breathing. It was a lovely sound. I had that peculiar, pleasant, and very personal sense of satisfaction that only another night nurse would properly understand. When our patients slept badly we not only felt responsible, at Martha's we were held responsible. All our sisters reacted to a bad morning report with much the same question and comment: 'What happened to your nursing, Nurse So-and-So? A good nurse does not allow her patients to sleep badly. Never give me a report like this again!'

Holland muttered in his sleep. Wrigley turned on his side, making his bed-springs creak. Rawson, close by me in Seventeen, altered the position of his splinted legs and set the attached weights jangling softly. I moved to still them, then to see if he had woken, or had disturbed the tension of his splint by his changed posture. He had not woken himself or done any damage. I moved to Fourteen, felt Curtis's toes. They were fine. He was flat out, his colour and pulse excellent. I glanced down to the little group of D.I.L.'s, all near the table, three on Tiny's side, two on the other. I had been glancing their way every few minutes all night. When I saw who was standing at the door end of the screened table, for a moment I thought I was having some sort of a night nurse's delusion.

Andrew had come in so quietly that he had passed the half-closed door of the clinical room in which Mary was cleaning the acid cupboard without her noticing or hearing. He stood very still by the table, his hands hanging limply at his sides, his head bent. He was staring at the table. He did not look up until I spoke to him. 'Good morning, Dr Lairg. Can I help you?'

'Morning? Already?'

'Twenty to four.' I showed him my watch.

'So it is. I've lost all account of time to-night. I'm sorry to disturb you at such an extraordinary time,' he said heavily, 'but I'm about to go home and wanted news about one of your patients before leaving. A man called Curtis. E. T. Curtis. Admitted this evening. I believe he went to the theatre?'

'Yes.' I had forgotten that first Night Ass.'s warning. I was now deeply grateful for our Mr Curtis's high-powered friends. 'Mr Briggs did a reduction and repair and has put him in plaster. He has come round. Would you like to see him, Doctor?'

'He's awake?'

'No. He's been sleeping since he came round. Would you like to see his notes?'

'I can't do that, thank you. He's not my patient. But he is a friend of mine and had dinner with me here to-night, which makes me feel very responsible for his accident. I'm glad it wasn't too serious. I'd have liked to look in before, but couldn't manage it. He's'—he looked over the screens and up the ward—'engaged to my sister-in-law. I've not yet told her about his accident. I thought I would wait until he was over the anaesthetic. I'll ring her in the morning.'

I expected him to leave then, but he went on looking up the ward, so I was able to look at him properly. His face was lined with fatigue, and even in that light nearly as grey, if not as yellow, as that night in his flat. I was used to weary men drifting into Albert in the small hours and leaning against the table as if they did not know how they were going to raise the energy to walk out of the ward. That was how he looked. And judging from those other men, something grim had just happened somewhere in Martha's. His eyes were as bleak and defeated as George's after that ghastly night in Matilda, and as so many other men's on so many other nights, when they could not bear the thought of their own rooms and own company and came in to cadge a hot drink and borrow a temporary shoulder.

Momentarily I forgot he was a pundit. 'Doctor, would you like some tea—or coffee—before you drive home?' As I spoke I noticed his suit, and remembered he was not just another resident.

He turned to me. 'If you can spare the time to produce either I'd be very grateful.'

I had to get Mary, as I could not leave the ward for more than seconds. 'Dr Lairg? I didn't hear him! Why is he here, Nurse Newenden?'

I explained briefly. I took the small tray of coffee and biscuits from her in the ward door a minute or so later. 'Thanks. That was quick.'

'The urn was boiling and milk hot. It hasn't brewed yet. Shall I watch the ward?'

'I'll do that. He's not here officially. He won't mind.'

She gave me a long, searching look. 'Thanks. My routine's all behind.'

I took the tray to the table. He was sitting on the edge. 'Aren't you having any, Nurse?'

I said primly, if correctly, 'Nurse Eccles and I will be having our tea shortly.'

He did not argue that. He knew as well as myself that while Night Sister might be prepared to look the other way on certain rare busy occasions if she found me having coffee in the ward with a resident, she would be horrified if I did that with a pundit, even in the small hours. 'Milk, Doctor?'

'No, thanks.' He helped himself to sugar. 'How's young Ellis? Mr Franks said he showed great courage.'

I told him the details. Added, 'He hasn't spoken yet. He

138

smiled at me a little while ago. He wasn't with us.'

'One wouldn't expect that.'

Fatso had told him about Tiny's parents.

I said, 'It's a pity his mother hasn't his courage.'

'Yes.' He folded his arms. 'But as she hasn't, it's illogical as well as useless to expect her to be capable of producing something she hasn't got. Would you expect a woman with a broken leg to walk, much less run, as well as a woman with two good legs?'

'No. But in an emergency she might try.'

'If the woman with the fracture tried she'd fall over and not be able to get up.'

Reluctantly, as I was furious with Mrs Ellis, I had to see his point. 'You don't think she can help herself?'

He shook his head. 'She's obviously got some personality deficiency that renders her incapable of accepting the burden of a crippled son. Of course, there's a cause for that; we don't know what it is, but the fact remains that it exists. It isn't her fault. And she certainly won't overcome it by having the extra burden pushed on her. If you push burdens on people who are mentally incapable of carrying them all you do is push them into mental hospitals.'

'But what about her husband? He could have come.'

'I would have thought so.' He paused. 'As he hasn't, I assume he doesn't want to.'

'Doctor! Tiny's his son!'

'All the more reason for the poor man being frightened. He may be sick, or faint, and then his son will despise his weakness. He may feel he must have time to adjust himself to having a son with one leg. His wife also. This is going to affect all their lives. From now on there will be certain subjects they'll have to avoid discussing, certain things they'll have to do for him, until he gets his tin leg. Very well-balanced people can take this in their stride, but this family don't strike me as that.'

I reminded him how well Tiny had taken to-day.

He said, 'That was very brave.'

His tone made me ask, 'You don't think he can keep it up?' This had been worrying me all night.

'I don't know him nearly well enough to give a straight answer on that, but from the little I do know, wasn't his behaviour to-day rather out of character?' I nodded. 'I always suspect any situation in which a person appears to act out of character. God knows I could be very wrong about this boy! I don't know all the answers. I didn't even understand all the questions.'

I poured him more coffee, wondering not why but what had

made him talk to me like this. I knew the why, because of those other men. They had also had to talk, or crack. Fortunately few of our doctors cracked. They all did a lot of talking in the small hours.

I had to do another round. 'Will you excuse me, Doctor?'

'Of course. I'm just going.' But he was still there when I got back. The little coffee-pot was empty. I offered to get more.

'No, thank you, Nurse.' He got off the table at last. 'It's more than time I left.'

'You've had a long night.'

'Yes.' He put his hands in his pockets. 'I'm glad it's over. Though glad is the wrong word.' He looked at but not through me. 'I expect you knew we had Dr Stone's baby in Christian? He died an hour or so ago.'

That explained everything. I wished I knew the words that might help him. I didn't. 'I'm sorry.'

'Yes,' he said, 'yes. It was bad. He was a nice wee boy. I wish——' He broke off, shrugged unhappily. 'There was nothing we could do for him. We can sometimes mend a heart. We can't yet begin to replace one. That alone could have saved him.' He gave a queer little grimace. 'Such a nice wee boy. His parents brought him half across the world to us—and there was nothing we could do.'

He sounded defeated. That had upset me for other men. Now it hurt like a physical pain. 'I know this is trite, but you did what you could.'

'It wasn't enough.'

'Unhappily not, Dr Lairg. But no man can do more.'

He inclined his dark head in acknowledgment and for a few seconds was silent. Then he thanked me for the coffee, said good night and he would see himself out.

Mary came into the ward as he was leaving. She waited until the outer door closed. 'He was here ages.'

'Yes.' I told her about the baby.

'Nurse, how pathetic! After all this time. No wonder he looked upset. But how odd that he should tell you! I didn't think pundits talked to nurses about such things.'

'Pundits are men,' I said more sharply than I could have wished, 'and the Stones are his friends. And every one talks to night nurses at this hour. It isn't only the patients whose resistances are lowered now. That happens to the whole human race —including pundits.'

That would have slapped Player down. Mary was a very different type. 'I hadn't forgotten that. I only thought it odd that a pundit shouldn't mind showing a nurse that he liked her enough to unburden to her.'

'I wouldn't say that came into it.'

'Nurse,' she said firmly, 'of course it does. You can't unburden to people you dislike, any more than you can to people who gossip. He must know you don't.'

'Not always. Sometimes. I've just told you.'

'I won't talk. You know that.'

She was right about that. It was not until morning that I realised she could also be right about Andrew. That was because I could not let myself dwell on her words and keep my mind wholly on Albert, so I refused to think on them until I was off duty. Then I could not think of anything else.

CHAPTER TWELVE

A PICTURE IN A NEWSPAPER

CHARLES'S letter said he was back in circulation, must see me as soon as possible, and would I be sure to ring his flat before I went on duty?

He was waiting in his car when I got back that morning. 'We on speaking terms, darling?'

I was in no mood to be on bad terms with anyone. I apologised for biting his head off. 'What's the problem? Like to come up and tell me now?'

'You can't guess?'

'No,' I lied. 'Sorry.'

'I think you could if you tried. We can't go into it now, as I've got to get to a meeting and I'm sure you have to sleep,' he added impatiently.

I did not bother to remind him I had been up all night. He was obviously in a bad temper, and now reminding me very much of Francine. 'I'll be off in two nights. Any use?'

He said he supposed his problem could keep until then, as it would have to. 'Dine with me on your first evening. Promise?'

Albert was much busier for those two nights, but by my last morning only Tiny and Marcus Cohen, in Twenty-three, were left on the D.I.L. And Tiny was well enough to be offering through Stan odds of five to one on himself, tens on Cohen. 'If we come off together the book takes all.'

Mr Cohen was a tailor and one of our few non-road accidents. He was a gentle, grey-haired little man with very high blood-pressure. He had had a black-out while waiting for a tube, fallen from the platform as a train was coming in. His back and both legs had been broken. He was an excellent if gloomy patient. 'Ai, ai, ai, very weak, very weak. Weak like a baby I am Nurse.'

'That'll pass, Mr Cohen, when your bones start to heal. You'll soon feel a new man.'

'So I should live so long!'

Tiny was continuing to behave and do well. Almost too well. The S.S.O. said if he was not such a bloody cynical surgeon he might believe in miracles. 'I don't know what to make of that boy. I just don't know.'

Sister Albert was more sanguine. 'Youth is a great ally.'

Meg was due back that day. George told me she was off nights and taking Carr's place on days in Casualty. 'No point in her moving in with you now you'll be on opposite shifts. How much longer have you got in the flat?'

I had a hunch that was going to depend on my date with Charles. 'Probably not much longer.'

'Francine coming back?'

'Who knows, with Francine!'

Bridie's nights off for once matched my own. The Stone baby's death had upset her very badly, and she had scarcely spoken at meals since. We all knew how she felt, having all at some time worked in Christian, so we did not bother her with conversation. At breakfast that morning she roused herself to tell me she was going to spend all her time off with a married sister in Birmingham. 'Honest to God, Cathy, I can use the break.'

'I know. Poor old thing! I was going to suggest if you weren't going away you might like to spend them with me.'

'No hard feelings, but I don't even want to see you. Or even that decent man Andrew Lairg. I've had enough of doctors and nurses for the moment. No doubt at all I'll be glad to see you all when I get back.' Then with a flicker of her old self, she added, 'Hugh tells me that wedding's near.'

I stiffened inwardly. 'Our Dr Lairg's?'

'And who else? He was showing his young woman round the hospital yesterday. He left her with Hugh when he had to see some man in William. She told Hugh she's now given up her job and is having a fine time choosing furniture and curtains. It went to Hugh's head. What did the foolish man do but walk into Christian last night and ask me to marry him? As if I could marry a man with no more sensitivity than that.'

I said, 'You might feel differently after your nights off.'

'I will not. I've other plans.'

I glanced at her determined face. 'Sister Christian? After—this?'

She said simply, 'I love that ward, Cathy. It hurts like hell, but I love it. It's for me.'

'Yes. I would say it is.' I thought back to our time in the P.T.S. when she had been the craziest member of our set, and next to Francine the girl we all thought would be the quickest to chuck nursing. We would have laughed our heads off at the idea that Bridie Sullivan had a genuine vocation, and she would have laughed loudest. It had taken us and her a long time to discover that was exactly what she had. Sister Matilda had spotted it. She had given Bridie a 'rave' first-ward report. Bridie

143

had gone on collecting similar reports on her nursing from ward sisters, even though the Sister Tutors had sighed over her examination results. Yet she had done fairly well on the whole, as her excellent practical marks made up for those she lost on written work. I had now no doubt at all she would one day be Sister Christian, but never a Matron. She loved pure nursing too much to roll down her sleeves and put on her cuffs for good. She would make a wonderful Sister Christian.

I did not sleep well that day, and was awake and getting dressed for my date long before my alarm went off. I kept thinking about Ann MacDonald, wishing I had known last night that she had been in Martha's. She had probably visited Mr Curtis. He was a friendly man. I could have asked him casually about her, found out the details for myself. That might not have made me feel any better now, but it would have stopped me looking down the ward so often and getting so disappointed when all the wrong men came in. I had not seen Andrew since that night the baby died and after Mary had given me that foolish surge of hope. What, I now asked myself, had I been hoping for? That we could be friends? A pundit and a nurse? And even if he had not been a pundit I did not want him as a friend. I knew what I wanted as clearly as Bridie, but she could do something about her plans. I could not do one single thing.

Charles had booked a table in a roof-top restaurant with a superb view of London. The head waiter bowed us to our seats, advised Charles on the menu, while two table waiters and the wine waiter, with a chain any Lord Mayor might covet, brooded over us anxiously.

Eventually we were alone. Charles raised his glass to me. 'A most elusive young woman.'

'Not so much elusive as a working girl.'

'Darling,' he drawled, 'don't pretend you have not been trying to avoid me. It's very naughty of you, as you know how much I have wanted to have you to myself.'

I smiled weakly as our first course arrived. Then some of his friends coming in to dine stopped by us. Charles introduced me, was as polite as ever, while managing to give the impression he could not wait for them to leave us alone. That happened three times. As the tables filled, a number of interested glances came our way. Then an elegant, ageless lady with silver-gold hair bore down on us.

'Dearest Charles! How wonderful to see you back among us! You've been neglecting us all shockingly!'

He stood up, kissed her cheek. 'Angel one, you must forgive me.' He smiled at me. 'My cousin Cathy likes quieter places. And I like what Cathy likes.'

Angel one flashed me a keen glance. Charles introduced us. I did not catch her name.

'You are cousins?' she purred. 'Dearest—how disappointing! But a new approach from "just good friends."'

'Why?' he queried smoothly. 'Is there some law that says cousins can't be good friends? Or a law that cousins can't marry? I don't believe so—I am thankful to say.'

'Are you, indeed?' Her eyes sparkled. 'Dearest! Can I quote you on that?' She was now beaming at me. 'Miss Newenden—it is Newenden? Imagine that! Do tell me about yourself!'

'It's useless trying to get Cathy to talk about herself, angel,' retorted Charles before I could open my mouth. 'She's a nurse. You know what trained nurses are like, whether they come from St Martha's Hospital or anywhere else. They never give anything away!'

'But never! And you are nursing, Miss Newenden?' She sounded as if that made life a song for her. 'Wonderful work—dedicated—you have to be born to it! Nurses are an inspiration to us all! I expect it will be an agonising wrench to—but I mustn't say more! Lovely to meet you—lovely to see you, dearest,' she gushed and swept on.

I was gaping. 'Charles! What was all that about? And who is she?'

He shrugged lightly. 'Only Pristine, darling. You must know of her. Every one knows Pristine.'

'I don't. Who is she?' I demanded again. 'And what was that about quoting you? Is she one of your P.R.O. pals? Or a journalist?'

'She has a column. Does it matter? Why so peeved? I enjoy being with you, and I couldn't care less who knows it. You are very lovely, very sweet, and I am very fond of you. Do you seriously object to that?'

'No. I'm fond of you. But'—I hesitated, then, as it had to be said, I said it—'Charles, I'd better tell you—I'm sorry—but I'm not in love with you.'

He flushed very faintly. 'Your honesty does you credit, darling, even if it does nothing to my manly ego. If it's any consolation this isn't news to me.'

'You guessed?'

'I knew. When I kissed you.' He refilled our wine-glasses. 'I had suspected it previously.'

'You don't mind?'

'The truth? Sweetie, I'd be a liar if I said I enjoyed having it pushed down my throat, but on the whole I would much rather have things that way. Do you realise you are a most unusual person?'

145

'I don't think so.'

'I don't think,' he replied drily, 'I know. It may interest you to know you are one of the only two genuinely honest women I have ever met. And by some strange coincidence both of you have told me to my face that you don't love me.' His crooked smile was not touching his eyes. 'There must be a moral there somewhere. Let's not go into it now. Let us talk of other things.'

'Things like your problem?'

'It's taken care of, thanks.'

He was giving me such a guilt-complex that I spent the rest of that date exuding charm in compensation. He did the same, I was much afraid for a different motive. I was very relieved he did not suggest another date when we said good night.

My relief did not last long. An enormous basket of early-spring flowers arrived in the morning. Mrs Shaw switched off the vacuum cleaner to lean out of the window. 'Where did your young man find those this early, dear? Must have cost him a pretty penny! Aren't you the lucky one!'

'That's me, Mrs Shaw! How's the family?'

Half an hour later I was free to ring Charles. 'I don't want to seem ungrateful, but you must stop giving me things.'

'Darling—I haven't upset you?'

I had fully intended to be firm. I ended by accepting his invitation to see a new play that evening which we had discussed the previous night. I thought of old Marcus Cohen. Weak like a baby—that was me as well.

The play had split the dramatic critics into violently anti and violently pro groups. It was news. and the audience was bursting with celebrities. In the intervals Charles said I mustn't miss the famous and infamous elbowing each other out of camera-range.

The foyer was packed. He took my arm, and a flash-bulb exploded right by us. I started. 'Charles, this is unnerving! Shall we go back inside?'

'If you are hideously bored. I find it very amusing. Well worth the small bribe for our tickets.'

I could not insist on our retreating after that. 'So that was how you got hold of them so quickly?'

'Quicker than you know, my love. This afternoon. Any objections?'

I had. I kept them to myself, as he would neither understand nor believe them. Like Francine, when he wanted something he just bought it. As practically everything was for sale if the price was right, and he could afford the price, he got what he wanted. But money was the only answer he knew. If he ever had to find another he would not know where to start looking, or what he was looking for. And since he was convinced that whatever it was did not exist, it was unlikely that he would find it.

Andrew's car was sitting outside when I left the flat to go back to work. 'Nurse Newenden!' He pushed up his front window. 'I am about to go back to Martha's. Want a lift? The car's unlocked, so get in. I'll be down in a minute.'

He did not keep me waiting much longer than that. It was long enough for me to wonder what it would be like to have a right to get into his car as I had just done, a right to wait for him. It would, I thought, be like having a right to the keys of heaven and earth. Then he joined me, and we talked about the weather, and Christmas.

'Are these your last nights off before Christmas Day?'

'Yes. I'm off on Boxing night for one night. Then I'm back for two, off for four. All the nights off get switched around for Christmas.'

'Boxing night your dinner?'

'Yes.'

He had to stop in a traffic jam. 'I've forgotten the form. When do the sisters have theirs?'

'Christmas Eve night with the staff nurses. The first- and second-year nurses have theirs Christmas night.'

'Of course! And the day staff nurses take over on the one night all you night seniors are off.'

He was making polite conversation. I did the same. 'You on over Christmas, Doctor?'

He nodded. 'I'll move in for a couple of days. Dr Petrie and Mr Jameson are doing the same to let our married colleagues see something of their own families. It suits me well, as it means I'll be free to get away the following week-end. Weather permitting, I want to fly north. I'm looking forward to that,' he added with unusual warmth.

I guessed he would be seeing in the New Year with Ann MacDonald. I said something trite about all Scots wanting to get home to Scotland for New Year's Eve.

'It's not only that. I haven't been out of London for more than twenty-four hours since I came back to Martha's. I feel like a change of scenery.'

Suddenly he was sounding as he had back at the beginning. He was being very polite—and giving me this lift—but his politeness had a cold edge.

Unfairly, I switched the subject to Mr Curtis. I knew it was a low trick to remind him of Curtis and, I hoped by association, of the night Curtis had come into Albert, but it seemed my ace, and so I played it.

It did no good. 'Did you know he was discharged yesterday. Curtis was sorry not to have said good-bye to you. He seems to have enjoyed Albert.'

'It is a nice ward, Doctor,' I said flatly.

Staff Nurse Carr came out of the Night Home as he dropped me at the front steps. She raised her eyebrows as he drove off. 'You seem to be moving in very exalted circles, Newenden.'

'His flat is next door to my cousin's.'

'So I've heard. And—about your cousin. It must be quite a come-down for you, having to join us working girls at night.'

I was on edge with disappointment. 'Doesn't bother me at all, Nurse Carr,' I snapped back. 'I'm a very good mixer.'

She looked startled and scuttled off. I did not know what she said to the girls at our table, but at supper they treated me with a most extraordinary mixture of wariness and respect. When a girl who had come in late announced she had heard I had been living it up, plus, plus, she suddenly jolted as if some one had kicked her under the table. I had no intention of talking Andrew with them, so pretended not to notice and looked round for Bridie. 'Sullivan overslept?'

'She's got an extra night off. The Office rang her in Birmingham this morning to say she needn't come back until to-morrow.'

There were three empty beds in Albert that night. Staff Nurse Jenkins said there was nothing like empty beds to make us feel a teeny, weeny bit nervous, but as we were not on take-in and were discharging as many patients as possible home for Christmas, perhaps we could relax a little. 'Take-in or not,' she added, 'we are much afraid we will be overflowing by Boxing Day. We all know what happens after all those Christmas office parties. We never learn, do we?'

Mr Cohen and Tiny had come off the D.I.L. together two days ago after one of Fatso's rounds. On my own first round I asked, 'Wouldn't that be described as quite a turn-up for the book, Tiny?'

His smile was strained. 'As if I'd know, Nursie!'

His parents had started visiting him again, and now came in every day. Martha's visiting hours for adults were from 2 until 4 P.M. on Wednesdays and Sundays, from 7 until 8 on all the other evenings. From Jenkins I heard Mrs Ellis had to soothe herself with tranquillisers before and after every visit. 'We are trying very hard to conquer ourselves. We come loaded with flowers, fruit, books.'

Tiny was having nightmares again. The S.S.O. was convinced there was a direct connection between them and his parents' visits. 'What can I do? They are his parents. I can't turn them out. I tried suggesting tactfully that the journey must be exhausting for Mrs Ellis, but her husband wasn't having any. He said the boy had been very sensible about their leaving him in peace while he was getting over his post-op. shock, now looked forward to seeing them, and as his wife was being very brave, he felt their daily trips could only do good all round. I just hope to God he's right. Certainly, what's left of Tiny's leg is now making strides. The sepsis has gone. His temp. has settled.' He frowned at Tiny's chart. 'This thrashing about in his sleep may even be good exercise. You just cannot tell. Every patient ends up by forcing you to accept he's a law unto himself. All the same—I don't like it.'

Nor did I. 'Can he have stronger sleeping tablets?'

'We won't cure him by turning him into a drug addict, Nurse Newenden. Still—let's try a change.' He wrote up a new type of sedative, of similar strength to those we were already using. 'See what these do.'

They made no difference. The nightmares went on, and Tiny now dreaded them so much that he often tried to keep himself awake to avoid them. The only way to get him to sleep then was to sit on his locker, hold his hand, and talk quietly until he was relaxed and could then drop off. It would not have been easy to fit in the time for that had we been on take-in; as we were not we managed it.

I had seen nothing of Meg since her return. Day and night nurses in Martha's never met unless they happened to work in the same wards. She came into Albert early on Christmas morning, that being the one morning of the year when any nurse could walk unquestioned into any ward in the hospital. 'Cathy, the ward looks wonderful! And where did you get that holly in your cap? I can't find any with berries anywhere!'

Our splendid holly had been produced by Mr Cohen. One of his sons worked in Covent Garden. I gave Meg a sprig to pin in her cap, then took her round to meet the men. Stan Gould had a bit of mistletoe fixed to his hair with a hair-grip. 'Just hoping, Nurses. I ask you, no harm in hoping, is there, see?'

Tiny had needed a pillow-case to hold the many presents his parents had left for him. He had not yet opened them. They were stacked high on his locker. Meg asked, 'How can you stand the strain of waiting? I should want to open the lot at once.'

'I like to choose the right moment, Staff Nurse. Dead fussy— aren't I, Nursie?'

Meg said she had masses to tell me, and ask. 'I suppose you won't have a spare moment this morning?'

'Not a chance. Sister Albert's staff coffee party'll go on until it's nearly time for the patients' Christmas dinners. Then I'm flopping into bed in a spare room in the Home, as I'm working to-night. Oh—Lor! Here's Sister Matilda with mistletoe in her cap!'

Meg's jaw dropped. 'Now I've seen everything!' All our ward sisters gave coffee parties for their day, night, and resident staffs on Christmas morning. We all got presents from Sister, and, this year, from the men. Tiny had organised this before his operation; Mrs Stan, Mrs Cuthbert, and Mrs Cohen had done the secret shopping, then called on Sister Albert in the Sisters' Home and sprung them on her last night. Every Albert nurse had a powder-compact, lipstick, and card signed by all the men. The Orthopaedic Unit surgeons had after-shave lotion and handkerchiefs. Fatso had an old-fashioned cut-throat razor as an extra. Albert demanded a penny from him in return.

Fatso was delighted. He disappeared to the hospital kitchen, came back in a striped butcher's apron and straw hat, smelled strongly of after-shave lotion. George said we could have trusted Tiny to use his loaf. 'We all pong so beautifully that no one'll be able to smell the gin.'

George was on top of the world. He kissed every nurse who came near Albert. He had kissed Meg four times before I vanished with the other night girls at half-past eleven. Matron was in Central Hall, surrounded by two Office Sisters, Night Sister, Dr Petrie, Mr Jameson, and Andrew.

'Going to bed, Nurses?' Matron advanced on us smiling. 'Night Sister has told me how hard you all worked last night to get all the cleaning finished before the day staff came on duty, in addition to filling and hanging up all the stockings, and your ordinary ward work. You must be very tired, but, I am sure, very happy. Sleep well.'

'Thank you, Matron,' we chorused.

I glanced at Andrew. All the others were smiling at us. He was looking at the floor.

Albert was a quiet ward when we got back on duty, Christmas Day in hospital being nearly as exhausting for the patients as it was for the staff. The men were more than ready to settle, and half were asleep before I finished my first round. Only Tiny was wide awake. He was still awake when Val Gower went to first supper. She was working as junior for the night, as it was the junior's night off.

I sat on his locker. 'Too many visitors at this afternoon's party?'

'I'll say. Every relative I possess turned up to see the new family freak.'

'Tiny, that's unfair. And stupid. They came because it's

Christmas Day. All families get together on this day, unless they include doctors and nurses.'

He reached for my hand. 'Don't nark, Nursie. It's not my fault you girls have to work over Christmas—or maybe it is. If I hadn't been driving that bloody car I wouldn't be here now.'

'No. There'd just be another man in this bed. As for our working over Christmas, you may not believe this, chum, but we enjoy it. This is one of the high spots of our year.'

'God-awful years you must have!'

'We like 'em.'

We were silent. Yesterday the decorations had gone up. Above our heads a cluster of silver-paper stars hanging from the ceiling swung gently in the current of rising warm air. The dim night lights softened the harsh colours of the paper flowers and chains. They looked like real flowers and garlands of real leaves.

'Tiny. Phantom hurting?'

'Not the phantom. The fact. And for God's sake,' he added bitterly, 'don't tell me I'll soon have a nice tin leg, and aren't I bloody lucky as my tin foot will never get chilblains, or ingrowing toe-nails, or corns? And you can skip the bit about the wonders of science, and how they now make such splendid artificial limbs that you can't tell the difference unless you happen to be wearing one. I've been hearing that bloody tripe the whole afternoon and evening. I can't take any more of it, Nursie.'

'I won't give you any.'

'Skip the understanding patter! I know you are all lovely girls and it's the flaming festive season, but I've had a surfeit. I'm a-weary, Nursie. I'm a-weary of the lot.'

I said nothing. I was desperately sorry for him, but to say so, as I had learnt on other occasions with him, only made things worse. I held his hand in both of mine as he went on: 'The other chaps thought it a hell of a good day. They were all so bloody cheerful and trying to be brave—they always are! God's in His Heaven and all's bright and beautiful, and even if we are all busted up in small pieces and every piece hurts there's nothing like a smile, and you can see the poor bloody nurses are doing their best, and if the sisters turn bitchy it just shows their hearts are in the right places, but it doesn't do to wear your heart on your bloody sleeve.'

I spoke then. 'Keep your voice down, dear. Your bloodies don't worry me, but they'll shock Stan out of sleep.'

He smiled reluctantly. 'Poor old Stan! He's not a flaming fraud like most of the others. He really has got guts. Did you know Mrs Stan brought her husband up to the tea-party?'

'No!' I could have kissed Mrs Stan for this lead. 'How did they get on?'

151

'So well that if Stan hadn't been strung up by both legs I thought they'd all get into bed together.'

'Some party.'

'It was. I thought it would never end.' He took a long breath. 'Only one bright spot. Everything ends.' He stared up at the swinging stars. 'We had an English master at school who was a nut. He had a fixation for Swinburne. He was always spouting chunks. I didn't dig it then. There's one I like a lot now.' He paused. 'Know this:

> *'From too much love of living,*
> *From hope and fear set free,*
> *We thank with brief thanksgiving*
> *Whatever gods may be*
> *That no life lives for ever;*
> *That dead men rise up never;*
> *That even the weariest river*
> *Winds somewhere safe to sea.'*

He turned his face my way, but it was in shadow and I could not see his expression. 'I wish I'd written that.'

Suddenly I was scared. 'Is that how things are with you, Tiny?'

'I don't want to talk about me. I'm fed to the back teeth with me.'

'It might help.'

'I don't want help. I want to talk about you.'

'Not much to say.' I stalled to give myself time to think of a way of getting through to him. So far I had always managed to do that eventually. Now he seemed to be moving out of my reach. 'What do you want to know?'

'The lot. It'll be something to think about.'

If that was true he could have my life's history. I told him about the flat, where it was, Francine, my home, Luke, my parents.

He said, 'You've left out the cousin in that newspaper picture with you.'

'With me? In a paper?'

'Sit forward.' Quietly he took a torn-off piece of newspaper from his locker. 'Here.'

I switched on my torch. The photo was of Charles and myself in that theatre foyer. It was set in a gossip column above a paragraph giving our mutual backgrounds, and if not the fact that we were engaged, the impression that the wedding invitations would shortly be in the post. Pristine had a double-barrel surname and a style that gushed even worse than her conversation.

152

Tiny asked if I was going to marry soon.

'I certainly am not! This is sheer rubbish! This female's another nut! I can't think why she had to write this——' Then I remembered exactly why. 'What on earth made him do it?'

'What?' He was now genuinely interested. 'Tell all.'

'I must go round again—then I will.'

The ward was sleeping. In a few minutes I was back on his locker. Sisters P.T.S. said no nurse should ever confide the details of her private life to a patient. But if it kept Tiny's mind off himself I would almost have told him about Andrew.

When I finished he said, 'That chap wanted this to get round.'

'Obviously. Why?'

'Is he jealous of another character in your life? Would he want to rock that boat? Or—that other little number of his own? I guess you know about it?'

'Know—what?'

He took my torch, switched it on my face, then off again.

'You don't know.'

I bent close to him. 'What?'

'That La Belle Eccles in the not-so-far distant past was a hot favourite as the future Mrs Charles Newenden.'

'Eccles? Our Nurse Eccles?' I demanded in astonishment that was instantly followed by an even greater astonishment at my own thick-headedness. I should have guessed from that night in Cas. There had been so many pointers. I simply had not bothered to see them. Now I did. 'How do you know this, Tiny? And does the whole ward?'

'Only yours truly.'

'And you've not told them? That is big of you!'

'A noble nature. Besides, the chaps are too young. They'd be shocked at nurses having sex. Not that La Belle has lived with him—and don't ask how do I know! I know everything. I am the eyes and ears of Albert, the comic relief, the laddie with the right stuff up here.' He patted his head as he mimicked Fatso. 'What I don't get from you night nurses I get from the day nurses, the cleaning ladies, the gentlemen who electric polish the floor, the window-cleaners, the newspaper man, the students, the physios, Fatso and his lads—and the lady who comes round with improving tracts and lavender-bags.' His voice was a murmur—a self-derisive murmur. 'You name it, I know it. I don't have to talk about it. La Belle Mary has been bloody good to me, even if she does love another, and so, my favourite blonde Nursie, have you. So I've said nowt about your well-heeled cousin. I had the whole works from one who shall be nameless—and not a night girl—weeks ago.' He paused. 'Your cousin seems to have it all ways. La Belle may have departed from him in high dudgeon, but she's still sold on him.'

I wasted no breath asking how he knew that, or doubting him. When Mary and I worked together she still looked and behaved like a silent ghost.

He asked how I was going to square things for her.

'I don't know yet.'

He said, 'Before you do anything it might be an idea to make sure you aren't going to hurt her more.'

'If Charles isn't serious about her?'

'You have said he is not exactly the marrying kind.' He was thoughtful. 'And she's not the mistress kind. If he wants her he'll have to marry her, but if he tries to buy her she won't marry him. I suppose he's always bought his women. That'll have him clean out of his depths when making a play for our Mary.'

'Tiny, I always knew you were bright, but not this bright! You're brilliant. You don't even know Charles, but you've got his number.'

'Sheer genius.'

'Not far off. May I now say something about you?'

'I may tell you to belt up.'

'I'll risk it. Now, listen to me, and this isn't patter. You may have a tricky—no—more than tricky, a very tough immediate future. But in the long run you will make out very well. You've got terrific brains, insight, imagination—and don't throw things —a very kind heart. You can't miss!'

He yawned. 'No comment.'

'My dear, I'm being honest!'

'I believe you.' He blew me a kiss. 'I adore you, Nursie. I adore all my nurses, but particularly my night nurses.'

Again he had slid out of my reach, but he was now very sleepy. I gave him a drink, turned his pillows, smoothed his sheets. 'Try and sleep now. We've been talking ages.'

'God bless Albert for snoring its head off. I wanted to talk to-night. I'll make up all my lost sleep when you are off to-morrow night. Who are we having, incidentally?'

'I don't know. One of the day staff nurses and Player. I'm sorry to leave you with a stranger, but I'm sure she'll be very sweet. Player'll look after you.'

'I don't need looking after. I'm a big boy now. Even if I can't go to the bathroom by myself.' He took my hand and kissed the palm. 'Thanks a lot for everything, Nursie.'

He slept through until morning. He did not have a nightmare. Sister Albert was very pleased. 'This could be a turning-point, Nurse Newenden. Off you go—and I hope you and

Nurse Gower have a very happy time to-night. Is there a party after your dinner?'

'Yes, Sister. The Registrars are entertaining us.'

She smiled. 'I must remember to warn my relief night nurse that all to-night's rounds will be done by the most senior residents, and the consultants. Right, my dear. Thank you.'

CHAPTER THIRTEEN

TINY WRITES ME A LETTER

I HAD never been to Charles's flat. The hall porter was doubtful. 'It's early, miss. Mr Newenden may not be up yet.'

'Then if you will kindly ring him to say I am on my way up he'll be awake by the time I get there. Miss Catherine Newenden.'

He hopped round his counter and nearly broke his neck in his efforts to get the lift gates open before I reached them and back to his switchboard before I vanished.

Charles opened his front door. He wore a dark-grey silk dressing-gown over paler-grey silk pyjamas. 'Cathy, my love, this is an unexpected pleasure. And what can I do for you?'

I remembered something I had overlooked. 'Would you care to ask me in? Or—are you entertaining?'

He raised one eyebrow, held open the door. 'I stopped holding pre-breakfast parties when I was at Oxford. Please do come in.'

'Thank you.'

His flat was larger than Francine's, less ornate, but looked to me to be even more expensively furnished. And, unlike Francine, he had hundreds of books.

I went over to one locked glass-fronted shelf. 'These look like first editions.'

'They are. I've some etchings in my study. I don't generally exhibit them until after breakfast.'

I faced him. 'I'm sorry to be so early. I wanted to see you.'

He bowed. 'If I had known I'd have shaved. I apologise.'

'Don't bother about me. If there is one thing night nursing does it gets a girl acclimatised to unshaven men in the early mornings.'

'Another reason for my considered opinion that nurses must make excellent wives.'

'I remember your saying something about that. Do you remember my changing the subject?'

'Very well.'

'That was because I thought you were talking about me. Had you said the girl you had in mind was Mary Eccles I'd have been happy to discuss it for the rest of our date. Do you still

156

want to marry her, Charles? Or only to add her name to your little black book?'

For the first time ever, for a fleeting moment he could have been Luke. He looked me over exactly as Luke did some one who had affronted him. 'Angel one,' he drawled affectedly, 'you'll have to forgive me. I have my nasty habits. They do not include discussing one woman with another.'

Once that would have made me want to crawl into the ground. I answered now as I would have done Luke. 'Charles, don't be so damn silly! I'm not one of your women. I'm your cousin. Don't blame me because you've been trying to pretend you own me! I'm still not dead clear why you gave that Pristine female all that blah, though I guess it was to show Mary that you aren't losing any sleep—or time—because she walked out on you. You got me into Francine's flat, you've been building up a nice pretty little picture round me, and as I've had a lot of fun I'm not holding that against you for my own angle. For myself, I'm grateful. But that's not going to make me say I like what you've done to Mary. I like that girl. Even if I didn't I don't like seeing anyone kicked when she's down.'

He said coldly, 'I see no reason for you to assume she is down—or point in continuing this conversation.'

He had much more control than his mother and sister. By now both would be throwing tantrums. He was very very angry. I hoped that was a good sign. I decided to find out. I had never tried to needle him before, but I knew the right technique for Luke.

'So you just wanted her as a mistress? That's why you used that corny absent-friends routine in Scotland. And poor pretty Mary nearly fell for it.' He was silent. 'Not that I blame her. It's so impossible to see a man clearly when one's in love with him. And being very intelligent, she always had a hunch you were just playing around. I hope that was some consolation on that ghastly trip she had down from Scotland. You did know she hitched her way home in all that snow? It took her two days to get to Manchester, and an obliging lorry-driver who brought her down the M1 in the small hours. She finished up walking from Covent Garden to Martha's.'

'She did—what?' he snapped.

I repeated myself, added how exhausted she had been that night. 'But why should you care? You only wanted to make a play for her, she wouldn't play, so all you have to do is cross out her name. She'll get over loving you. With her looks she won't be allowed to brood alone long. And Martha's is stiff with young men. They mayn't have much lolly, but most of us settle quite happily for marrying them.'

That did it. He asked how I dared say Mary loved him when she had told him to his face and in writing that she detested him and never wanted to see him again. She had returned all his non-perishable presents, refused now to answer or even read his letters, or talk to him on the telephone.

'Since Scotland? What else did you expect? You didn't follow that up with a handsome present?'

He flushed faintly. 'And if I did?'

'Oh, dear!' I sat down. 'Charles, I think you would probably be generous even if you were broke. But you aren't broke. So people can't help thinking that all a present means to you is filling in another cheque. You buy things with cheques. Not people.'

'Don't you believe that, my love.'

'I should have said—not people worth having. Those sort of people don't like being bribed. They aren't even all that interested in money.'

'And where do these paragons exist, Cathy?'

'Around. For a start, I don't know how many hospitals, schools, or churches there are in this country. I'm very hazy on the total number of probation officers and district midwives. Would you say any of those jobs—and there are dozens of others—are generally regarded as a short-cut to riches? Yet people do them.'

'Possibly.' He sat by me. 'Perhaps I've not met enough of them.'

'Perhaps. Might be a help if you married into the breed. Don't you want to?'

He said, 'So much that I haven't even wanted to look at another woman since I met her. That was at a party eight months ago. I didn't want to go to it—it sounded deadly—but I had nothing much else on, so I looked in and saw her.' He stopped speaking for a little while. 'I'd never seen such a wonderful face. It's perfect. Yet it's not the big thing in her life. She can talk. Until I got to know you, recently, she was the only girl I knew who could talk. Know what I mean?'

'Yes.' I thought of Francine and her debbie friends. Nice girls, some. Conversing with them was heavy going even for another girl. 'I know.'

He went on: 'That was why I wanted you in the flat. I thought as you and she worked together, if you and I got along you might be able to get her to believe I was not merely playing around with her.'

'Surely you could have proved that by asking her to marry you? Preferably, being you, in writing.'

Again he flushed. 'Being me, I had to be sure it was me.'

158

I remembered Francine on gold-diggers and all those women who did not know the word no. 'Yes. You had to. Are you sure about yourself? Then what are you waiting for?'

He showed me the letter Mary had written him the morning she returned from her hitch-hike. 'Understand?'

I read it again. 'I can understand this hurt your pride. It's fierce. She's hurt and hitting back. But if she genuinely wanted to finish with you I don't believe she'd have written at all. I think from the moment she walked out on you you'd have heard not one more word from her. Your presents would have been returned without messages.' I gave him the letter. 'Did you write and apologise? Or just send that soothing token?'

'I wrote. It came back unopened with the bracelet.'

'But you do want to marry her? Then write and tell her so.'

He said gloomily, 'What's the use? She won't open the letter.'

'Charles, don't be gormless! Let me deliver it. I'll see she reads it.'

He brightened. 'Darling, can you? How?'

'I don't know yet. I'll think of something.'

I made us tea while he wrote, and wondered whether I was really doing Mary a kindness. Luke would say not. Oh, well, I thought, she doesn't have to marry him, she does know how to say no, so it will be up to her.

Charles dressed and walked back with me to my flat. 'I know I must seem to have used you, darling. Face it, I have. But I always knew that you wouldn't mind. You're so understanding, Cathy. What would the family do without you?'

Pick up its own pieces, I thought wearily after he had gone. Solve its own problems. And not only the family. George. Meg.

I knew it was mainly my own fault for being such a busy little do-gooder, for enjoying giving advice, and running a private lonely hearts' bureau. I was still happy to go on doing that for anyone in a hospital bed, but not any more in my private life. 'Cathy won't mind,' they all said. I had news for them. I minded like hell. I was relieved Charles did not love me, but the thought of the mental chess he had been playing with me as a pawn made me feel slightly sick and very tired. Then as I was so tired and my resistance was down, I could no longer hold off thoughts of Andrew. How long would I have to go on loving him? Without any encouragement, or hope? I had not wanted to love him. I did not want to now. I could no more stop than I could stop breathing. But I still had to call him Dr Lairg, and I always would. I ought to be grateful for one thing. At Martha's no nurse was allowed to 'sir' any doctor.

The mews was horribly quiet. Mrs Shaw was not around, and

the garage at the far end was closed, as it was a Bank Holiday and a Saturday as well as Boxing Day. The Americans had apparently vanished for ever, and Andrew was in Martha's. There was nothing to disturb my sleep, but by mid-afternoon I had had enough of my own company. I had to be in uniform for our dinner, and then to change into mufti for the Registrars' party. I packed a suitcase, went back to Martha's, and asked the Night Home Sister if I could use the same spare room as last night as a dumping-ground, since Bridie was asleep. She said I could use it until seven, but not after, as it was booked for the night by another non-resident senior.

I had to wait until the night nurses woke up to see Mary. She was working in Matthew that night. My reception was icy. She tried not to believe what I had to say, but as she wanted to believe me, in the end she did. She then endeared herself to me as a future cousin-in-law by not asking for my advice. She said she would read Charles's letter and then decide what to do next.

Our dinner went on until half-past ten. The party was officially supposed to end at midnight, because of Sunday morning. Joe Briggs, my immediate host, suggested some of us moved on and continued the party in one of the married Registrar's flats in a block belonging to the hospital five minutes' walk away. It was after 3.30 when he drove me back to the mews. The lights were on in Andrew's flat.

'Neighbours celebrating likewise?' he asked.

I told him who lived there. 'Not the party type?'

'Lairg? God, I'd forgotten! He's not the party type indeed! And do you wonder? He must have had a bellyful in the old days. They say his wife was a great party girl and used to get hellish mad with him because he had to work. You know what people are like who don't work in hospitals. They think because a chap's off he can get away. Apparently she was always turning up and making scenes in Cas., because he kept her waiting. You knew she was stoned the night she killed herself and that other chap? *De mortuis nil nisi* and so forth—but they say she had it coming to her, poor kid. Wasn't much fun for him, before or after. Not surprised he's kept clear of rep. mist.'

The party had loosened my tongue as well as his. 'Joe, he's about to. He's engaged to some ex-ward sister. Her name's Ann MacDonald.'

'Ann MacDonald?' he echoed. 'Am I drunk or are you? She's his sister-in-law. Step sister-in-law. His wife's father married twice. Joanna Lairg was his first wife's daughter. Ann's mother is his second wife.'

I said mechanically, 'That makes them half sisters.'

160

'Does it? Right. And this Ann woman is engaged to that chap with the os calcis we had in Albert. Curtis. Lawyer chap. Went out a few days before Christmas.'

'Joe! Are you sure?'

'Of course I'm sure. I put him in a walking plaster, and they've asked me to the wedding. Mid-week, so I won't be able to make it. Nice of them to ask me.'

'Very.'

He laughed. 'How much have you had to drink? You are not with me.'

He was so right. It was not alcohol. I blamed my pet whipping-boy—night duty. 'I had better go in, Joe. Thanks for driving me home and a wonderful party. I'd ask you in, but'—I jerked a thumb at Andrew's windows—'he knows I live here.'

'He'll know this car. It's Fatso's second best. He lends it to us. And since we are in one pundit's car, with another pundit breathing down our necks from on high, we will say good night with the dignity and decorum that are the hallmark of St Martha's Hospital, London!'

I let myself in in an enchanted trance. I noticed the envelope in my letter-box and removed it absently. I was too wrapped in my own personal happiness to remember there had been no afternoon post, or notice it was unstamped. The handwriting of the address was vaguely familiar. The message in pencil across the back of the envelope had been written by someone else. I squinted at the signature, being too lazy to get my glasses. I could read very well without them once I got my eyes in focus, but as that generally gave me a headache preferred not to. I did not worry about getting a headache now. I would not have worried over a fractured skull. Andrew was not engaged and about to remarry, and nothing could worry me now! I refused to face the fact that that was unlikely to make any difference at all to his attitude towards me, being too content to wallow in the difference it made in mine towards him. To think I had once been furious with him for jumping to conclusions! Mrs Shaw was a honey, but I had nursed dozens of Mrs Shaws. She was a kindly, very sentimental soul who loved a good gossip. The doctor was single, so of course she had to provide him with a young lady! Hadn't she provided me with a passionate admirer in Charles—aided by him? As for Bridie's inside information—when, outside of a ward, did Bridie ever get her facts right? 'Cathy, my girl,' I said aloud, still squinting at the pencil writing, 'you are another nutty Newenden.'

Then I realised the signature was 'Mrs Stan.'

'Tiny asked me to pop this in the post for you,' she had

scribbled, 'but seeing as there won't be one till Monday I got hubby to drive me your way.'

I shouted with laughter all by myself. Bully for hubby! I was not sure my father would agree, but Stan, Mrs Stan, and hubby were most truly an inspiration to us all! They were experts at peaceful coexistence! She must have taken hubby for another jolly evening's visit to Stan. Tiny probably felt he had to let off steam again and had given her the letter, rather than put it in the ward post-basket which Sister or Jenkins took round every evening. Sister Albert was a broad-minded and sensible woman, but the rules that forbade any nurse becoming too involved—or, indeed, involved at all, emotionally—with any male patient were so strict that Sister would have had to query my name on that envelope.

Clever Tiny, I thought, opening the envelope at last. Trust him not to slip up.

Then I read what he had written.

'God!' I gasped. 'No!' I hurled myself at the telephone and rang Matron's Office. There was no ringing sound. In an agony of impatience I tried again. That time I could not even get a dialling tone. My telephone was dead, and I had to get to a telephone. There might still be time. They might still think he was just having a good sleep. The strange staff nurse would not know his sleeping habits. Player was a good kid, but she was not as observant or experienced as Mary. As Tiny had known.

I raced down to the mews. Andrew's lights were still on. I would have kept my finger on his bell, as I did, had they been out.

He answered the door immediately.

'Can I use your phone?' I asked without explanation. 'Mine's bust.' I thrust the letter at him, rushed by him and up his stairs without waiting for his answer.

'Hold on——' He followed me up quickly.

'I can't!' I was dialling. 'I must tell Night Sister.'

He said quietly, 'She knows,' and took the reciever from me. I stared at him, frozen with horror. His expression answered my unspoken question. 'Come and sit down, and I'll tell you.'

I had underestimated Player. She had told the staff nurse she had never seen Tiny sleep so heavily. As the staff nurse had not nursed him previously, knew about his many bad nights, and had herself noticed he seemed extremely sleepy when she came on, she not unreasonably assumed he was simply worn out. He was no longer a D.I.L., and not even on a four-hourly pulse, as his temperature had been settled for the past few days. Mainly to soothe Player, she put him on a four-hourly for the night. She was having a busy night. The Christmas road accidents had finally filled Matthew to capacity and overflowed into Albert. The ward now had no empty beds and three new D.I.L.'s. Player had not been soothed. She had kept an unofficial watch on Tiny's pulse, and when the rhythm seemed to her to be doing odd things three times running she had risked being told to get on with her own routine work and leave the ward to her senior. The staff nurse had been impressed by Player's persistence and checked Tiny's blood-pressure. The first reading made her wonder if the machine had broken. She took it again, and rang the S.S.O. This was just after midnight. Ten minutes later the S.S.O. rang for the S.M.O. Andrew had been with Dr Barnes when he got that call and went with him to Albert.

'He was then in coma. His heart held out fairly well for about forty minutes, then it went into acute failure. The S.S.O. opened his chest in the ward, and we tried cardiac massage. We couldn't get him going again.' He sighed. 'We didn't then know where he had got the dope. We found the empty half-bottle of whisky hidden in his locker behind the bag of strong pepper-mints. He had been very clever. There was no scent of alcohol on his breath. Just the peppermints. The junior said he liked them.'

'Yes. He did.'

He went out to telephone. He left the door ajar. He talked to Fatso. 'Yes,' he said, 'from his mother's handbag. Yesterday. Her spare bottle of tranquillizers. Apparently she always carries a spare. Yes. Replaced them with aspirin. What? Hold on, Franks.' He came back to me. 'Where would he have got those aspirin?'

I said wearily, 'Not from the ward. We seldom use aspirin in Albert. Mr Franks isn't very keen on it. But any of his visitors could have brought them in.'

'Like the whisky. Right.'

He returned in a few minutes. 'Mr Franks is going to ring me back. His parents are still in Martha's.'

'How have they taken it?'

He sat on the arm of a chair. 'Badly, I'm afraid. They didn't bring the whisky. At the moment they blame the hospital. They are convinced he somehow got the drugs from the ward.'

'That's impossible! We have to account for everything we give.'

'Mr Franks explained that. To double-check he has had the dispenser on call, and one of the night sisters check the contents of Albert drug-cupboard against the Dangerous Drug Book. There's not so much as half a grain of Luminal missing.' He frowned to himself. 'His father suggested he must have hoarded his nightly sedatives.'

'No. We have to watch them being swallowed.'

'Sister Albert and the Night Superintendent said that.'

'Sister Albert? Was she called up?'

'There was no alternative. A major inquiry had to be started at once. That question had to be asked. It would certainly have been asked at the inquest if he had not written you this letter. If it's true I don't see any blame can be attached to the hospital. One can't blame his mother for not realising what she had in her handbag. But I am not the only man in Martha's who would very much like to get hold of the maniac who gave him that whisky, probably as a Christmas present. An amputation patient. And a boy of twenty-one. From his condition when I saw him I would have said he had been taking the whisky in little doses all evening, and then the tranquillisers in one go. The combination would be disastrous.'

I was not really listening. I was remembering last night, and how, had I not been at that dinner and the party, I would have had that letter hours ago.

'I wish I hadn't gone out to-night! He might be alive now.' I had left the envelope in my flat. I told him of Mrs Stan's message. 'If only I had been in!'

'You can't possibly blame yourself for that!'

'Doctor, I must! I should have guessed! I should have guessed what he meant last night when he said he would make up all his lost sleep to-night. Why am I so blind?' I demanded bitterly. 'It all makes sense now!'

The telephone was ringing. He said, 'We'll go into this directly,' and went out to answer it. He was not long. 'Mrs Ellis's spare bottle of tranquillisers is full of five-grain aspirins. The tablets are the same size as her tranquillisers. She took two of them this morning. She didn't notice the difference.'

CHAPTER FOURTEEN

ALBERT SOUNDS LIKE ALBERT AGAIN

'YOUR tea is getting cold,' he said a second time.

'Sorry. I forgot it.'

'Do you smoke?'

'Occasionally.'

He took a new packet of cigarettes from his desk and shook one out. He had to go into the kitchen for matches.

'Don't you smoke, Doctor?'

'Not now. You should give it up, but not at this moment.' He sat by me on the sofa. 'I don't know what Mrs Shaw has done with the ashtrays. Use the saucer.'

It was very quiet. There was no sound from the mews, and the pre-dawn Sunday traffic was sparse on the main road round the corner. The quiet would have been restful had I not been haunted by the thought that if I had stayed in this evening Tiny might be alive now.

Andrew broke the silence. 'What else did he say to you last night? Can you remember?'

'Yes,' I said, 'yes. Do you want to know, officially?'

'Why? Did he specifically mention suicide? I'm afraid that would have to come out.'

'No. I should have guessed it was in his mind from his conversation, but he didn't put it into words then, or at any other time. He was often very depressed. I thought last night was just another black night for him. The feeling that I couldn't get through to him should have made me suspicious.' I frowned at my thoughts. 'I'd always had his wavelength. Not last night.'

'Is that why you want this off the record?'

'Oh, no.' I hesitated, looking at his pundit's suiting. Then I saw the kindness in his face. 'A lot of our conversation had no connection with him. It was utterly unprofessional, but as it gave him something else to think about, I didn't mind. And it didn't only concern myself. Tiny wasn't just a patient, he was my friend. But I'm afraid Matron wouldn't approve of my discussing the things I did with him.'

'I see. Would you prefer not to tell me? You don't have to, but it might help to talk.'

I told him everything. The only thing I left out was Mary's name. The telling was agony, and a relief.

He did not interrupt or hurry me when I had to stop because my voice shook too much to go on. He sat still, watching me thoughtfully.

I even told him how I had followed up Tiny's lead. 'If Charles and this other nurse do marry—and I think they will—it'll be largely thanks to Tiny. He said this nurse was still sold on Charles. He was right. I saw that this evening.' I paused again. 'If only I had had his insight I could have done something about it last night, and he'd be alive now.'

'Possibly. But if you had saved him for to-night it would have happened on another night. You must believe that. It's true.'

'I wish I could. I wish I could.'

He said, 'I am not merely saying this to give you peace of mind. It's an unhappy fact that any person really determined to kill him or herself always succeeds. No-one, no-one at all, can stop them. It makes no difference if you remove all the obvious and unobvious means. You can use religion, love, responsibilities, money—every argument under the sun. You can even lock them up in a padded cell and have them under a twenty-four-hour watch. They'll find a way.'

'But some suicides are prevented.'

'In my experience, only those in which the intention was not a hundred per cent serious.' He went over to the bookshelves and came back with a stack of standard medical textbooks by assorted authors, found the place in each, and handed them to me. 'Read these.'

Everything I read matched what he had told me.

He said firmly, 'There's no question of any blame being attached to you, as he has carefully explained in that letter. Nor is it your fault you were out to-night. It was pure chance that letter was delivered and not posted. He didn't intend you to get it before Monday. His letter was not a hysterical action based on the hope of causing a fuss and getting attention. It's as detailed and matter-of-fact as a case history sheet. He had it all planned.' He replaced the books and sat down again. 'He knew what he was doing. He did it because that was what he wanted to do.'

'Why? Why?' I demanded. 'Now he was at last getting better? He was doing very well. Physically. And he had been so good about consenting to his amputation.'

'Didn't you once tell me he was very frightened of that?'

I nodded. 'He thought it would kill him.'

He said gently, 'And when he found it didn't he killed himself. Don't ask me why. I can only speculate. I can't properly answer you. But you know very well one cannot start asking why in any hospital ward, and remain sane. And not only in a ward.' He sat back, locked his hands behind his head, and looked at the wall opposite. 'I expect you know what happened to my wife?'

'Yes.' Momentarily, I forgot even Tiny. 'I'm very sorry.'

'It was bad,' he said, 'it was bad. It was so pointless. She wasn't driving anywhere special. She was at a party. I meant to join her, but there was a crisis in William and I couldn't get away. I didn't even know the man who died with her. They had only met at that party and decided to have some air and then go back.' He was silent. Then: 'If I hadn't stayed in William she wouldn't have taken that drive—or if she had I'd have been driving.'

'It wasn't your fault you got held up in William.'

'I know that now. It was no help at the time. It took me a long time to accept it. I felt so responsible. In a way, I still do. But being ten years older I have now discovered that though we are often responsible for other people's actions, up to a point, the main responsibility for anyone's actions rests with his or her self.' He looked at me now. 'Did Tiny Ellis ever tell you why he originally crashed his father's car?'

I was startled. 'No. It was an accident.'

'An accident isn't an act of God. It's the result of human carelessness, or intention. You must be aware some people are more accident-prone than others. Was it his first?'

'No.' I began to understand. 'He had two smashes in his own car. That was why he was driving his father's.'

He nodded as if he had expected this. 'My wife had been in three before the last. She was driving in all four.'

He did not speak for some while after that. I was very moved by what he had said, and above all by his saying it. His expression showed what it had cost him to open up his past to help my present.

I said, 'I am sorry you had to tell me. But thank you.' He roused himself. 'I didn't have to tell you. I wanted to tell you. I expect you can guess why.'

'Yes. I'm grateful.'

'You don't have to be that.'

'Oh, yes, I do.' I looked round the room. 'It would have been even more hell if you hadn't been here to-night. I would have had to find a call-box—and then hear it was too late. Then I would have had to go back to my flat and be alone.' I shuddered. 'I'm used to the night. I don't mind the dark in a hospital. Not alone. Not to-night. If I hadn't had you to talk to I wouldn't have known how to face Albert to-morrow. Before you told me all this I felt as if I never wanted to nurse anyone again. As if I had lost my nerve. If you had not been kind enough to help me I would have had to cope with all that alone, and that letter. I suppose I would have had to take it back to Martha's. I don't know. I do know I have to thank you very, very much. I am so very glad you didn't stay on at Martha's to-night.'

'I had intended staying, though I was off from midnight.' He got up and walked over to a window to look out. Then he came back and sat on the arm of a chair. 'Then I was in Albert. After, as there was nothing more for me to do in the hospital, I decided to come back here. I guessed you'd be at the Registrars' party and thought you might have heard about Tiny.'

'We moved on at midnight.' Then I realised what he had said. 'You came back—for me?'

He nodded calmly, as if nothing could be more natural. 'This mews is lonely. I didn't care for the idea of your being quite alone on this specific night. Please don't say that was another kind thought on my part, or I shall have to remind you that even hospital pundits have a few human instincts. To-night you lost a friend. To-night you needed a friend. The circumstances being what they are, I can't pretend we ever can be genuine friends.' He smiled a queer little smile. 'But we are neighbours.'

For a few moments I could not say anything. I loved him so much; he was being so wonderful to me; and yet he had so hurt me by reminding me of our jobs and the stupid conventions that ruled our working lives.

Then, at the back of my mind, I found myself wondering if that had really been what he meant? Now? When he knew I was shattered by Tiny's death—and had been so honest about coming back. I knew he was a pundit, but every nurse who had worked with him knew he had not even a trace of the typical pundit's Jehovah-complex. His attitude when he met red tape was to reach for scissors.

I had to be sure. Last night I had missed an opportunity and lost it for good. I was never going to do that again.

I asked bluntly, 'Why can we never be genuine friends? Because you're a pundit and I'm still in training?'

'That could be one reason.' He folded his arms. 'There are others. I'm not disturbing you with them on this night of all nights.'

'Because of Tiny? Because it's so late?' I insisted in a voice that did not sound like my own.

'Neither—no'—he corrected himself—'that's not true. Both come into it, but they aren't the main reasons even though they are the cause of your turning to me to-night. You look so tired, my—my dear girl. So dazed with shock and distress. In that shock and distress you told me a great deal about yourself. What kind of a man would I be to take advantage of that now? When I now know that you had one emotional shock to-day before this blow to-night?'

'Shock? You don't mean Charles?' His expression answered me. 'I wasn't shocked about Charles! I've never been so relieved! I've been foolish enough to be worrying because I thought he was falling in love with me, and I couldn't possibly marry him as I don't love him. That's true! To-day was a good day, until I got Tiny's letter. I was so happy when I read it— I'd seen Mary—our dinner and the party were fun—and then Joe Briggs told me about——' My voice faded out as I realised what I had nearly said.

He took me up on it at once. 'Was it Briggs who brought you home in Franks' car? What did he tell you?'

I nearly lost my nerve. Not quite.

He did not move, and when I finished speaking he just looked at me. Then he stood up, and walked over to the window. With his back to me he told me how, under the terms of his father-in-law's will, he managed Ann's affairs. 'He left her a considerable sum, and, having decided very young women were unfit to have too easy access to a lot of money, made me responsible for her affairs until she reaches thirty. I've recently been arranging for her to buy a house. Possibly I mentioned it in Martha's—I don't remember. Of course, she's visited me there often and wore an engagement ring. I should have recollected that would be more than enough for any hospital grape-vine to fix the date for us.' He turned. 'Has it?'

'Just "soon." Joe Briggs will stop that.'

'Good,' he said, 'good.'

We looked at each other in silence, and the silence was electric with unspoken words.

'Do you have to work to-morrow night?'

I did not know what I had been expecting. It was not that. 'Yes. For two more nights. This is just an odd night off. Like— like the first night we met.'

He inclined his head gravely. We might have been in a ward, and I might have been telling him about a patient.

I went on: 'That first night—I honestly didn't know about your keys.'

He said, 'I realised that when I saw you in Albert. I came back to Albert the following night to apologise for my disgracefully high-handed behaviour towards you on our first meeting. You weren't there.'

'No. At supper. I thought you came back for your pen. My junior said you'd lost it.'

'I didn't lose it. I left it in Albert on purpose. In my present job I can walk unquestioned into any ward, but I don't totally ignore ethics. Albert belongs to Franks, I'm thankful to say.'

Outside the early morning was black as midnight, but in that room the light was coming fast. It was a lovely, lovely light, not harsh and blinding, but gentle as a winter sun. I could see it, yet I dared not believe in it. I had to be sure. 'You don't like orthopods?'

'I obviously prefer medicine, but that wasn't what I meant.'

'Tell me, please. Don't say I'm too tired. Of course I'm tired, and sad for Tiny, but only for him.' I stood up. 'Can't you see that?'

'Now.' He came closer. He did not touch me. 'Can't you see that had you been working in one of my wards I would have found our relationship even more intolerable than I have? God knows it's been bad enough as it is.' He was looking at me as no man had ever looked at me before. He added almost casually, 'Did you know I was at Martha's when we first met?'

'No. Your name rang a bell. I couldn't place it. I rang Henry.'

'Trust Henry to know the answer. What was your reaction?'

'I got a bit het up that night. Then I decided it probably wouldn't matter, as we shouldn't see much of each other here, and nothing at all in the hospital. The Professor was the first coronary Albert's had in years.'

'So I've gathered.' He went on to say he had then decided to apologise to me outside the hospital, then he noticed how I was trying to avoid him in the mews, and felt I would prefer him to say nothing and appear not to have recognised me. 'You didn't give the grape-vine that story.'

'I can't take any credit for that.' I explained taking Meg's advice.

'Did she also tell you to keep quiet about saving my life?'

'No. I couldn't have told anyone about that night.' I shivered. 'I still can't bear to remember it. Twice, I was afraid you might be dead.'

The light was not only in the room, it was in his eyes and illuminating his whole face. 'I had been dreaming about you that evening. When I woke and saw you standing by the window I thought I was still in the dream. The cold, the gale, added to the unreality. I was packed with quinine, and at first I couldn't think clearly. I wanted to touch you—to hold you. That was why I forgot the carbon monoxide. I don't usually make a mistake like that. But even without quinine as an excuse,

170

I don't find it easy to think clearly when I am near you. Which is why I am very thankful you've not been working in one of my wards.' He put his hands on my arms, and as he gently drew me towards him I felt the faint tremor in his hands. 'I love you beyond belief. I haven't known you long, but it seems a very long time since the one thought uppermost in my mind when you were near was to hold you like this.' His arms tightened round me. I felt as if every bone in my body had melted and I would have fallen to the floor but for his arms. 'I was attracted to you from the first. I didn't want to be attracted. You reminded me too much of your idiotic cousin, and I was annoyed with myself for wishing you were different. That was why I was so bloody to you until we met in Albert. It was then I knew why you had attracted me, and that I had been looking for you for a long time. I didn't even realise I had been looking. I had come to enjoy being alone. I was not lonely. I liked my solitude. I haven't liked it since that night in Albert. It was then I began to love you. I saw your affection for that old man, and the way you refused to accept defeat for him as everyone else connected with him seemed to be doing. I saw we looked on that in the same way, and despite the absurd conventions keeping us at arm's length from each other, we spoke the same language. Then I remembered Charles. I wondered what there was between you. Later, I was sure you loved him. Even that didn't stop me loving you. I did try. I reminded myself I was so much older than you, and of my own views on pundits when I was your age. Wasn't any good. I love you. I desire you. I want to marry you. And, dearest'—his voice shook badly—'I can't hold out much longer.' And then he kissed me.

Later, we had breakfast together, then he took me back to my own flat. Before we left his I rang my parents to ask if I could bring him home on my next nights off on Wednesday. My mother did not sound surprised. 'Darling, how nice! Luke told me you had a very pleasant neighbour. Your father and I will love to meet him.'

Andrew was amused. 'I thought your twin had an intelligent face that morning he asked me where to buy a paper.'

'How did you spot he was my twin? He's so dark. No-one ever takes us for brother and sister as a rule.'

He took my face in his hands. 'He has different colouring, but he walks like you, he talks like you, he has the look of you.'

'And I was worried you must have got hold of the wrong impression.'

'For once, no.' He kissed me lightly.

He went back to the hospital that morning while I was asleep. I had rung the Office for permission to skip supper. He returned to have it with me in my flat, and then drive me to work. He did not talk of Tiny until we turned on to the embankment and saw the lights of Martha's on the far bank. 'His parents have seen that letter. They've accepted it.'

'They don't blame us any more?'

He shook his head. 'Only themselves.'

'Andrew, no!'

We were stopped by traffic lights. He took my hand. 'My darling, have they any alternative?'

I could not answer that. When we drove on I said, 'I feel awful to be so happy.'

He said slowly, 'I didn't know him. You did. Do you honestly —and I mean honestly—believe he would mind?'

I had been refusing to think of Tiny and still dreading the thought of Albert. That made me think of him. I thought of his smile, his quick laugh, and I could almost hear his rather light voice, 'So I brought you together, Nursie? Bully for me! Call me Cupid and have done! A noble nature, that's me!'

'No,' I said at last, 'I know he wouldn't mind. He'd be very pleased. He wanted to help Mary. I think he would have wanted to help me too. He was always helping the other men. He did their pools, sickness benefit claims, advised them on income tax, and, of course, the Albert "book." He gave them such fun through that. He made them laugh. He was so gay.'

'Remember him,' he said, 'like that.'

Mary was on with me. As we left our cloaks an empty theatre-trolley was whisked up our flat. One of the day nurses put her head round the changing-room door. 'Sister Albert says can you be quick as Nurse Eccles will have to go straight down with the theatre case.'

'We busy?' Mary and I asked together.

'Busy! God! We haven't drawn breath all day! Haven't you read the Christmas accident figures?'

Albert was very subdued, but we were too busy to be more than aware of that at the back of our minds. We had six D.I.L.'s and, as our theatre was working until past midnight, the men's rounds were still going on when a Night Ass. came up for the 2 A.M. report. The ward was not really quiet until after three.

Stan woke as I was attending to the new D.I.L. in Tiny's bed. 'Filled up again, eh?' said Stan as I turned his pillows. 'Reckon that's always the way of it. Mind you, I'll miss him same as I seen you are, Nurse. But it don't do no ——— good fretting does it? He wouldn't want that.' He considered his strung-up legs. 'Shame he didn't look at it right. But there, maybe it looked right to him. He had a good head on his shoulders, he had. And the things as he'd say! Gawd! It were a —— wonder we had any —— stitches left! Beg pardon—no offence, Nurse.'

'Of course not, Stan. I know how you feel.'

'Reckon you do, Nurse.' He jerked a thumb as if Tiny was still in the next bed. 'He always said as you always understood. Thought the world of you, he did. I'm not saying as he hadn't an eye for a bit of skirt, but it weren't that with you. You was his nursie—if you see what I mean?'

I touched his hand. 'He told me you really had got guts, Stan. He was so right.'

He gripped my hand fiercely. 'Ta, Nurse,' he mumbled, 'ta.'

He was asleep again when Mary came into the ward with an envelope. 'This was in the clinical room. I didn't see anyone leave it. It's for you.'

I waited until I was alone at the table to read Andrew's note. It had been written at midnight.

I was worried about you, so I came back. I have just looked into Albert and seen how busy you are. I'm sorry for the new customers, but glad for you and the old patients. I'll fetch you in the morning. Look out for me, my darling. I'll be there.

Yours, in every sense,
ANDREW

It was time for another blood-pressure and pulse round. All the D.I.L.'s were safely round from their anaesthetics and sleeping. The other men were flat out. Stan snored loudly. Mr Cohen made little chirping noises without his teeth. Johnson, by the balcony doors, grunted in sleep. Toms, across the ward from Johnson, shifted his position without waking, and his weights jangled. The new man in Tiny's bed slept soundlessly. I stood by him and found I was tense, waiting for the start of a nightmare. It was only then I properly realised Tiny had had his last nightmare.

I listened to the night sound of Albert and began to breathe more easily. Tiny had been so terrified by those nightmares, and they had been getting worse. They would have gone on, he would have had to be moved to another ward, and almost inevitably, another hospital. He must have known that, and how he would probably end. I still did not believe he had done the right thing, but, as Stan said, it must have looked right to him.

Around me Albert snored, sighed, grunted on. Albert had

gone to sleep with a heavy heart, but in sleep Albert was sounding like Albert again. The night was nearly over. In a few hours the light would be back. In a few hours I would see Andrew again. I touched his letter under my apron bib and went on listening to my peaceful ward. It was a lovely sound, and though my heart was still heavy, slowly I felt the peace.

THE END

RING O' ROSES *by* LUCILLA ANDREWS

After a year spent in Canada, Cathy Maithland returns to England to be bridesmaid at the wedding of her old school friend, Ruth. That evening, when Cathy and Joss, Ruth's elder brother, meet after the reception, they find that instead of their former indifference, each experiences a new and overwhelming attraction to the other.

But on her return to St. Martha's Hospital the following Monday, Cathy is told to report to the Accident Unit, where she learns Joss is already working as S.A.O. And although this seems a happy coincidence, things just don't work out as expected. Against a background of crisis and emergency, a dedicated team have to cope not only with human tragedy and suffering, but with the problems of their own tangled relationships.

552 09288 6—35p   T30

THE NIGHT PEOPLE *by* KATE NORWAY

Sister Alison Ford kept telling herself to forget Dr. Tom Redgate—but forgetting him was not the easiest thing to do . . .

Dorothy Fenn, newly qualified as a doctor, waited—and waited—for a word from Chris Welland . . .

Lewis Stein and Nurse Millie Robinson seemed to have something in common—but what part did heiress Mandy Hodderson play in his life?

These were the Night People, in whose hands lay the responsibility of the hospital . . .

552 09417 X—30p   T31

A SELECTED LIST OF CORGI ROMANCE
FOR YOUR READING PLEASURE

☐ 09195 2	NURSE ERRANT	Lucilla Andrews	30p
☐ 09196 0	THE NEW SISTER THEATRE	Lucilla Andrews	30p
☐ 09197 9	THE SECRET ARMOUR	Lucilla Andrews	30p
☐ 09198 7	A HOUSE FOR SISTER MARY	Lucilla Andrews	30p
☐ 09199 5	HIGHLAND INTERLUDE	Lucilla Andrews	35p
☐ 09200 2	FLOWERS FROM THE DOCTOR	Lucilla Andrews	35p
☐ 09564 8	THE PRINT PETTICOAT	Lucilla Andrews	30p
☐ 09565 6	THE QUIET WARDS	Lucilla Andrews	30p
☐ 09566 4	MY FRIEND THE PROFESSOR	Lucilla Andrews	30p
☐ 09567 2	EDINBURGH EXCURSION	Lucilla Andrews	30p
☐ 09208 8	BRIDAL ARRAY	Elizabeth Cadell	30p
☐ 09207 X	THE GREEN EMPRESS	Elizabeth Cadell	30p
☐ 09166 9	THE CUCKOO IN SPRING	Elizabeth Cadell	30p
☐ 09133 2	THE YELLOW BRICK ROAD	Elizabeth Cadell	30p
☐ 09329 7	CONSIDER THE LILIES	Elizabeth Cadell	30p
☐ 09426 9	MONEY TO BURN	Elizabeth Cadell	30p
☐ 09470 6	THE SECRET MAN	Nora Lake	30p
☐ 08725 4	LOVE LETTER	Hilary Neal	25p
☐ 09537 0	THE GREEN LIGHT	Bess Norton	30p
☐ 09662 8	THE QUIET ONE	Bess Norton	35p
☐ 09664 4	THE WAITING ROOM	Bess Norton	35p
☐ 09663 6	NIGHT DUTY AT DUKE'S	Bess Norton	35p
☐ 09228 2	THE SEVEN SLEEPERS	Kate Norway	30p
☐ 09183 9	JOURNEY IN THE DARK	Kate Norway	30p
☐ 09148 0	MERLIN'S KEEP	Kate Norway	30p
☐ 09415 3	THE LAMBS	Kate Norway	30p
☐ 09561 3	TO CARE ALWAYS	Kate Norway	30p
☐ 09539 7	THE DUTIFUL TRADITION	Kate Norway	30p
☐ 09538 9	GOODBYE, JOHNNY	Kate Norway	30p
☐ 09469 2	THE GINGHAM YEAR	Kate Norway	30p
☐ 09528 1	TO LOVE A STRANGER	Barbara Perkins	30p
☐ 09312 2	NO SINGLE STAR	Alex Stuart	30p
☐ 09517 6	DOCTOR MARY COURAGE	Alex Stuart	30p
☐ 09516 8	DOCTOR ON HORSEBACK	Alex Stuart	30p
☐ 09555 9	DAYBREAK	Jean Ure	30p

All these books are available at your bookshop or newsagent; or can be ordered direct from the publisher. Just tick the titles you want and fill in the form below.

CORGI BOOKS, Cash Sales Department, P.O. Box 11, Falmouth, Cornwall.
Please send cheque or postal order. No currency, and allow 10p per book to cover the cost of postage and packing (plus 5p each for additional copies).

NAME (block letters) ....

ADDRESS ....

(APRIL 75) ....

While every effort is made to keep prices low, it is sometimes necessary to increase prices at short notice. Corgi Books reserve the right to show new retail prices on covers which may differ from those previously advertised in the text or elsewhere.